Split Decision

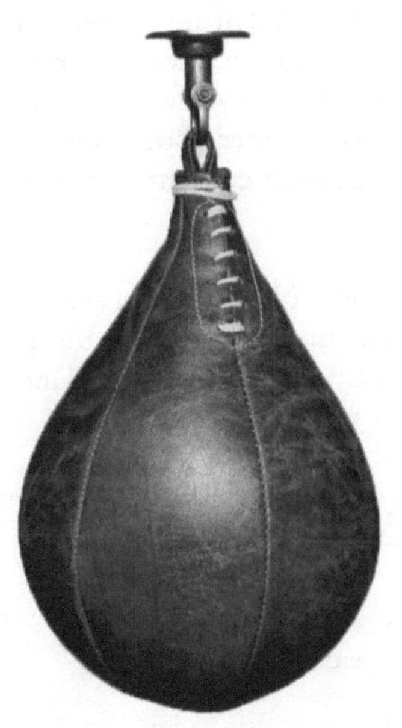

Marc A. Beausejour

S.H.E. PUBLISHING, LLC

SPLIT DECISION

Copyright © 2019 by Marc A. Beausejour

All rights reserved. Printed in the United States of America with simultaneous printings in Australia, Canada, and United Kingdom. No part of this book may be used or reproduced, stored in a retrieval system, or transmitted in any form or by any means or any matter electronic or mechanical or by photocopying, recording whatsoever without written permission of the publisher, except in the case of brief quotations embodied in critical articles or reviews. Exclusive worldwide content publication/distribution by SHE PUBLISHING LLC.

This book is a work of fiction. Names, characters, businesses, organizations, places, events, and incidents either are the product of the author's imagination or are used fictitiously. Any resemblance to actual persons, living or dead, events, or locales is entirely coincidental.

For information contact : www.shepublishingllc.com | info@shepublishingllc.com | Tel: 219.515.8032

Edited by D.A. Goodwin | Front Cover photo by ID 48584570 © Ammentorp | Dreamstime.com

Library of Congress Control Number: 2024932580

ISBN: 978-1-953163-94-3

Second Edition : February 2024

1   2   3   4   5   6   7   8   9   10

This book is dedicated to my late great-godmother and surrogate grandmother, Sencia Charles Pierre. Thank you for taking my mother under your wing and fortifying her faith in the Lord and her family. Continue to rest in peace, beautiful angel.

Prologue

With his broad shoulders glistening in the moonlight, Sylvio Dominique finds himself in the throes of passion, kissing and licking his lover as her sounds exude the euphoria she feels in his arms. It is a sweet escape from both of their realities—the false pretense that neither of them is meant to be together at that very moment. As she slowly slips off her nightgown, exposing her bosom, she proceeds to kiss him more intensely.

Oblivious to their surroundings, the two are completely in a trance as they continue to work their way down each other. Valentina Cruz kisses Sylvio's chest as she proceeds to his naval. She does not rush at all, taking her time for her lips to reach his midsection. He begins to undo his pants as he feels himself stiffen. Squeezing her supple breasts, Sylvio kisses Valentina more intently. He needed this. He needed her. He was weary of fighting. He was tired of contending for survival. His body yearned for her softness...her tenderness...her delicateness.

Sylvio guides her to the bedroom, where they continue.

With a sly grin, Valentina pushes Sylvio to the bed, as only she could, and she begins to mount him. Massaging his sore muscles where she had rubbed soothing oils earlier, she continues to use her tongue as a form of foreplay, drawing patterns all over his bare chest.

Closing his eyes, Sylvio caresses Valentina's hair with his hands. Her hair feels so good. She feels good. I shouldn't even be here. But I need to be here.

"I know what you need," Valentina whispers seductively in Sylvio's ear before licking his earlobe and driving him out of his mind.

"Oh, really? What you think I need then?" Sylvio teasingly kisses Valentina's lips again.

"You need my sweet wine, papi." Valentina lowers her body and gyrates on top of Sylvio's waist.

I love when she calls me "papi."

Sylvio continues to work on Valentina. The room temperature starts to rise with their body heat as their nature begins to rise. He turns her over on the bed and licks her wet crevices. After a few minutes, he feels her body convulse as she begins to climax. I'm hittin' her spot. Sylvio is confident as she moans out in pleasure.

As soon as Sylvio has her dripping, he moves up and slowly inserts himself inside of Valentina. Moving in rhythmic motion, her moans get even louder, and he continues to pleasure her. But as he continues to move, he also feels a sharp pain on the side of his ribs, a reminder of the dreadful punishment his body took over the last twenty-four hours. Attempting to mask the pain from Valentina, Sylvio strokes her body, but unfortunately, he can't hide his pain.

"Baby, you okay?"

"Yeah, I'm good. You know me. Just got some battle scars from the fight." He hopes this does not kill the mood.

Valentina runs her hands over the swollen, red marks around Sylvio's rib cage, which causes him to wince again. "Are you sure?"

"Yeah, I'm good. Besides, you're makin' the pain go away."

But this does not appease Valentina. "Sylvio, I'm serious. Every time you step in that ring, I get so scared for you. I mean, I know you can take it. But how much can you take?"

Blaming himself for not keeping his injury discreet, Sylvio laid down on the bed beside Valentina. "I can take whateva they dish out. I ain't scared of no one. I've been fighting my whole life," he replied, although he'd never told her that he had pondered stepping away from the sport.

Having fought one of the toughest bouts of his life, Sylvio wondered if it was worth permanent injury. But boxing was his livelihood, his income. It was all he knew for more than thirteen years, and he didn't see quitting as an option. "I can't stop now. I'm on da' top, and I don't care what or who I have to go through to remain there."

Valentina seemed to understand although concern still showed on her face. "I feel you. But promise you don't forget me when you start blowin' up on commercials and shit," she said, kissing the back of his hand.

Sylvio held Valentina's hand as he smiled at her. "Girl, you goin' to the top wit' me, best believe that," he reassured her.

Suddenly, he heard a sound coming from his sweatpants that were lying a few feet from the bed. Someone was trying to call him. Reaching into the pocket, Sylvio took his cell phone out and answered. "Yeah, what up?"

"Yo, you still at ole' girl house? You betta get the hell up outta thea dawg. Her brothers are on their way to da crib right now," a voice frantically warned him.

Recognizing the voice as one of his friends, Sylvio took a second to gather his thoughts. He knew that Valentina lived with her brothers, but he also knew her brothers had no love for him. "Aight, dawg, I'm comin' out. Meet me at the end of Corona and 144th," Sylvio replied, before hanging up the phone. Rising from the bed, he frantically began dressing.

"What's wrong?"

Sylvio turned to face Valentina. "I thought you said your brothers weren't gonna be home all night."

"They're not. They supposed to be in Jersey."

"Yeah right. My boy just said they 'bout to roll up in hea any minute. I gotta bounce." Sylvio knew how dangerous her brothers, Bruno and Juan, were, especially with all their connections to drug and weapons dealers in New York.

"Okay, baby, I'll walk you out." Valentina pulled on her robe and began to walk with Sylvio towards her front door, but no sooner did they approach the door, did they see the headlights.

Bruno and Juan were pulling into the driveway.

"Shit, they hea. Sneak out through my back window," Valentina frantically ushered Sylvio to her room. Opening the window, she shifted its outer screen, just wide enough for him to get his body through.

"I'll hit you up lata," he said, kissing her goodbye. Sylvio hated sneaking out the house like a thief, but he wasn't armed, and he wanted to live to fight his next bout. Walking onto a warm Queens Street, he made his way over to the corner to meet his friend.

Upon arriving at the corner, Sylvio saw Omar Keaton leaned against a light post. Shaking his head, Sylvio walked to him and shook his hand. "Why you gotta stand hea lookin' obvious?"

"Cuz I ain't even 'spose to be out hea, you feel me? I had to leave my girl at the crib to come wit' yo ignorant ass," Omar replied.

As a longtime resident of Queens, Omar knew the game of the streets. A former high school and college basketball player, he had finished his collegiate career, but his bid to enter the NBA draft had fallen short. Moving back to Queens, he rented an apartment in Hollis, where he worked a steady warehouse job while figuring out his next move. Years prior, he had met Sylvio in Richmond Hill High School in Queens, and their friendship had grown. And although their careers had taken them along different paths, they'd remained good friends.

"My bad, dawg, but she was worth it. Goddamn, she was worth it, homie," Sylvio smiled.

"We keep tellin' you she suspect, man. How you know she ain't settin' you up? You could have any bitch you want, especially after the work you put in last night at MSG." Omar was referring to Sylvio's match against top middleweight champion Felipe Maximo.

"You know how I do, dawg."

As they headed to the opposite end of the block, Omar slowed and looked at Sylvio. "They asked you to throw the match?"

Sylvio didn't answer for nearly two minutes. "Yeah, but I wasn't gonna do that shit. It's about respect. Even if it cost me my life, I gotta protect my rep. I'll go to the grave wit' that," he added as they continued walking the block.

A small black Mazda that had been silently following the friends pulled up onto the curb next to them. Sylvio and Omar stared curiously at the car and then each other. It wasn't until the window rolled down that the young men realized their lives were in peril as they noticed the .45mm gun tip pointed out from the partially rolled window.

"SHIT, RUN!" Sylvio shouted to Omar, and they both darted across the empty intersection, but not before three gunshots blasted in their direction from across the street.

Chapter 1

Fourteen Years Earlier | Crashing to the asphalt, nine-year-old Sylvio attempted to break his fall, but it ended up costing him as he scraped his hands and arms. A hard shove to his back had sent him sprawling, and before he could turn to face the perpetrator, he'd already heard the cruel laughter behind him.

Brandon Mills, a burly fifth grader, stood over Sylvio, laughing. "Aw, is Sylvia 'bout to cry?" he asked sarcastically, as his friends Kerrell Davis and Robert Johnson laughed alongside him.

Slowly, Sylvio rose up from the ground but not without silently blaming himself for not taking the back route to school.

The sun's early rays shone from behind the trees as kids made their way over to Public School 55. It was only the third week of school, and Sylvio already knew it was going to be one nightmare of a year. Brandon had tormented him for the past two years, and as much as Sylvio hoped that he would eventually get tired of teasing him and jumping out from behind walls or trees to push him, it seemed the more Sylvio ran, the more eager Brandon was to torment him.

When he was in the third grade, Sylvio had managed to avoid Brandon on more than one occasion by entering the school through the back doors. Brandon never caught him during the school day because he was in a grade higher, so he was always on the next floor level with the other kids in his grade. Yet, that didn't stop Brandon from occasionally catching Sylvio before or after school.

God forbid if Sylvio ever had money on the days that Brandon picked on him because Brandon was especially keen at detecting money, whether it was dollar bills or loose change. Rumors swirled about Brandon robbing another kid for his high-tops. He shook the poor boy to the point where his parents immediately snatched him from the school. Thus, Brandon earned the reputation of being able to literally chase kids out of P.S. 55. There were days when Brandon even bragged about it, and that's what raised his profile.

It wasn't too soon after the sneaker-less kid transferred out that Brandon turned his attention towards Sylvio and focused on making his time at school miserable. But unlike Brandon's previous target, Sylvio didn't have the option of transferring to another school, partly because it was a decision that both his parents would need to agree on. His parents couldn't even agree to stay married.

Sylvio's mother, Anne Dominique, left him with his father when Sylvio was only four years old, taking his baby sister, Rebecca, with her. His father told him that she moved out of New York and decided to live in Philadelphia, where she remarried. So telling his mother about the abuse he faced from Brandon wasn't an option for Sylvio.

And Sylvio's father, who grew up in Gonaives, Haiti, would give the same advice he always gave Sylvio whenever Brandon messed with him: "You have to stand up for yourself. Nobody's gonna fight for you. Ou we' ki jan mama'ou kite ou?" That was his way of saying, "Did you see the way your mama left you?"

It was another way of Jacques Dominique verbally hammering home a point to his son: even family won't save him all the time, and he had to fend for himself sooner or later. This lesson was already painfully administered by Brandon every week until Sylvio finally found a shortcut to avoid his enemy altogether.

Unfortunately, this time Sylvio had become distracted as a few girls with African braids gracefully tied in their heads pranced by, almost hypnotizing him. He decided to gather the courage to introduce himself, but upon following them, he forgot to take the alternative route he normally took to avoid his bully.

Spotting him from just a few feet away, Brandon ran behind Sylvio and shoved him hard as he could. If Sylvio's reflexes had not been as swift as they were, he might have shattered his face and teeth on the ground.

"C'mon, Brandon, what I do this time?" Sylvio attempted to use a deep voice, but a low whine was all that came out.

"You got in my way, son," Brandon said, smiling devilishly.

Sylvio got up to check his hands. They were scraped and bloody, but nothing too serious.

Maybe if I turn my back and walk fast towards the school, a teacher might come out and stop him before he has too much fun. It was only wishful thinking. As soon as Sylvio turned to walk away, Kerrell and Robert grabbed him by his arms and held him in front of Brandon, whose smile was instantly replaced with malice.

"I ain't done wit' you yet, punk." Brandon snarled as he approached Sylvio.

"C'mon, Brandon, I gotta go. I'm gonna be late for school," he whined.

"C'mon, Brandon. I gotta go. I'm gonna be late for school," Brandon mocked in a high- pitched voice as his friends laughed.

Deep within the recess of his heart, a wave of anger swept through Sylvio, but he was trapped and unable to move, despite struggling to escape.

"How much money you got? I left my cash at da' crib, so you gonna be my new bank today," Brandon said, menacingly.

"I ain't got no money." Sylvio knew that wasn't true. The night before, he had asked his dad for a dollar to buy snacks at the corner store after school. When Sylvio felt Kerrell and Robert loosen their grip, he hoped Brandon had bought his lie, but Brandon didn't give up easily.

Lunging forward, Brandon plunged his hands into Sylvio's pockets, snatching out the lint and small pieces of paper. Finally, he found the dollar that was crumpled in Sylvio's pocket. "Look at this, ya'll. He must think I'm stupid." After Brandon pocketed the stolen dollar, his cronies loosened their grip.

Sylvio began to breathe a sigh of relief until, without warning, he felt a sharp blow to his gut that sent him doubling over in pain as he held his breath.

"Next time, you betta have more, and you betta run me my shit, or else they gonna need a body bag for you when I'm through," Brandon threatened as he and his boys walked away.

Waiting for the pain to subside, Sylvio slowly began to make his way toward the school doors. As he entered, he happened to look in the direction of the school fence. And there stood a man, staring at him intently.

How long had he been there? Sylvio hoped the man hadn't witnessed the beating he had just taken. He half-expected the man to suddenly break down laughing. But instead, the gentleman just nodded his head, almost encouragingly, as if he sympathized with what Sylvio had gone through. Sylvio just shook his head and turned his attention to the door. As much as he knew, no one was going to feel sorry for him, not even a stranger.

As soon as the final bell rang, signaling the end of the day, Sylvio made a dash for the back doors so he could cut through the thin walkway that led to his street. It was the best path for him to walk through because he knew Brandon and his friends would leave through the front doors with all the other students. Although he had just spent seven hours at school, Sylvio could still feel the pain from Brandon's blow to his stomach. Figuring that he needed to sleep it off, Sylvio ran across the street to the OneStop store.

Luckily, Sylvio had managed to scrounge up quarters, dimes, and nickels from his school desk that added up to be about eighty-five cents, just enough to buy a juice box and a small bag of Wise potato chips. After easily locating his chips, Sylvio searched through the beverage section to find the juice grenade as he heard the bell chirping when another customer entered the store. Sylvio paid the customer no mind at first, but as soon as the man made his way over to the section where he stood, Sylvio realized it was the same man he'd seen outside the fence after he was accosted by Brandon.

The man appeared to be in his late thirties to early forties. When Sylvio walked up to the line to pay for his items, the man, with a couple of cigar stogies and a newspaper tucked under his right arm, got in line behind him.

Sylvio paid for his items and left the store, at first unbeknownst to him that the man followed. *Maybe he lives close by. It would be kinda creepy if he was following me for no reason.*

But it wouldn't be too long before the man caught up to Sylvio. "Yo, kid." To his surprise, the young boy continued walking.

Maybe if I ignore him, he'll go away.

But he was persistent. "C'mon, young man, I know you heard me."

Finally, Sylvio turned around. He might be skinny and short, but he knew Richmond Hill was no place to talk friendly to strangers. "You talkin' to me?"

"Course, I'm talkin' to you, brotha. What's up?"

"What's up?" Sylvio replied before deciding to walk away, even quickening his pace to distance himself from the stranger.

But the man was not to be deterred. "Is that how fast you plannin' to run away from big boy tomorrow?"

At once, Sylvio knew that he was referring to Brandon. "What you mean?" Sylvio slowed down to look at his follower.

"I ain't stupid, son. I saw what went down this mornin' before school. It's messed up how they did you."

Sylvio carefully eyed the man, wondering if he was just playing around with him or if he was serious. For the moment, he seemed to have genuine concern.

"It's just Brandon being stupid. You know, kid stuff. He was just messin' around, no biggie."

"That don't look like he playin' around, son. Trust me, I know. I've been there. I've been pushed around by every big kid on da block, and believe me, nobody knows more about these shortcuts and alleys than I do."

Sylvio hung his head, a little embarrassed that the man saw him avoiding Brandon. "I just don't want any trouble. Brandon is gonna be Brandon, and I just gotta find a way to stay away from him."

"But for how long, brotha? How long can you keep duckin' and dodgin' him? If you keep givin' power to him, he's gonna keep fuckin' wit' you till the day you die."

"Did you see his posse? You know how many dudes he got wit' him? I don't stand a chance with all three of 'em."

"All a mind game, son. He know dem boys scared of him too, so they gon' do what he says, so they don't end up in yo place. All he doin' is protectin' his rep."

Sylvio started backing away, fearing the stranger had devious intentions. "Look, I know what I'm doing, sir. I don't need your help."

"I'm sho' you do. But I can help you defend yourself," the man said, pulling out a small business card and handing it to Sylvio. "Name's Jim Shaw. I work at the Steel Glove Gym down on Liberty Ave."

Upon looking at the card, Sylvio saw that Jim was a boxing instructor and trainer. "Thanks, but I don't know. I mean I got school and everything, and my parents don't really have the money for boxing lessons. Besides, I'm too skinny for that."

"So? That ain't neva stopped nobody, son. With hard work, training, and certain habits, you'll be a natural. If you train yourself not to take nobody's crap, I guarantee you you'll earn all the respect at school. And trust me when I say this: Brandon won't be a problem anymore."

"Thanks anyway, sir, but I'm no boxer. I don't think it's gon' work," Sylvio started walking to his apartment building.

Jim remained persistent. "You know what's funny? I said the exact same thing when I was about yo age, give or take a few years," Jim said, chuckling. "I thought I wasn't cut out for boxing. But the sweet science of boxing is incomparable. I learned how to slip punches, how to block punches, how to duck, how to move, how to adjust my footwork. I parlayed all that into a Golden Gloves championship and twenty-six amateur bouts, winning twenty-four of them."

"Really?" Sylvio was suddenly more interested in the career that Jim once had.

"Yeah, man. I was just like you at yo age. Getting' jacked fo' my money and hiding behind bushes and corners until danger passed. After all, it was all about survival back in them days. But I see potential in you. You might be skinny, but we can work on your speed and strength. It ain't gonna be easy. You gon' have to dig deep and work if you want respect out hea. As a matter of fact, I got so much confidence in you, I'm willing to train you—free of charge—and I don't normally do that for just anybody."

Sylvio's eyes lit up. "For free? You'll really do that?"

"No doubt, young brotha. Okay, let's do this. After school tomorrow, I'll take you to my gym, where we have over eighty members. We can do some basic drills. Then we'll learn the fundamentals of boxing. Just give me a few weeks, and I can transform you into a machine."

Sylvio thought about it. He wanted Brandon to stop tormenting him, and he didn't want to tell the teachers or his father because it would paint him as a coward. This was a problem that he was going to figure out on his own. "Let me think about it, and I'll get back to you tomorrow."

"Aight, son, think it ova. But remember, how long are you gonna be able to hide and stay away from him? There's only so many places to hide. You can find every shortcut and alley in the borough, but don't be surprised if he finds out you're hiding from him in those alleys. Running away never guarantees safety. But defending yourself and earning respect out here is the best thing you could do," Jim said, before turning around to walk in the opposite direction as Sylvio made his way home.

Chapter 2

After spending the whole night wide awake, Sylvio finally decided to check out Jim's boxing gym, so before he left for school the next morning, he packed his deodorant and P.E. shorts. He didn't have any other shorts or a lot of clothes to choose from, so he took what he had. He brushed his teeth and hair and then made his way over to the kitchen where his father, Jacques, already sat, eating his usual: a toasted bagel with whipped butter spread and a banana on the side. And it was never complete without his cup of decaf.

Jacques stood about five foot nine with short black hair receding at his hairline. He was already dressed for work, donning a MTA uniform. Jacques worked at the ticket booth in one of the subway stations on Farmers Boulevard, and he often worked such long hours that there were days when Sylvio didn't see his father at all. Yet, Jacques did his best to provide for his son, cooking small meals like soup or making batches of rice and frying plantain, which was an island delicacy. He and Sylvio never prepared large meals. Unfortunately, that was the talent Sylvio's mother possessed before abruptly moving out with Rebecca.

Jacques was not home when Sylvio returned from school the day before, so Sylvio never told him about Jim or his offer. And it wasn't by accident that Sylvio decided to keep the meeting a secret. He knew his father was strict and traditional and didn't allow him to participate in any extracurricular activities if there was no educational merit behind them. Going to a boxing gym wasn't Jacques's idea of a beneficial activity.

More often than not, Jacques demanded that Sylvio keep his head in the books and not focus on sports, entertainment, or any other activities that normal nine-year-old boys enjoyed. Many other boys had parents that brought them video games, new shoes, new clothes, and new jackets, but to Sylvio, those items came at a luxury, and his father made but so much money to pay for necessities. Anything outside of Jacques's budget was considered unimportant until Sylvio worked for himself.

As he approached the table, Sylvio realized he had to find a way to talk his father into letting him go to the gym after school. "Good morning, Pop." Sylvio casually opened the fridge to grab a pack of waffles, which were also considered a premium in his father's budget.

"Good morning, Sylvio," Jacques replied in his strong Creole accent. "How was school yesterday?"

"School was okay," Sylvio replied, placing two blueberry waffles in the toaster.

"Did you finish all your homework?"

"Yeah, I finished it." Then after a moment, Sylvio decided to take his shot. "Hey, Pop, after school, there's an afterschool program, where the teachers are gonna take some of us to the library to study. They'll also take us to gym right after. Is it okay if I go?" Sylvio hated lying to his father, but he didn't see it as lying. He saw it as skating around the truth.

Jacques raised his eyebrows suspiciously. "Where is this program gonna be? Ki le' wap fini?" He also wondered if it was going to end.

"It's gonna finish at five o'clock. I'll come right back home. I promise," Sylvio's mind was racing wildly. *Who am I kidding? I don't know when I'm gonna come back. Hopefully, I make it back.*

Jacques normally worked at the booth until six or seven o'clock, so if Jim didn't finish teaching him all the tricks of boxing by five o'clock, Sylvio still had a couple of hours to beat his father home—even rush to a quick shower—so Jacques wouldn't expect anything.

Squinting his eyes as if he was trying to study his son in case he was trying to pull one over on him, Jacques thought about it.

Sylvio started to drop his head in disappointment. *It ain't lookin' too good. He's gonna say "no."*

But what Jacques said next surprised Sylvio. "Okay, you can go. But make sure you're back by 5:30 sharp. Or else, w'ap gen pwoblem ave'm," Jacques warned his son about the consequence of not returning on time.

"Yes, Dad. Thanks," Sylvio said as nonchalantly as possible, although internally, he was rejoicing. It may not be much to celebrate for others, but Sylvio knew, as all kids of Haitian descent knew, how victorious it was when a child was able to persuade his or her parents to participate in activities that did not include the three L's as they call it: "L'ekol," "L'egliz," and "L'akay," for school, church, and home.

After finishing his waffles, Sylvio grabbed his bookbag and headed out the door. Checking his stopwatch, he managed to make it to school about twenty minutes before the doors opened. Brandon wouldn't be there yet. After studying his nemesis' movements for more than a year, Sylvio knew Brandon came from the opposite end of the street and didn't normally arrive until five minutes before school opened. And Sylvio made sure to avoid the road where his burly rival would emerge with his buddies.

Sylvio could see other kids making their way to the doors. He knew he had to get to the back, so he cut through the side pathway that he took to leave school, but not before turning into the street.

Sylvio hadn't seen Jim this morning. He would normally be walking by on his way to the gym, so the fact Jim hadn't appeared yet made Sylvio uneasy. What if Jim never showed up again? Would he make me look like a complete idiot for hanging around waiting for some imaginary boxing lesson that would never take place while I have to continue to hide from Brandon?

Sylvio couldn't allow those thoughts to consume him. As he made his way to the back, he encountered his friend and classmate, Kyle Green, who lived about two blocks from the school.

"What's up, Sylvio?"

"What's up, Kyle?"

"You ight, man? Why you lookin' like somebody 'bout to jump you?"

"Nah, it ain't nothin' like that. Just walking around this way. Mr. Mitchell's class is closer to this part of the school anyway."

"Still sweatin' Brandon, huh?" Kyle chuckled. Nothing got past him.

Sylvio looked at Kyle. The last impression he wanted to leave upon Kyle was that he was intimidated and fearful. "It ain't just him, man. He rollin' wit' Kerrell and Robert this year. I thought you had my back. Where were you at?" he asked, hoping to divert the blame to his friend.

"Well, see what had happened was, I overslept, and I didn't get hea in time. But you know if I was there, I would've popped Brandon's big ass." Kyle balled his hands into fists and started playing punching Sylvio.

"Yeah, right. Okay," Sylvio said as they entered the corridor to head up the flight of stairs to their floor.

After school, Sylvio went downstairs and proceeded to cut through the back as he normally did. He had even made sure he was the first person out of the math class. As he reached the doors, he took out the card Jim handed him. The name on it read the Steel Glove Gym, located on the corners of Liberty Avenue and 102nd Street, about a ten-minute drive from Sylvio's school, or thirty minutes if he decided to walk.

But as Sylvio was leaving the schoolgrounds, he felt a hand roughly grab his shoulder. Believing it to be Kyle joking around, Sylvio turned around to greet his friend but quickly realized he was in for a rude awakening.

Brandon's large, beady eyes glared at Sylvio. In the split second that Sylvio tried to run for it, Brandon grabbed Sylvio by his shirt collar and spun Sylvio around to face him. "So, this is where you been going all this time, huh?"

Sylvio looked around, watching all the kids pass by, oblivious to what was going on.

"What, you thought you could hide from me with your skinny chicken ass? Boy, I'mma be all ova you this year. You ain't eva getting away from me. You got it?"

Trapped in Brandon's grip, Sylvio noticed that Kerrell and Robert weren't with Brandon this time. Still, it offered little consolation for the predicament Sylvio was in. "Where your boys at?" he managed to choke out.

"I don't need 'em to stomp you," Brandon replied confidently. "So, I see this why I never see you once school is ova. You be tryin' to take them shortcuts. How much money you got?"

"I ain't got nothin', man. I'm broke as a joke."

"Nah, you just a joke. I know you got money around hea somewhere," Brandon said, freeing one hand from Sylvio's collar to search his pockets. Finally, his hand fished out the loose change Sylvio had—the last of his saved allowance money.

"Boy, you gon' learn not to lie to me again," Brandon said, raising his huge right fist menacingly.

Sylvio closed his eyes as he braced himself for the impact.

"Hey! What's going on ova there?" a voice yelled out.

Sylvio turned around and saw that it was Mr. Wilder, the school health teacher, who had just walked out and noticed the commotion.

Brandon dropped Sylvio and looked up at the teacher, surprised. "Nothing, Mr. Wilder. We're just playin' around."

"Is that true, Sylvio?"

Sylvio looked at Mr. Wilder before turning back to face Brandon, which he instantly regretted. Brandon gave Sylvio a grimacing stare, as if to say, "You betta say 'yes' because if you don't, I'll jack you up."

"Yeah, Mr. Wilder. Brandon was just jokin' around. We just playin' a scene from a movie we saw. No big deal."

"Alright, but no funny business. I got my eyes on you, Brandon. I don't wanna see you back in Principal Gutierrez's office. You understand?" Mr. Wilder asked, sternly.

"Yeah, sir. I understand."

Once Brandon finally let him go, Sylvio was able to blend in with the throng of kids exiting the school.

That was a close call.

Had Mr. Wilder not reappeared, Brandon would have smeared Sylvio's face all over the asphalt. The worst part of it was that Brandon finally found out where Sylvio had been sneaking to escape him.

As Sylvio walked, he heard a car honking rapidly. Believing it to be a parent of one of the students, he kept walking. But he heard someone call his name.

"Sylvio! Ova here!"

Turning toward the street, Sylvio realized that it was Jim Shaw sitting behind the wheel of a green Ford Coupe. Beckoning to Sylvio, he opened his passenger seat. "Get in, brotha."

Sylvio didn't think twice before hopping inside the car. By this time, Mr. Wilder would have walked back inside the building, leaving Brandon to his own vices. Sylvio figured the quicker he got out of dodge, the better. "Whew, that was a close one."

"Yeah, luckily for you, your teacher was there. But how long can you depend on 'em? At some point, you're gonna have to stand up to him and defend yourself."

"Yeah, I know," Sylvio confessed.

"Don't worry though. Before long, he won't be messin' with you again. So, you ready to check out the gym?"

"Yeah, let's check it out," Sylvio said excitedly.

As they made their way to the gym, Jim asked. "Do your parents know where you goin'?"

"Yeah, they know. Well, actually my dad knows. I didn't tell my mom about this."

"Why not?"

"Well, my mom and dad divorced when I was four years old. She moved outta state somewhere, so I ain't seen her. She never visited me or my dad. But my dad said that if I come back home at 5:30, it's all good."

"Well, I'm just lettin' you this now, son. Learning how to box is gonna take more than just two hours a day. It ain't gonna come easy. It's gonna take hard work, persistence, dedication, and commitment because, in this world, there are more Brandons than Sylvios out there, and your father, mother, and close friends won't always be around," Jim said as they continued driving.

Ten minutes later, they finally arrived at the gym. Stepping out of the car, Sylvio looked up at the two-story brick building with the large round letters: STEEL GLOVE GYM.

"Yo, this is dope!" Sylvio exclaimed excitedly as Jim led him through the front door.

A young black slender woman was sitting behind a small desk, filing papers. Upon hearing the doors, she looked up and smiled when she saw Jim.

"Hey, Jim, what's up?" she greeted.

"What's goin' on, Angie? Just stoppin' by to check things out. I got someone I want you to meet. Angie, meet Sylvio Dominique. Sylvio, this is Angelina Peterson—our receptionist, bookkeeper, and backup security," he introduced, laughing slightly.

"And what is so funny, boss? Don't play with me. I got enforcer skills now," Angelina replied in a sassy voice, before turning to Sylvio. "Nice to meet you, Sylvio. Welcome to Steel Glove," she said, shaking Sylvio's hand.

Sylvio couldn't help but observe how beautiful Angelina was. "Nice to meet you too, Angelina."

"Boy, don't call me that! Please call me Angie. Everybody else does," she said, laughing.

Sylvio looked at the wall behind Angelina, where dozens of photos of different boxers hung, seemingly from every nationality.

"This is one of the biggest boxing clubs in Queens," Angie said, pointing to the pictures. "Each one of them started out hea. Some of them grew up to be regular police officers, firefighters, but others became real boxing champions." She walked over to one of the pictures, pointing at a light-skinned black man with eyebrows raised and a mouth and jaw tightly shut, as if to instill fear through the photo. "This one's named Ricky Styles, but we called him 'Rick Da Brick' cuz every punch this cat dished out felt like you was getting hit wit' bricks. He started out real young, maybe only a couple years older than you. How old are you anyway?"

"Nine," Sylvio replied.

"Oh, yeah, Brick was about eleven or twelve," Angie said.

"Remember how skinny he was?" Jim asked.

"Who you tellin'? Boy was a twig when he started, but once he came here, and Jim and the others worked on him, he was a machine," Angie replied.

"Wow, that's cool," Sylvio said, but he was struck by a thought. All the boxers he saw in the photos had at least fifty to one hundred pounds on them and were much bigger than Sylvio was.

"Okay, Angie, we're gonna step inside. Don't worry, he on my dime," Jim confirmed as he and Sylvio walked inside the gym.

Loud music was blaring from the speakers as young boys, ages thirteen to eighteen, were involved in different boxing activities. Some were jumping rope or shadowboxing, and others were performing strength conditioning, lifting weights, or working on TRX ropes. On the other end of the gym, Sylvio saw a row of about seven boxing bags. Three of those bags were occupied with boys working on punching combinations.

In the center of the gym, there were two huge rings where other boxers were sparring. Sylvio's eyes lit up. The energy in the gym was like no other as he felt pumped with adrenaline. He would soon realize that Jim wasn't the only trainer in the gym. He was introduced to the other trainers in the gym: Will Timothy, Brian Conrad, Stan Reese, and Jose Delgado. Each was already working one-on-one with a boxer. But after Jim introduced Sylvio to the crew, he could hear snickering from one of the trainees.

"Shorty's a bit too small. This hea's a man's game. Come back when you lose all ya baby teeth," one of them cracked, causing some of the other boxers to laugh.

"He'll lose 'em all hea. That's fo' damn sure," another boy cracked.

"Pipe down, A.D. Give me two left jabs and a hook," Will replied, holding up his hands.

Impressed by the combinations thrown by the boy, Sylvio didn't think too much of the barb that he had made just a few minutes earlier. A.D. was quick, landing all his punches in the center of Will's glove pads with amazing dexterity and speed.

It was during this exercise exhibition that Jim began talking to Sylvio. "Okay, I want you to watch what A.D. is doing. You see how he's throwin' them jabs? Straight out—no curves, no leaning. He's poppin' it fast and retracting."

Sylvio continued to watch. "What does 'A.D.' stand for anyway?" Sylvio whispered to Jim.

"It's short for Alfred DeMarr. He's been boxing here since last September, and he's a natural. He's more of a hook fighter than a jab fighter, which is dangerous because it leaves his interior exposed. I keep tellin' that boy to work on his jabs, but he still needs more work. He'll get there though. All it takes is patience and perseverance. Those are gonna be the key words as we begin your training."

Sylvio could barely contain his enthusiasm. He was witnessing the sport of pugilism in its purest form, and he couldn't wait to get started. "So, when do we start training?"

"Oh, we're starting today. Go to the locker rooms in the back, and change into your gym gear. I already have it laid out for you outside your own locker. After that, come back out hea, and we'll get to work."

Sylvio ran to the locker room, where he saw a pair of shorts and a medium T-shirt that read "STEEL GLOVE GYM" in large letters followed by a picture of boxing gloves. Oddly enough, when he tried on the shirt and the shorts, he was surprised to find they fit him.

I don't think I told him my size. How does he know how much I weigh? Maybe Jim had an eye for shirt and shorts sizes. After five minutes, Sylvio emerged from the locker room.

"Alright, you ready to start your training?" Jim asked.

"Yeah, I'm ready to go." That's what Sylvio said, but he was not ready for what would happen next.

Jim reached into a storage closet, grabbed a broom, and handed it to Sylvio.

"Alright, so let's sweep around the gym a little bit. Make sure you get the corners and the sides. Then I want you to run to the back of the storage room, grab a bunch of small white towels, and bring them out," Jim instructed.

Reluctantly, Sylvio took the broom and started sweeping the gym. Maybe he just wants the floor clean. No big deal. I'll probably start boxing as soon as I finish.

It wouldn't take Sylvio too long to realize that he was mistaken. What he thought was going to be a few chores turned out to be a daily two-hour grind of manual labor—sweeping the gym, fetching the towels, cleaning the washrooms, and the most despicable job of them all: having to clean the spit buckets that were used by the older boxers whenever they had sparring sessions. On top of that, Sylvio wasn't even getting paid for his services.

Although Jim dropped him off at home on time so that he wouldn't miss his father's curfew, Sylvio was starting to grow impatient with Jim. He certainly did not sign up to be anyone's maid or butler. Sylvio still wanted to learn how to box, and although he managed to avoid Brandon during that span, he was beginning to grow weary of his role at the gym.

After two weeks, Sylvio had finally had enough. He was going to tell Jim that he quit. Between occasionally being abused by Brandon or having to do manual labor, Sylvio would take the school bully any day. On Friday, Sylvio decided to leave school through the front door. He was able to alternate between going through the back doors and leaving through the front of the school to keep Brandon guessing. Brandon had not made it his personal agenda to torment Sylvio as of lately, but Sylvio figured that he just didn't want to risk being caught by a teacher or another staff member.

Instead of looking for Jim's car, Sylvio decided to walk straight home. After a block or two, he heard a car horn behind him.

"Hey, son, where you going? You not going to the gym today?" Jim asked.

"What for? So you can work me like a slave? I don't wanna go anymore. I quit!" While Sylvio was angry, for a moment, he feared that Jim would be too.

Jim was investing in Sylvio and using his resources to help him. Sylvio knew his father couldn't afford the membership at the gym or the clothes he needed to train. But it was all cold comfort for Sylvio, who felt like he had a whip on his back. "Why don't you make the other kids work? You always have me do all this extra stuff. If I wanted to work, I could've been doin' all that at home."

Instead of getting angry, a concerned Jim parked his car and looked at Sylvio. "Look, son, I know I've been on your case, and it seems like I've been hard on you more than anyone else, but I see potential in you. Even if boxing is a sport, I want you to learn the value of hard work."

Then Jim stepped out of the car. "Sylvio, a lot of these cats out here are talented. Hell, the ones that are training in the gym are talented. But boxing is more than just talent and skill. You gotta work to be the best that you can be out there. It's a life value. I see it like this. Life is like a boxing ring. Every day is another round. You get up, not only to live life but to attack life—even if it means doing the things you don't wanna do. Sometimes life requires you to get yourself dirty and to work twice as hard because that's the society we live in. Young black men such as yourself sometimes lose focus on what it takes to succeed in life, and they think that they could just skate by with just talent. I don't want you to get the impression that life is a free ride. It's going to knock you on yo ass and force you to play your hand. But with hard work, you can achieve anything."

"Do you really see potential in me?" Sylvio asked.

"Man, you're gonna be a champion one day. Believe me."

Sylvio looked at Jim once again, wondering if he was just toying with his emotions, but again Jim seemed sincere.

"But if you wanna quit, I'll understand. I don't think Brandon and guys like him are gonna quit though. You can quit and run for the rest of your life, or you can stand up, do the work, and earn your respect."

After thinking it over for a few minutes, Sylvio opened the door to sit on the passenger seat. "So, what do you want me to do today? Take out the garbage? Clear the storage closet? Clean up A.D.'s spit bucket again?"

Without replying, Jim reached into the back of his car and took a couple of seconds to search underneath the seats. Before long, two brand new, medium-sized, red boxing gloves fell onto Sylvio's lap. "Box. That's what I want you to do today. These are for you to keep. Ready to go to work?" Jim smiled.

"Hell yeah," Sylvio replied as they drove to the gym.

Chapter 3

It was the first time Sylvio tried on a pair of boxing gloves, but while he was elated, he also felt a sense of dread. *What if I'm too clumsy? What if I swing wildly at a sparring opponent or a punching bag and end up hitting nothing but air?*

Having arrived at the gym, Jim witnessed the apprehension on the face of his young student and immediately went over to help Sylvio. "Here. Put 'em on like this," Jim said as he helped Sylvio with his gloves.

Once on, Sylvio looked at his reflection in the large mirror facing the opposite end of the gym. Wearing his tank top and school gym shorts, Sylvio looked at the image of an unsure, slight boy with large red boxing gloves. Raising his hands slightly, he realized the gloves were slightly heavier than he'd anticipated.

"What up, B.? I see you got dem gloves on today. Shaw finally took you off cleanin' duty?" A.D. asked as he walked out of the locker room, wearing his own boxing gloves.

"Yeah, I guess I finally get to box today," Sylvio replied.

"That's what's up. Don't sweat it, dawg. It's easy when you get the hang of it," A.D. reassured Sylvio as he walked over to Will, who had his pads ready for their training session.

After checking the gloves, Jim walked Sylvio over to one of the huge punching bags.

"Okay, Sylvio, this is what you wanted. Today, your training officially begins. Remember, you don't have just two gloves in yo hands. You have two pistols in your hands. Your punches are bullets that are swift, penetrating, and powerful and can be used to strike or block," Jim explained.

Sylvio nodded, acknowledging that he understood.

"The purpose of this bag is to increase your power and strength. The smaller punching bag, also known as the 'speed bag' is used to work on your speed. Once you master this bag, we'll move on to the speed bag. We will also work on cardio exercises in between training, some which will include jumping rope, running the treadmill, and in due time, swimming."

"Swimming?"

"Oh yeah. You'll be surprised at how many boxers swim to strengthen their muscles and improve their coordination. Trust me. After a few minutes of throwin' hands underwater, punching above ground will be cake. Okay, so here's what I want you to do. We're gonna start with straight left jabs," Jim continued while demonstrating the boxing technique to Sylvio as he listened and observed intently. "Okay, give me ten left jabs," Jim said, holding the bag.

Sylvio started punching the bag with straight, but ineffective jabs.

"Good job. Jabs are straight and direct. The only thing we need to learn is to apply more force to the jab. I know you got more strength than that in you," Jim said.

Jim instructed Sylvio to give him more left-handed jabs, and Sylvio obeyed. He punched the bag ten more times, applying more force than the first round. Looking at Jim, Sylvio expected him to be pleased, but he saw that his trainer had a wry expression on his face.

"Still weak, brotha. Look, if that was Brandon, do you think those punches would affect him? He wouldn't even move an inch. In the ring, every punch you throw must be effective. Speed with impact. Remember that. You force your opponent to react to you. Keep him guessing. Try it again."

Sylvio looked at the bag. Almost instantly, it transformed. Legs sprouted out from the bottom, and short black hair plunged from the top. As Sylvio watched the bag, a sneer began to form across its front. Brandon stood before him now, but instead of running, Sylvio zeroed in on his enemy. He could still feel the pain from Brandon's blows to his body and the scars from scraping his hands on the asphalt after Brandon had shoved him in his back.

"Everything that you feel—all the anger, all the pain—I want you to channel it all into your arms and your hands. "When it's time, let it out with every punch," Jim's voice said, but it was distant in Sylvio's head because all he saw was Brandon.

Sylvio resumed punching the bag, applying more power. He could see Brandon wincing under his blows, his body breaking down as he doubled over. Sylvio buried his gloves into Brandon's wide face, and as he zoned out, he hadn't realized that some of the members of the gym had stopped to watch his display with the bag. Sylvio had gone beyond ten punches, but Jim didn't warn him, and when the round was over, out of sheer exhaustion, Sylvio finally stopped punching the bag. It wasn't until the gym got quiet, that Sylvio realized all eyes were on him. Even A.D. and Will had stopped training to watch the small skinny boy working on the bag.

"That's more like it," Jim said, smiling at Sylvio.

"Yo, how old did you say you was?" another boxer named Lance asked.

"Nine," Sylvio replied.

"Yo, on da' real, I ain't neva seen no nine-year-old punch hard as he does," Lance told Jim.

"Word, I gotta give you props on that. Good shit, homie," A.D. said, giving Sylvio a gloved fist bump.

From that very moment, Sylvio became more comfortable in the gym. He felt that the other trainers and boxers respected him. For the rest of the afternoon, Jim ran drills with the right jab, and they even worked on ducking and the art of the right hook.

At the end of his boxing session, Jim drove Sylvio back home. Once Sylvio arrived at his apartment, he ran to his room and fell facedown on his bed. He had never felt more exhausted in his life. But at the same time, he'd never felt the confidence that he felt at the gym earlier. He looked at his dresser mirror and raised his fists in a defensive stance. He threw a right jab, followed by a left, before his body protested again, and he fell back onto the bed.

As the days passed, Sylvio began learning the finer points of the boxing game: how to duck properly and how to slip jabs. Jim had him warmup on more than several exercises, and easily his favorite warmup was jumping rope. At first, Sylvio felt awkward, and his lack of coordination did not help the slightest bit.

But Jim taught Sylvio how to jump rope without losing balance. "It's all a rhythm, Sylvio. The rope is a great tool to improve your stamina and speed," he would say. There were days when Jim would ask Sylvio to run a few laps around the gym, and by the time training ended, he would be sore from head to toe. But Sylvio also felt a different vibe; he was beginning to get stronger and would often work on pushups during the night or early in the morning before he departed for school.

Surprisingly, Brandon did not encounter Sylvio in the mornings, and Sylvio believed that he might have finally decided to leave him alone and pick on somebody else. There might've been a chance that he transferred out of school.

But it would all come to a head during the second week of October.

One day as Sylvio began to walk towards the side of the school, he saw a girl carrying a huge poster board and holding a plastic bag with supplies for a geography project. When the bag fell to the floor, and as Sylvio got closer, he recognized it was Tia Monroe. He didn't know her personally, but they'd had several exchanges in the past. And he didn't want to openly admit it, but he had a crush on the beautiful girl with the long, jet-black hair and thin, petite frame.

As soon as Sylvio saw her plight, he rushed to her. "Hey, what's up? You need some help with this stuff?" Sylvio offered as he reached for the bag.

Tia smiled. "Thanks, my teacher would assign us a project this early into the year. It's mad stupid," she complained.

"No worries. I got you," he said, handing her the bag. As they entered the building, they started to ascend the stairs to the top floor where the fifth graders had class. After a few minutes, they finally arrived at Tia's homeroom class. But to Sylvio's horror, his nemesis sat in the same room, talking to a friend.

It wouldn't take long for Brandon to realize that Sylvio was only a few yards away. "What you doin' here, shorty? I see you been hiding from me lately. Well, that means that the bank is open!" Brandon sneered as he approached Sylvio.

The class suddenly stopped talking and watched the scene unfold.

"I ain't yo bank," Sylvio said in a low voice.

"Nigga, look around you," said Brandon, menacingly. "Do you know where you at?"

Doing his best to ignore him, Sylvio turned to Tia. "You good? Is there anything else you need help with?"

After Tia confirmed that she no longer needed help, Brandon turned to face her. "Must be nice havin' your own slave willing to do whatever it takes."

"Shut up, Brandon. Get out my way!" Tia snapped as she attempted to pass by the small throng to get to her seat.

But it was apparent that Brandon wanted to stir up trouble. Without warning, he shoved Tia, causing her to lose her footing and fall on top of the plastic bag that contained paper-mache models of Puritan settlers.

"No!" Tia yelled in anguish as she removed the mashed figures from the bag. She turned to Brandon. "Look what you made me do, you jerk!"

Brandon seemed unfazed by the incident. "Whateva. Just hop off mine. You started it. Besides, I'm tryin' to get to this faggot ova hea." Brandon began pointing at Sylvio, who had been watching the whole scene unfold while trying to back away at the same time.

"Just let him go! Leave him alone," Tia sobbed, distraught over her ruined project.

"Brandon, I don't want no trouble," Sylvio protested, and he turned to head out of the classroom.

Suddenly, Brandon charged his way through the other students and grabbed Sylvio by his right shoulder. At that moment, a well of emotions ran through Sylvio, but not fear. Not anymore. It was bottled-up anger and rage. All the times that Brandon had used him as a punching bag had resurfaced in a sea of red in Sylvio's eyes. What Sylvio did next, he couldn't explain. As soon as Brandon grabbed his shoulder, he turned around and jabbed Brandon in his abdomen.

Sylvio's bully, not realizing what hit him before the sudden impact, fell back into a group of desks, holding his stomach in shock and pain.

Hearing the "oohs" from the other students, Sylvio pointed at Brandon. "I'm warning you. Leave me alone!"

For the first time in Sylvio's life, he saw a different look on Brandon's face. It was no longer frightening or menacing. This was the look of fear. Sylvio could hear Jim's words at the gym: "Look at your opponent's eyes. There are times when the fights are more mental than physical. If you see fear in his eyes, you've already won."

But it was only for a fleeting moment before Brandon's scowl returned. He was not used to being shown up by a kid who was in a grade below him. He had a reputation to keep. "Now, I'mma whup yo ass!" Brandon charged at Sylvio in hopes of tackling his smaller frame.

But Sylvio's reflexes had vastly improved. He easily dodged his much larger, slower opponent. Brandon swung wide left with an open hand, but Sylvio ducked his blow and retaliated with a right jab to the side of Brandon's head, sending a sharp pain shooting down Sylvio's hand. However, with Brandon holding the top of his eye, Sylvio knew he inflicted pain in his enemy as well.

Brandon lunged at Sylvio again, but Sylvio ducked out of his grasp and followed the first jab with more blows to Brandon's body as his opponent was unable to avoid the hits from his attacker.

With the class yelling, "FIGHT! FIGHT! FIGHT," Sylvio realized that he was in a bad spot. He had to return to his floor before the teacher arrived.

But Brandon was not finished. Quickly recovering from the body blows that he had taken, he lunged at Sylvio again. This time he managed to wrap his arms around Sylvio's waist, but that left his face exposed to Sylvio's stinging jabs that were peppering his eyes and nose. Both boys fell in a heap on the floor, and by this time, students from the other classrooms had run into the room where the fight was taking place. And with the other classes, came the teachers as they fought through the crowd of kids to finally break up the fight.

Mr. Roddenberry, the fifth-grade teacher from down the hall, grabbed both Brandon and Sylvio. Brandon's face was covered in bruises and bumps, while Sylvio, apart from a sore leg when he fell after being tackled, was virtually untouched. Both boys were marched to the principal's office on the first floor of the school. To keep them separated, Sylvio sat in one room adjacent to the attendance office, while Brandon sat in the resource room.

Sylvio rubbed his sore knuckles. Despite the punishment that awaited him, he finally felt free. No more hiding from anyone, no more using secret passageways or backdoors, and if Brandon wanted to come after him, he would be ready. As far as Sylvio was concerned, Robert and Kerrell, who were normally with Brandon, didn't have his back during the fight, and if they wanted Sylvio, he would be ready for them too. He was sick of running away. He had finally earned his respect—the hard way.

After a couple of minutes, Principal Andrew Gutierrez entered the room, wearing his usual stern expression. Sitting at the desk opposite of Sylvio, Principal Gutierrez looked at him intensely as if he was studying him. Sylvio did not want to look his principal in the eye in case he showed fear.

"Well, Sylvio, do you want to explain what happened?"

"Not really."

"Sylvio, what you did to Brandon was borderline brutal. You're looking at three weeks suspension from school for your part in this."

"He started it. Brandon was beating me up and taking my money, and everyone let him do it. So, I just had enough."

"Well right now, Brandon's the one looking beat up, wouldn't you say? Now, I've called your father, and he's coming here to pick you up, and I've called Brandon's family as well. We're going to discuss a proper punishment for both of you."

Things could not have gone any worse for Sylvio when his father rushed to the school after receiving the phone call from the principal. As soon as Jacques arrived and saw Sylvio at the office, his son raised his head slightly. By the look on his father's face, he knew he would be in for it within a couple hours.

Soon afterwards, Brandon's mother arrived. Upon seeing her son's disheveled clothes and bruised face, she began yelling about the "little bastard who beat her son up" and how he should be punished while her son should just receive a stern warning.

Principal Gutierrez gathered both parties and placed them in his main office while attempting to get all sides of the story. Sylvio explained how Brandon had abused him and robbed him on numerous occasions, and while he ignored and tried to get away, he was cornered with no option left but to defend himself.

Brandon, however, painted a different picture. He portrayed Sylvio as the aggressor, calling him crazy, and while he didn't deny bullying Sylvio, he stated that it was all just jokes, and he was never serious about his intent to injure or hurt anyone.

If only Tia was here, she would prove that I'm right, and Brandon's wrong. Nobody can possibly believe his story.

Once each boy told his side of the story, the punishment was that Brandon and Sylvio were both suspended for two weeks. While Jacques and Brandon's mother, Patti, were outraged over the suspension, the principal explained that Brandon had bullied other kids, so he deserved the punishment. Sylvio received the same punishment because Principal Gutierrez felt he should have approached him earlier about the bullying, in addition to the brutal fashion in which Sylvio had thoroughly thrashed Brandon.

As Sylvio and his father walked to the car, they didn't say a word to each other. Sylvio knew Jacques was trying to control his rage.

The drive home was quiet, and as Jacques parked his Honda Civic in a perfect parallel behind a Chevy Ventura, he turned to Sylvio. "You go straight to your room and wait for me there. No TV, no games, nothing. You hear me?" he said in his strong Haitian accent.

"Yeah, I heard you." Sylvio stepped out of the car, his head down because he knew what was coming next.

Anticipating what was about to happen didn't make it sting any less for Sylvio. Wincing in pain, he stretched out his legs and arms across the bed. His arms and the back of his hands were marked with the angry red welts where the leather belt struck him. Angrily brushing away a tear, Sylvio looked out of his barred room window. He felt trapped and imprisoned by his own father.

Nothing that he did was ever good enough for his own flesh and blood. Staring at kids playing without a care in the world, Sylvio envisioned himself playing stickball outside or riding his bike miles and miles away from the prison that was his home. Most of all, he wanted to box. He needed to release frustration, and he wanted to feel free to express himself. Boxing got him out of Brandon's clutches, and he had it in his mind that it was going to get him out of his father's hands.

Over the course of the next few days, Sylvio never left the house. Jacques punished him, so he couldn't watch TV or do anything fun. Going to any after-school programs, including the gym, was out of the question. His father wanted him to stay in the apartment and read. It didn't matter what he read, whether it was the dictionary, encyclopedia, or anything he had laying around. Sylvio read some of the books he checked out from school, but once he finished them, he was bored again.

To make matters worse, when Jacques left for work in the mornings, he would ask his aunt Miriama to come over to the apartment and babysit Sylvio. He knew she was only doing her younger brother a favor, but while Miriame was there, all she did was watch TV, oblivious to what Sylvio was doing. At night when Jacques returned home, Sylvio would finish eating leftovers from the previous evening and would walk into his room without saying a word to his father.

As the streetlights would come on, Sylvio often turned off his lights. With his room illuminated by streetlights, he'd look across the room at his shadow. If he couldn't go to the gym, he would bring the gym to him.

There, in the still of the night, Sylvio began shadowboxing. Jab, uppercut, left hook, right hook, slip, duck, slip.

One night, while Jacques was watching TV and eating dinner, he heard a knock. Sylvio opened his bedroom door and curiously peeked down the hall as Jacques went to look through the peephole. After a few seconds, he opened the door.

"Hello, pardon my intrusion, but is Sylvio home?" a familiar voice asked.

Sylvio beamed with excitement upon recognizing the voice of his boxing coach.

Chapter 4

Jacques never moved an inch from the doorway, nor did he invite Jim inside the apartment. "Yes, I'm his father. Who are you?"

"Yes, my name is Jim Shaw. "I'm the boxing coach at the Steel Glove Gym," Jim stretched his hand out to shake Jacques's, but Jacques refused to shake hands with a stranger who was asking for his son.

"Boxing coach? What does that have to do with my son?" Jacques raised his eyebrows, suspiciously.

"Well, Sylvio's been training at my gym for a few weeks after school, and I saw that he was making progress. But he stopped showing up, so I was just checking to make sure he was okay."

Jacques turned back to face Sylvio at the end of the hall, staring at him with laser-like intensity as he attempted to digest the new information.

"Boxing gym? My son was going to an afterschool educational program. At least that's what he told me."

"No, I was taking him to my gym where he began a training program with us. I thought he told you this," Jim said, but Jacques didn't appear to be listening, his eyes still trained on his punished son.

Man, I'm looking at another ass whuppin'. Sylvio still winced from his father's previous round of lashes.

After a few seconds of silence, Jacques turned back to face Jim. "My son was involved in a fight at school a week ago, and he was suspended," he said slowly.

"Did he fight a student by the name of Brandon?" Jim asked, but Jacques abruptly spoke before he could get another word out.

"The name of the student he fought with does not even matter. He should not have been involved in the first place."

"I agree, sir. But this young man, Brandon—assuming it was Brandon that he fought— was victimizing your son. He was scared to walk through the main door because he didn't want to run into him. I saw this, and I took it upon myself to help Sylvio defend himself. Boxing teaches discipline, character, technique—"

"No, it teaches him to be an animal and to react to every single action. That's not how I raised my son!" The Haitian patriarch was now raising his voice. "I raised him to resolve problems using his mind, not his fists."

"Mr. Dominique, with all due respect, sir, I completely understand where you're coming from. I take it that you're from the islands—Puerto Rico, Dominican Republic, maybe even Haiti. It's a different culture, and maybe the environment where you grew up didn't require you to use self-defense tactics."

Jacques raised an eyebrow, cynically.

"But I would like to ask you to take a look around. We're living in an age where most of our children disregard the law, so much so that out of their hate breeds jealousy. They see someone who was raised with principles, such as Sylvio, and they take advantage of him because of it. I'm sorry to be the one to say it, but simply having a mind won't be enough in this society. We have an obligation to teach our sons and daughters to stand up for themselves. We don't advocate starting fights, but we want our kids to be prepared if they have to fight."

"That's not why I sent my son to school! I want my son to learn to talk to someone when he has problems with them. If Brandon was bothering him, why didn't he come to me? I would've spoke with that young man and his parents, and that would've been the end of it."

"Would it be the end of it?" Jim asked calmly. "You won't be in Sylvio's life all twenty-four hours. Neither will Brandon's folks. I promise you, if it was Brandon that Sylvio fought, then Sylvio rightfully defended himself, and

Brandon learned a harsh lesson." With that, Jim threw a sly wink toward Sylvio's direction as if he knew who won the fight.

"I wanted my son to have a productive year, and now, because of your interference, you caused him to get suspended. Don't you understand that this suspension will be on his permanent record?"

"Would you rather have a stained permanent record on your hands or a death certificate?" Jim hollowly asked.

Perhaps, he went too far because it was the final straw for Jacques. "I think it's time for you to go, Mr. Shaw. My son will no longer be a member of your gym, and I don't want you communicating with him."

"But, Dad!" Sylvio protested, but Jacques wasn't hearing any of it.

"Pe' bouche' ou!" he replied angrily, suggesting Sylvio shut his mouth.

Taking the hint, Jim decided to call it a day. "I understand, Mr. Dominique. For what it's worth, I do apologize for Sylvio being suspended from school. That was never my intention. But although he won't get the credit for it anywhere else, I commend your son for finally standing up for himself." With that, he walked off.

Jacques closed the door and firmly locked it before turning to Sylvio. "You can forget about any afterschool programs from now on. It's going to be school and home. Do you understand?"

"Yeah, Dad, I understand," Sylvio said somberly, sulking on the way back to his bedroom.

A couple of days later, Sylvio sat in his room reading The Autobiography of Muhammad Ali. He'd read the book more than five times, but he found it more interesting since he started boxing. He was intrigued by how Ali mentally psyched out his opponents before they fought. It's a strategy that I can use someday if I can ever get back in the gym.

Suddenly, without warning, Jacques walked into the room, carrying a couple of boxes. Throwing them down in front of Sylvio, he said, "Start packing all this stuff now. Hurry up."

"Wait, what are we packing for?"

"We're gonna move out of here, so get to work now."

"Moving? Where to?" Sylvio asked, but Jacques had already left the room.

Once he recovered from the shock of the realization that he and his father were leaving their current residence, Sylvio began packing his belongings, folding up his New York sports team posters and stacking his books in boxes. Jacques wanted to start packing earlier so that the movers who were scheduled to come out would not have much trouble loading the truck. With the help of a family friend and neighbor, Jacques and Sylvio were able to fold up their bed springs, stand their mattresses upright, and pack all their books, cassette tapes, and other belongings into storage boxes.

Later that day, the movers finally arrived. Sylvio read the words on the side of the truck. "Cruz Movers Inc." Attempting to save money on their behalf, Jacques had opted to go with a small private company. Fortunately, one of his co-workers referred him to Luis Cruz, one of the owners of Cruz Movers.

The truck parked, and two Dominican men stepped out and shook hands with Jacques. After giving him his receipt, the men started working, loading the truck with the Dominiques' belongings. As for Sylvio, he found himself occasionally helping, but he knew he wasn't obligated to lift the heavy boxes.

When Sylvio walked outside with his small box of posters, he saw one of the men looking into the passenger seat of the truck as if he was talking to someone, although Sylvio couldn't tell right offhand who he was addressing at the time. But the man seemed to be giving instructions to whomever was in the passenger seat.

"Sientate por favor!" the man ordered as he walked back into the building to resume loading the truck.

"Sylvio! Come here, and get this box for me!" Jacques yelled out to his son.

Sylvio went to get the box from his father. Anticipating a light load, he lifted the box before finding out quickly that it was unusually heavy.

Forget the stairs. I gotta take the elevator for this. He walked to the end of the hallway where the elevator was. Upon stepping out of the elevator, Sylvio lugged the box outside before fatigue took over, and he had to slowly place the box down.

What is in this box? Finally, curiosity got the best of Sylvio, and he peeped inside the box through the opening flap. There was a bevy of his father's old dress shoes, work boots, and tennis shoes. Shaking his head, Sylvio closed the box and proceeded to carry it to the truck.

When he approached the truck to load the box, he heard a loud "Hey!" coming from inside. The greeting was so shrill and loud that it startled Sylvio, causing him to drop the box, which landed on his foot.

"What the hell?" Sylvio shook off the pain and walked to the front of the truck. It didn't take him long to find the source of the voice. It belonged to a little girl, about age eight or nine, sitting in the front passenger seat. This was the person the male worker had been addressing earlier.

As he took a closer look, Sylvio also realized that the girl was Dominican as well with a light-skinned complexion and curly brown hair that partially covered her pretty face.

Smiling mischievously at Sylvio, she said, "Scared ya, didn't I?"

Sylvio shrugged his shoulders. "Not really. I just ain't know someone was in hea."

"Don't lie. You know you was scared," the girl said smugly.

"I just told you. I wasn't scared. What, you can't hear me or something?"

"Sure, and you just dropped the box fo' no reason, right?"

"You got a smart mouth. You know that?" Sylvio bit back.

"Whateva. What you gon' do about it?"

This chick's bold. She lucky she a girl, or I might have knocked her lights out. But there was one thing he couldn't deny: the girl was beautiful. She had a tone that sounded as if she was teasing Sylvio, but he had a strange feeling that she was flirting with him. "What's your name?" He was eager to change the subject.

"Valentina Cruz."

"Cruz?" Sylvio asked, looking at the front of the truck. "So, you mean Mr. Cruz..."

"...is my dad? Yeah."

"Oh, well, I knew that."

"Right, sure you did," Valentina said, laughing.

He noticed Valentina holding a small pinch device, no bigger than a keychain. Every couple of minutes, Valentina diverted her attention toward the miniature contraption. Sylvio recognized it immediately. "Is that a Gigapet?"

"Yup, it's my kitty, Ms. Whiskers." Valentina leaned her virtual device to the window so Sylvio could see her electronic kitty. "I just finished feeding her, and now I'm petting her so she can go to sleep."

"Cool. I used to have a Gigapet too. Mine was a goldfish."

"What happened to it?"

"Uh, well, it kinda died after a couple days."

"Oh no! What'd you do to it?" Valentina laughed again.

"I don't know. I thought I was takin' care of it. I was feedin' it and lettin' it swim freely. Then, before I knew it, I came back from school one day, and he was just floating upside down with X's in his eyes. He went to the big tank in the sky."

"You're a terrible pet owner! Shame on you!" Valentina jokingly scolded Sylvio.

"I know, I know, but it's all good. Besides, I ain't got no time for pets anyway. I gotta get my muscles up. I'm gonna be a boxer one day," Sylvio boasted proudly, hoping that declaration would impress Valentina, but he received a different reaction.

"Really? You don't look that strong to me."

"So, what? I'm stronger than you."

"Maybe, but you ain't stronger than my brothers. I bet if they were hea they would beat the shit outta you."

Sylvio scoffed. After taking on the world's most menacing fifth grader, he didn't feel that anyone could challenge him. "I ain't scared of yo brothas. Where dey at?"

"They're at home playing their Sega Genesis. They're always playing that stupid Sonic game."

"Lucky them. At least they got video games to play."

"You don't have any games?"

"I wish. It's just that my dad—"

"SYLVIO!" There was no mistaking the accent.

"There he goes. It's cool meetin' you, Valentina."

"Wow, he's really strict, huh?"

"You have no idea."

"My dad's like that too. I mean, I like going to work with him and stuff, but sometimes I wish that I could just..." Her voice trailed off.

"...run away?"

Valentina looked towards the setting sun in the horizon, and in her eyes, Sylvio saw someone who shared his pain. Walking back towards his apartment, Sylvio looked back towards the truck, wondering if he would ever see Valentina again.

The Liberty Avenue Apartments down 105th Street came with an unusually cold disposition for Sylvio. After he and Jacques settled into their new apartment, they spent the next couple of days unpacking items and arranging them. Life became a drag for Sylvio, and without any outlet or entertainment system to keep him occupied, he would wait until nightfall when Jacques finally fell asleep to turn off the lights in his room and shadowbox as the moonlight shone through the window.

Right jab, left jab, right hook, left hook, uppercut, slip, slip, block, duck, and double jab.

Working on the combinations that Jim taught him, Sylvio continued fighting imaginary opponents. Sometimes the opponent would be Brandon again, but other times, Sylvio would find himself fighting a man he never thought he'd had to fight. The man that raised him with an iron fist...the man who ultimately broke his family apart. Sylvio would go round for round with his father, and he imagined his father falling in a heap, lying in a puddle of his own blood. Such thoughts were disturbing, but Sylvio knew what was driving the power behind his fists. It was anger and rage.

"Boxing is a combination of controlled rage and passion," Jim had told Sylvio during their previous training sessions. And although Sylvio didn't understand what he meant right away, he finally realized what Jim was telling him.

By the third day after moving, Sylvio was becoming desperate to return to the gym. He needed to find a way to get back to his comfort zone. Jacques had already registered him at Public School 50 about ten minutes away from where they lived, and Sylvio was scheduled to start school the upcoming week. It would be a battle all over again, from becoming familiar with the school, to making new friends, and it was quite unnerving.

On Saturday afternoon, Jacques was at work, and Aunt Miriame was unable to babysit her nephew because of other obligations, which caused Jacques to leave Sylvio at the apartment on his own. With his punishment lifted, Sylvio was finally granted permission to watch TV. While watching an episode of Nickelodeon's The Strange Case of Alex Mack, he heard a familiar voice outside the apartment near their first floor window. When he looked out, he realized the voice was coming from A.D., one of his friends from the gym.

Sylvio's heart skipped with excitement. Opening the window, he called out, "Yo, A.D.! What's up, man?"

A.D. looked for the source of the voice before his eyes landed on Sylvio's window. "Yo, Sylvio! What up, dawg? You good?" A.D. dapped Sylvio through the window. "We ain't seen you at da gym in weeks, son. Jim said yo pops had you on lockdown or something."

"Yeah, it sucks. I wanna go too, but I can't."

"I'm actually going there now. One of my boys is givin' me a ride. You comin'?"

Sylvio thought about it before answering. "I don't know, man. My dad said I couldn't go."

"Is yo pops home?"

"Nah, he at work."

A.D. smiled mischievously. "Ight, let's go," he said. Noticing the look of doubt on Sylvio's face, he added, "Man, don't sweat it. Yo pops ain't gotta know. Just go there for an hour, and I'll drop you back hea."

"And how you gon' do that?"

"Cuz I live hea, fool," A.D replied, laughing. "Second floor. I got you. So, put yo gear on, and let's go."

Sylvio ran to his room and dressed in his Nike shorts and gym T-shirt. Grabbing his spare key, he locked the door behind him and ran out to join A.D. and his friend as they drove to the gym. Elated was an understatement to describe Sylvio's return to Steel Glove Gym.

Although Jim was not pleased that Sylvio had snuck away from home, he was genuinely pleased to have his pupil return. As they began training, Sylvio went to work, punching the power bag with speed and power.

Impressed, Jim walked over to Sylvio. "Man, you are aggressive. You got the speed and power, and you got what it takes. You ready for this ride?"

"Yeah, I'm ready. Let's do it," Sylvio replied as they resumed training.

Chapter 5

oxing fans from all over the tri-state area made their way toward Prudential Center on a cool March evening. The air was buzzing with excitement and commotion upon the upcoming boxing match. Closed within the confines of their locker rooms, two middleweight boxers prepared for their upcoming bout. As the area began to fill up, the boxing analysts and commentators prepared for their broadcast from the skybox that overlooked the boxing ring in the center of the arena. Two of the commentators, George Redman and Lee Skiers, were waiting for the cue from the cameraman. As soon as it was given, the two elderly white reporters began their coverage of the event.

"Hello, boxing fans around the world, and welcome to the Prudential Center in East Rutherford, New Jersey. Today, we have two of the best fighters in the middleweight division facing off against one another, and I'm sure we'll all be in for a great fight," George said.

"That's right," Lee replied. "Now these two middleweight boxers are both fighting for a shot at the middleweight division crown, which is held by current champion Felipe Maximo. Now, let's look at our fighters today, George," Lee added as he pulled up a comparison chart of both contenders for the viewing audience. "One of the contenders in this fight is no stranger to this stage. Kenny 'Kamikaze' Brown, with a record of twenty-four wins and three losses in his professional career, has been on a tear as of late. In his last match against Leroy Misick, he wore down the taller Misick in the tenth round with a flurry of body shots and left hooks that ultimately gave him the decision in the twelve-round bout."

"Kamikaze is a devastating puncher and has shoulders so wide that the moment he gets his opponents on the ropes, it makes escape virtually impossible, and he's able to rack up the points once he renders his opponent defenseless. With six knockouts and the ability to inflict damage with either hand, it's no surprise that he's favored to win this match," George remarked.

"Absolutely, George, but today will be a real test for Kamikaze because, while other opponents seemingly throw the towel against him, tonight he'll be facing a fighter who is as relentless as anyone in the division. Young Sylvio 'Wolf' Dominique, will pose a threat to Kamikaze due to his counterattack," Lee said.

"That's right, Lee," George replied as they pulled up Sylvio's comparison chart. "This young man has a unique, deadly combination of speed and power. His knockout power has been a subject of criticism as he's only knocked out three opponents in ten bouts. But with a record of ten wins and two losses on his resume, there's no denying that The Wolf is a force to be reckoned with, especially in the first five rounds," he added, observing Sylvio's last fight.

"As you can see on the screen, during the last bout with Mexican fighter Pedro Hernandez, Dominique was able to evade the wide right and left hooks thrown by Hernandez, and while ducking, he was able to get inside and get some clean shots at Hernandez's midsection. He continued applying pressure to Hernandez in the seventh round, setting up that devastating right hook, which sent Hernandez to the canvas. Hernandez was unable to rise on his own accord, giving Dominique his tenth victory and his second knockout. So, for Kamikaze Brown to be successful in this fight, he must use his experience, his reach, and his size to his advantage," Lee concluded.

As the two commentators continued providing coverage for the bout, both fighters received the ten-minute warning from the referee in their locker rooms. In one of the locker rooms, Kenny "Kamikaze" Brown was focused on his upcoming fight with a younger, brash opponent. Brown's trainer, 45-year-old Oswald Satch, sat on the stool across from his fighter as he stretched his hands and neck and then got his hands taped and wrapped in gauze. Finally, Oswald helped Brown put on his gloves.

After testing the fit, Brown threw a couple of jabs in the air. "You saw how much shit he was talkin' at the weigh-in?" Brown asked his trainer, referring to the weigh-in a day earlier.

Sylvio walked into the facility. Before he encountered Brown, all he heard was how much he had to respect Brown because he was older and was a very humble man of a few words. But Sylvio didn't intend to bow down to anybody. He certainly wasn't going to begin that night. Looking at Brown, Sylvio chuckled. "Well, this fight finna be ova in six rounds," he said, just loud enough for photographers, beat writers, and journalists to hear. Sylvio thought Brown wouldn't respond, but he took the bait.

"Yeah, it is. Wit' yo ass lying in the canvas. You betta quit talkin' boy. You 'bout to deposit some checks that yo mouth can't cash."

"Boy? This boy's gon' be whuppin' yo ass, and you gonna be my boy when I'm done. You gon' be callin' me Daddy."

Brown, who had been fighting a few years longer than Sylvio, knew that Sylvio was trying to use reverse psychology to get him off his game. "See you tomorrow night. Then we'll find out who's da Daddy," he told Sylvio, looking him straight in the eye before walking off.

It was ten minutes before the fight, and Brown's rage returned. Now more than ever, he wanted to shut that boy's mouth for good.

"Yeah, and you know what? He asked for this, so now you 'bout to show him wassup. No mercy," Satch replied, grimly.

In the other locker room, Sylvio already had his gloves on. With the bright lights glistening from his muscled shoulders and pectoral muscles, he walked over to Jim Shaw, his cornerman and trainer. Sylvio even kept it within the family, entrusting Jim's brother Kevin Shaw as the fight manager and financial advisor. With a balding head and short stature, Kevin sat at the opposite end of the locker room.

Sylvio's friends, Gary Williams and Kyle Green, were in the locker room as well. Sylvio looked at the boys who rode with him through elementary, junior high school, and high school. As a part of the "Wolf Pack," which he'd dubbed his entourage, they knew the real Sylvio Dominique. Everybody outside of Sylvio's circle saw the brash, loud-mouthed boxer who was talented yet enigmatic.

Sylvio felt the familiar sick feeling in his stomach whenever he prepared to step out into the ring. He was nauseous, but he quickly swallowed the bile down into his stomach. Excusing himself to the bathroom, he looked at the mirror. Brown was just another obstacle in his way. Sylvio had his eyes set on one goal: the middleweight title belt. And it wasn't just about the money. He was out to prove that he wasn't just an insignificant being in the world, despite what anybody thought, whether it was his father, his aunt, or the leeches that he thought were his friends throughout high school who only stuck around when they wanted someone with status to associate themselves with. But the belt would legitimize Sylvio among his peers and among his contemporaries in the middleweight division.

Jim walked into the bathroom. "Everything okay, son?"

Sylvio smiled at the man who had groomed him from childhood and prepared him for every fight, from amateur bouts to the professional ranks. "Yeah I'm good."

"It's almost time. Don't worry. You've been hea before. Breathe," Jim advised his young fighter.

Sylvio took a couple of deep breaths. "You don't think I took it too far at the weigh-in, right?" Although Sylvio had berated his opponent, deep inside, he respected "Kamikaze" Brown as a fighter and just hated the media hype that surrounded him.

"Nah, forget about it. It ain't like ya' was gon' be fuckin' wit' each other afterwards, anyway. Ain't no friends in the fight game. He wants what you got, and he's been in it longer than you, so you got all the odds stacked against you. But you've beaten the odds before. Just stick to our strategy. Use your quickness to move him around the ring. Make him use up his energy early. Don't swing wildly because you'll start tappin' out before the later rounds," Jim instructed as he led his fighter out of the bathroom into the locker room.

As soon as the referee came in to beckon them to proceed to the ring, Sylvio tightened his face into a stoic glare as he walked the corridor and heard his theme music playing. The song was a dated rap single, followed by the slow howling of a wolf. The crowd of Sylvio's fans loved howling along with the track because it prepared them for his entrance.

After entering the ring, Sylvio hopped around a few times, warming himself up. As soon as he removed his robe, revealing his black trunks designed with mini pictures of wolves howling on the side trim, Kenny Brown made his way into the ring. From their corners, the fighters glared at each other. As they approached the referee to touch gloves, Sylvio looked at Brown's eyes for any sign of fear, but he saw none. Brown looked determined and focused. The referee read the rules to both fighters, and after they touched gloves, Sylvio went to his corner.

"Okay, I want you to work on that jab this round," Jim instructed his fighter. "He has a longer wingspan, so you gotta find a way to get inside him. Keep him moving around the ring. You got this. It's just you and him. Nobody else matters around hea. Let's go," he added, and as he pushed Sylvio's mouthpiece in, the bell rang, signaling the beginning of the first round.

The fighters approached the center of the ring. With each wary of the other's counterattack, they started by throwing left jabs.

"In and out, Brown. Go to work on him," Satch said.

Early in the round, it became clear that Brown was the aggressor, throwing more jabs at Sylvio's head, hoping to catch him off balance. But Sylvio evaded most of them. Apart from the few that barely grazed his forehead, none of Brown's punches had any impact as both boxers continued throwing soft jabs, each opponent feeling out each other. Sylvio threw a few jabs and a hook at the side of Brown's head, but Brown partially blocked his punches, and very few blows landed.

After three minutes, the first round ended. "Okay, same game plan, Wolf," Jim advised. "Expect pressure from him. He's gonna pick up the pace. He's lookin' for the early knockout. When he comes in wildly after the clinch, get inside of him, and kill the body," he continued, as he gave Sylvio a swig of water.

Both fighters were virtually unharmed as they began the second round. Brown played right into Jim's hands, pressing the attack on the young upstart, but Sylvio withstood the onslaught before wrapping Brown up, causing the referee to separate them. In the split second that they were separated, Sylvio unleashed his five-jab combination. The first two jabs missed, but the third caught Brown squarely in his nose. Reacting to the shot, Brown responded with two quick right hooks to the body. Anticipating the blows as they bounced harmlessly off his arms, Sylvio came back with two hard right hooks to Brown's body, and Brown braced himself for the blows, but there was no mistaking the impact as Sylvio's glove smashed the side of Brown's midsection.

As soon as Sylvio saw Brown lean slightly to his right, he knew his punch had caused damage. He decided to up the ante, getting inside Brown's space and punishing him with body blows. Suddenly, the bell rang. Realizing the round was over, Sylvio began to let up, not seeing an overhand right from Brown as it made impact with his left temple.

"Muthafucka!" Sylvio yelled through his mouthpiece in rage as he lunged at Brown, but the referee stepped in the middle of them, directing Sylvio to his corner.

The crowd, especially those rooting for Sylvio, shouted and protested in outrage by what they saw as a cheap shot after the bell. Jim sat his enraged fighter on a stool to calm him down.

"Did you see what he did? That nigga hit me after the fuckin' bell! He dead now!" Sylvio exclaimed as Brown sat in his corner, receiving the warning for striking after the bell.

"Ignore that shit. He's tryin' to piss you off. Just continue workin' on the body. He knows you winnin' on points, so he's gonna try every dirty ass trick in da book to throw you off." After a few seconds the bell sounded, signaling round three. "Make him pay fo' that," Jim piped as he pushed Sylvio back into the ring.

Suddenly, the crowd disappeared as Sylvio focused on his opponent's movements and began zeroing in on his tendencies. Left arm's not up, which means that's his dominant hand. He must be a south paw. Step back, Wolf. Right hook's coming.

Sure enough, the right hook swung around but wildly missed Sylvio. Spin around and pressure him into the corner.

Then go off on his ass for that cheap shot.

Now Brown was really in trouble. Sylvio's punches were landing fast and often, and Brown felt himself being pushed against the ropes. With his trainers frantically yelling at him to get off, Brown threw jabs and uppercuts, fighting himself out the corner but not before getting tagged again, just above the right eye. Sylvio's punches were finding their marks, and by the end of the sixth round, Brown had red spots, and a small cut had opened above his eye.

When the bell rang for Round 7, Sylvio continued to pressure Brown. Brown, through his many defensive attempts, seemed unable to avoid the stinging jabs that flew out of every direction. The crowd was awed by the quickness and speed of Sylvio's hands as they continued to inflict blow after blow. Brown attempted to use his double right jab and left hook combination—his signature move—but unfortunately, Sylvio anticipated his combinations and easily maneuvered around him, tagging Brown in his ribs and chest. And as he glimpsed down, Sylvio saw his opponent's legs beginning to get rubbery. He knew that Brown was not going to be able to stand much longer. But before he had a chance to land the knockout blow, the bell rang.

Lucky, you was saved by the bell. Sylvio returned to his corner.

Jim looked at Sylvio with a twinkle in his eye. "Oh, he's ours now. We got him. It's over after this round," he said confidently.

Sylvio, although he remained focused, flashed a smile at his longtime trainer. "I was gonna take it easy on da chump, but because of that cheap shot, he's goin' to sleep next round." Sylvio's eyes glinted with the prospect of an eight-round knockout.

When the bell rang for Round 8, Sylvio burst out of his corner with Brown awaiting him. Although Brown attempted to throw counterpunches against The Wolf's attack, they were ineffective, and Sylvio knew it was time to put Brown out.

Finally, a left hook to the right cheek sent Brown onto the canvas as the crowd roared. The referee began the ten count, and Brown managed to get up by the time he got to number eight. But he was only delaying the inevitable, as Sylvio continued punishing him with body shots. Finally, a jaw-jarring uppercut sent Brown down, and the referee began counting again.

This time, Brown couldn't muster the energy to get back on his feet, and the bell rang, signaling the end of the fight. Sylvio raised his hands in victory as the Wolf Pack ran into the ring, celebrating the victory. As both fighters approached the center of the ring, the ref raised Sylvio's hand.

Immediately afterwards, Sylvio walked over to Brown and hugged him in a show of sportsmanship. "Good fight, dawg," he said.

"You too, brotha. Yo, fo' real. We'll meet again soon," Brown replied humbly.

"Aight, man. I'll be waitin'."

The fighters made their way out of the ring and walked into their respective locker rooms.

An hour after the fight, Sylvio was in the locker room, receiving a massage from a local masseuse. With Sylvio lying on his front, she rubbed different scented oils on his back and continued to softly caress his sore shoulders and back. It had become a ritual for Sylvio since his entrance into the professional ranks. As the masseuse continued to work on his back, Jim, who had been talking with the press after Sylvio left for the confines of the locker room, returned to his protégé's side.

"Great fight, bro. Stuck with the game plan. You countered his attack, and you dug deep. But there are some things you can improve on."

Sylvio rolled his eyes from under the massage table. "Here we go," he said in a fake exasperated voice as he rose up from the table and sat down across from his trainer.

"Yo, can't you just give me props just for once? Yo boy's eleven and two now," he smiled smugly at Jim, but his trainer didn't return the foolery.

"Sylvio, I'm serious. Every round, you start off slow, and at times, it's costed you. Matter fact, if you got off to a better start against Chavez, you might have won that fight."

"Yo, come on, man. Why you sweatin' me like this? I told you them crooked-ass judges gave Chavez the fight. If you look at the fight, I was taggin' him all night. I don't even think I got hurt that fight."

"Doesn't matter. He won on points, Wolf. He connected more punches than you did because he was able to pressure you at the beginning of every round. You've gotta learn to keep your guard up, pace yourself, and stay alert at all times, or else Brown wouldn't have thrown that cheap shot at you."

"He got lucky with that. But how good did it do him? The outcome was still the same. Yo boy still got the dub," Sylvio said confidently, dapping Gary.

"Sylvio, I'm tellin' you this for your own good. You can't keep underestimating your opponents cuz one day you're gonna come across that one that ain't got nothin' to lose, and they're gonna use your weaknesses against you. You think Maximo's gonna let you off with just a cheap shot?"

Sylvio marinated on what Jim said for a minute. "Nah," he finally replied.

"Look, I think you got what it takes to win that belt. But you gotta be a technician out there. You gotta strategize when you're in that ring. Boxing is not just about strength. It's about mentally figuring your opponent out. Good fighters like Maximo can use your weakness or even your strengths against you," Jim said, before turning to the masseuse who had stopped massaging Sylvio to listen to the conversation. "Anything I can help you with today?" he abruptly asked her.

"Whoa, whoa come on, man. Don't come fo' Tiffany like that," Sylvio replied, defending the masseuse who was unable to hide the blush from her cheeks.

She had massaged many people, but she had never massaged a personality like Sylvio, and he knew he had her eating out of the palm of his hand. "Don't listen to my hard-headed trainer. He be buggin' sometimes. But nah, I'm good for now, baby. By the way, you got a card on you? Maybe I could give you a call sometime, and we can chop it up on a more personal level. You know what I'm sayin'?"

Tiffany was taken aback that a professional athlete asked for her number. After giggling for a few seconds, she clumsily reached for her purse. "Yeah, I definitely have a card," she replied, handing one to him.

"Ight, cool. I'm definitely gon' holla at you, baby," Sylvio said, flashing his megawatt smile.

"Okay," was all Tiffany could say, clearly flustered as Kyle walked her out of the locker room.

Jim shook his head before looking at Sylvio. "What is that, like, the sixtieth girl you've asked for a number?"

Sylvio shrugged and smiled. It wasn't his fault that he was adored by the opposite sex. "Maybe."

"You a dog. You know that?" Jim laughed.

"Nah, I'm a wolf," Sylvio joked.

Chapter 6

Two days later, Sylvio drove up to Steel Glove Gym in his new black Escalade. As he carefully parked in the lot across the street, he reflected upon the wave of success that he had experienced over the past two years. He remembered the days he'd gone to sleep with an empty stomach, not to mention how he'd grown up with a man who was an authoritative disciplinarian that sometimes bordered being abusive.

While initially enraged that his son returned to boxing after they moved, Jacques realized that he couldn't keep Sylvio away from the gym and eventually allowed him to continue training as long as he stayed in school. Sylvio didn't disappoint. Throughout the years, Sylvio had managed to maintain his grades while still boxing, and he graduated high school with a 3.2 GPA. Jacques still resented Jim Shaw, but he was grateful that Jim never allowed his son to stray into the streets or get himself into trouble. Jim made sure that Sylvio had all the tools he needed to get through high school, and during those years, he began boxing amateur bouts, dominating his division.

The most controversial decision for Sylvio came after finishing high school. It was then that Jacques was at odds with Sylvio about his future. Jacques wanted his son to go to college and work on a substantial career, but Sylvio's mind was made up to continue his boxing career and hold off on college. They often clashed on the issue, and after one encounter led to a shouting match between the two, Sylvio packed his bags and left his father's apartment. He eventually moved in an apartment with A.D. They both worked day jobs as warehouse crew members in Brooklyn, but when A.D. eventually gave up boxing to focus on music production, Sylvio continued fighting amateur bouts and two years later, decided to fight as a professional middleweight boxer.

After filling out countless papers and passing the physical tests issued by New York's Boxing Commission, Sylvio's career finally took off. Jim remained by Sylvio's side as his trainer, and they took the middleweight division by storm, winning the first five bouts. Then reality hit as Sylvio lost his first match in a close decision to Chicago native Alvin Sanders, followed by two more wins, before losing another decision to Jose Chavez.

Needing a win to redeem himself, Sylvio finally re-asserted his dominance with his eight-round knockout of Ken "Kamikaze" Brown. Boxing had its pros and cons, but there was one advantage that boxing gave Sylvio: financial security. He was making money at a clip that no other boxer was earning at the time. With the earnings, Jim began investing in stock, even expanding his gym, opening locations in each of the five boroughs of New York. Of course, the main attraction in the gyms would be the days that Sylvio stopped by, signed autographs, and posed for pictures with his fans. It was a surreal experience for the boy who once thought he would be insignificant to society.

In the months that followed, Sylvio began to establish the Wolf Pack, which consisted of friends, Kyle and Gary. Then, there was his trainer Jim and his brother Kevin, who eventually became his manager. It was Kevin's responsibility to negotiate Sylvio's fights and make sure Sylvio and his crew benefitted from his boxing matches.

One day as Sylvio walked inside the Queens facility, he looked around. A new girl, Sarah Donnelly, was sitting in the seat Angie had occupied for so many years. Jim made some not-so-subtle changes to the gym. It didn't appear the same way that Sylvio remembered it. The old mirrors had been replaced by larger ones, and the gym was repainted and renovated. They had even added a second floor because of the vast expansion.

Jim informed Sylvio that Angie had finally received her qualification as a personal fitness trainer, and he had promoted her to manage the Steel Glove Gym facility in Brooklyn.

Walking inside, Sylvio was unaware that he was in for a surprise. Looking around, his presence created the normal buzz as boxers stopped their training and made a beeline toward the Wolf to shake his hand, dap him up, and pose for pictures and selfies. Sylvio greeted many of the trainers, including a few female trainers, and one of them who wasn't aware that he was approaching her. Sylvio couldn't believe she had come back to town.

He knew Angie from a mile away because her shapely figure was hard to hide. That figure had drawn him to her when he was a boy. I'd recognize that ass anywhere.

Angie had headphones in her ear and was sparring with a male trainer, so it wasn't until the trainer looked at Sylvio that Angie turned to look at him as well. "Oh shit!" Angie exclaimed, turning red as soon as she saw the casually well-dressed middleweight boxer. "Yo, you scared the hell outta me, kid!" she said, hugging Sylvio.

"What's up, Angie? It's been a minute. Yo, what you doin' back hea? I thought you was still out in Brooklyn," he said as he returned her hug.

He was visited by an urge to grab her toned backside, but he refrained. He had to stop being a dog for at least a minute, but Angie wasn't making it easy. Even though she was older, she would still put younger women to shame with her physique.

"I'm still workin' in Brooklyn, but I decided to stop by and get me a quick workout before I go work wit' dem' boys. But how you been? What happened to the short, skinny boy that I remember? I peeped that fight last night on Showtime. You took care of business."

Sylvio shrugged, laughing. "Well, you know how I do. Brown's a good fighter, but he just ain't betta' than ya' boy, you feel me?" he replied, laughing.

"Whateva." Angie laughed, rolling her eyes. "I'm surprised you was able to fit through da doorway wit' your bloated head," she joked, knowing that Sylvio had a big ego.

"Well, this bloated head is eleven and two, so what now?"

"Don't play with me, boy. You gon' be eleven and three fuckin' around wit' me. What you hea to do, anyway? You goin' to church or something?" she asked staring at Sylvio's Versace suit vest with the solid black T-shirt underneath, tucked into gray slacks and designer shoes.

"Nah, I'm here for a meetin' with Kevin. He in the back?"

"Oh yeah, he did mention something about you today. He in his office in the back."

"Aight cool. Appreciate it. Yo we need to chop it up again soon. Don't hurt nobody now. Tell your trainer to take it easy on you. Yo face can't take any more pounding," Sylvio joked.

"Yo mama," Angie fired back, laughing as she turned back to spar with her trainer.

Sylvio walked into the office, where he was greeted by Jim, Kevin, and a third man he hadn't met but remembered from boxing coverages in the past.

"What's up, champ?" Jim greeted, before introducing him to the stranger in the office.

The man had long black hair tied in a ponytail behind his back. What's up wit' this dude's dome?

"Wolf, this is Shareef James. He's a boxing promotor for Showtime and the International Boxing Network. He came to visit us to discuss a proposition," Jim said as Sylvio sat down across from the man.

"It's good to finally meet you, Sylvio 'Wolf' Dominique," Shareef said, shaking hands with Sylvio. "I gotta say I'm a huge fan. I've followed your career from the jump, and I like your style, your grittiness, and you're relentless. You're the type of fighter I can see getting major endorsement deals down the line. So, what's yo record kid? Ten and one?"

"Eleven and two," Sylvio corrected.

"Oh, you lost two fights? To be honest, I thought you got ripped off in that Chavez fight," Shareef said.

"See, I told you!" Sylvio said triumphantly to Jim.

"Anyway, I wanted to discuss promoting your next fight. We're talking about a fight that is expected to rake in at least $12 million dollars for both fighters," Shareef explained.

Sylvio's eyes widened as he looked at Kevin and Jim. Could they finally be setting the stage for his shot at the middleweight title versus Maximo?

"Okay, so what I was thinking is that we promote an inter-ethnic bout. Dominique versus Rosjan Bokavic. The hype machine is gonna be off the chain—" he started.

Sensing a miscommunication, Sylvio cut him off, "Whoa, whoa, whoa. Dominique verses who?"

"Rosjan Bokavic, the middleweight contender from Croatia. We think that we can draw a gate of about twenty thousand fans," Shareef explained, but Sylvio wasn't paying attention to him.

"What's this?" Sylvio asked Jim. "You called me here for a meeting to set up a fight for the middleweight title belt, and I'm being set up to fight some scrub?"

"Wolf, this guy is not just some scrub," Jim replied. "He's a tough opponent, and he lost his last bout a few months back to, guess who? Maximo."

"His trainer said that after his twelfth-round loss to Maximo, he didn't want his fighter engaging Maximo in a rematch right away. He wanted Bokavic to fight top contenders vying for the same title. He saw your match against Brown the other night, so he issued the challenge," Kevin chimed in.

"So, what? I worked my ass off to get this title shot, and now I'm bout to be nothin' more than a tune-up for some nobody? Nah, I ain't feelin' that."

Jim stood up from his chair and gestured to Sylvio to walk outside the office with him. "Excuse us for a moment, Shareef," he said as he walked out with the discontent boxer.

Once outside the office, Jim turned to Sylvio. "What's wrong with you, son? This is the first fight that Shareef has promoted for us. We got twelve mill in the bank, and that's not counting any endorsements. So I'mma need you to man up and take this fight."

"Hell nah! This is some bullshit!" Sylvio exclaimed, their voices slightly lowered so the people inside the office wouldn't hear them. "Just like I ain't gon' be nobody's charity case, I ain't about to be nobody's tune up," Sylvio added.

"Man, think about this, Sylvio. A lot of money is at stake. We got a chance to take this fight, and you can go out there and show the world that you ain't no tune-up. Show 'em that you a force to be reckoned wit' out there by gettin' this win on Bokavic. That'll legitimize you to get a shot at that title. Okay?"

Sylvio, still feeling slighted, reluctantly agreed. With that confirmation, Jim walked back into the room with Shareef and Kevin and whispered something in Kevin's ear.

After a few seconds, Kevin stood up. "After a brief discussion with my client, we agree to take the fight," he said.

"Good. The fight is scheduled to take place at Las Vegas two months from now. I'll let Bokavic's camp know right away that you agreed to do the fight. We start promotin' this baby in three weeks. This will be a bout that'll get all the buzz out. You'll see," Shareef said, as he left the office.

Sylvio turned to his trainer of fourteen years. "Let's go to work," he told Jim while he grabbed his gym clothes and headed to the locker room.

Later that afternoon, Sylvio was sitting on a stool in Jim's living room at his house in Laurelton, Queens. After a light sparring session and countless drills, Sylvio began to work on the strategy that he hoped to employ against Bokavic. With Jim sitting across from him, they were watching films of Bokavic's fights with the first being against the man who had defeated Sylvio: Jose Chavez. The fight started with both fighters searching for openings.

For the first few rounds, Chavez had the upper hand. But Bokavic appeared to be in better shape than Chavez because as the fight wore on,

Chavez began throwing ineffective punches, so Bokavic seized the moment. A boxer with a unique combination of speed and power, Bokavic wore Chavez down in the later rounds before winning the fight in the eleventh round.

In the next Bokavic fight, he was facing off against the current middleweight champion Felipe Maximo. As they stood toe to toe in the ring, Sylvio realized that Bokavic was a few inches taller that his opponent although Maximo had more muscle definition than the challenger. As soon as the bell rang, it was apparent that Bokavic was no match for the champion. Maximo punished him with a combination of stinging jabs and hooks. Easily getting inside Bokavic, Maximo's blows were coming at a quick pace, and Bokavic never had a chance. Yet, he showed extreme bravery, despite the onslaught he endured.

By the beginning of the twelfth and final round, Bokavic was cut above his left eye, and blood was oozing from his nose and mouth. But he bravely stood his ground, and when the bell rang, although the decision easily went to Maximo, the crowd cheered his efforts.

"So, anything that you observed from these fights?" Jim asked.

"Yeah, he's slow," Sylvio shrugged.

"That ain't what I asked, champ. Look at his style. What makes Bokavic one of our hardest opponents to date is his wear and tear style. He's not looking for a knockout early. He's trying to tire you out, so trying to out-speed him early plays right into his hands. He has the body mass to absorb shots and the force to return 'em twice as hard. Once your hands are no longer busy, you become a target to him."

"Aight, I'll give it to him. Ya boy got some power, no doubt. But I'm too fast for him, and I got my own power."

"It ain't gonna be a quick knockout. This ain't Hernandez or Brown. This man we're looking at here will literally pressure you from round to round. He's learned ring pace from his trainer, and he's perfected that for years. Fighters like that are dangerous," Jim warned, but Sylvio was already distracted, replying to a text message from one of his friends.

"Wolf, are you listenin' to me? If you ain't careful against Bokavic, he will wear you down and knock yo ass out."

"Whateva man. Look, I got it covered. He's big, he's slow, and not very coordinated, but he hits hard. You act like I can't avoid any punches, man," Sylvio replied. "I just wanna dust him off inside seven rounds so I can go for that belt!"

"That's another thing. I want you to ease up on all the trash talk in this one."

Sylvio stood up, believing his trainer had finally lost his mind. "What? Come on, man. That's my mantra. You know that. I go to the press conference, I talk some shit, piss the other cat off, go in there, and back my shit up and get another dub. You know what it is. Worked on Brown, didn't it?" Sylvio snickered, but Jim wasn't laughing.

"Look, man. I know you. I know your temperament, but Bokavic is not our enemy. He ain't with all the trash-talkin' mess."

"Anyone who steps in the ring with me is my enemy. I don't care who he is and where he come from. If he knew any better, he wouldn't have chosen to fight me as his tune up, but I guess he gon' learn the hard way." Noticing the exasperation on his trainer's face, Sylvio decided to appease Jim. "Lookin' at the video, I saw that Bokavic doesn't protect his head very much, especially on the right side. His reaction time isn't as efficient, and I saw moments where he never protected his body. I'm surprised his ribs didn't break against Maximo."

"So, what you gonna do? You got a game plan for him?"

Sylvio shrugged. "If it's a long drag-out fight he wants, I'm down to make it that kind of a fight."

"Are you? Because you haven't shown me the ability to last twelve rounds."

"Trust me. The fight won't make it that far," Sylvio returned, eyes still on his phone. "But anyway, I gotta bounce, Jim. I got things to do, so I'll catch you in the A.M.," he said as he left Jim's house.

Once Sylvio was gone, Jim looked toward a once-forgotten photo frame that not only mounted his wall but was also a big part of his boxing background. A ten-year-old boy stared back at him.

I should have done more that day, Dante. I should've gotten there in time. I know it's too late, and I can't change anything, but I would trade any time that I have in this world to spend it with you.

Angrily brushing aside the tear rolling down his face, Jim was determined not to relive the tragedy that broke his family apart and sent his life into a downward spiral.

After leaving Jim's house, Sylvio stopped to greet people and sign autographs outside Baisley Park. Before long he was joined by Kyle, who walked up with another young black man.

"What's good, champ?" Kyle said, dapping his friend before introducing him to the other friend alongside him. "This my boy, Omar Keaton. He just rolled back into town."

But no introductions were needed as Sylvio dapped his old friend, recognizing him immediately. "Oh shit. What's up, boy? Yo, I know him too. Went to I.S. 139 with him before he balled out at Richmond Hill! What brings you back hea man? I know you finna go to da league."

"Yeah, I killed it at Richmond and was eatin' at Iona, but now I'm takin' some time off, workin'. I'mma be ballin' in them summer classics though. Watch me do work at Dyckman next month," Omar replied confidently, referring to Dyckman Park in Washington Heights near Manhattan, known for its summer basketball tournaments.

"No doubt, playa. I'mma roll through," Sylvio said.

"I saw a clip of yo fight against Brown last week. I was tellin' my boys how my nigga Sylvio's doin' da damn thing, on da come up," Omar said.

"All day," Sylvio replied with equal confidence. "I'm training right now for my next fight. I got that bum Bokavic next month."

"Aw, you mean homeboy from one of dem European countries? Man's too slow fo' you. You got that in the bag," Omar replied, before turning to Kyle. "Yo, check it out. There's this new spot that just opened in Astoria— Club Apple Kim or something like that—named after da chick who own the place. Anyway, my dude told me they got some bad jawns up in there, so I'm bout to roll through and drop some bands this Saturday. You down?"

"Oh, hell yeah. You already know. I'm in there like swimwear, dawg," Kyle replied.

"And I know you gonna come through, champ. All dem bitches in there gon' lose they minds when they see Sylvio 'Wolf' Dominique roll up in there," Omar told Sylvio.

But Sylvio wasn't fully sold. "Eh, I've done the club thing too many times already. It be gettin' played out. But what the hell? I gotta have some fun before I train."

"That's my dawg," Omar replied, patting Sylvio on the shoulder.

"But I ain't drinkin', smokin' weed, or doin' none of that hookah shit. For all I know, the NYBC could call me up fo' a drug test the day after," Sylvio said warily.

"Yo, don't even worry about that, dawg, cuz I'mma get you stupid drunk," Omar said, laughing. "Nah, I'm just playin', B. You could post up, and let all the hoes flock to you, like you do everywhere else you go."

"Exactly. Believe me, I don't need to get lit. I still gets mine, you feel me?" Sylvio said smiling slyly. In the back of his mind, he remembered what Jim told him. He couldn't afford to relax for a moment because he finally had a shot at the middleweight crown. But Bokavic stood in the way, and if Sylvio ever got unfocused and lost the fight, he would lose his chance to face Maximo for the belt.

But chillin' fo' one night couldn't hurt, right?

That night at the Apple Kim Adult Entertainment Club women dressed in scantily-clad garments, bikinis, and thongs danced seductively on rows of poles lined throughout the club. A haven for both the hardworking man and woman to the celebrity personalities, the Apple Kim Club had been the hottest spot in town since opening its doors some weeks earlier. While the dancers swayed their bodies to the songs, bartenders and waitresses were working diligently to serve its patrons and strike conversations with the men who came there to escape the pressures of work and, at times, life at home.

Stacy Nicole Redding, the head bartender and assistant manager of the club, called waitresses into the kitchen where a diverse team of chefs prepared orders. Apple Kim Club boasted the best food and catering selections in Queens.

As she grabbed an order of chicken wings, fries, and two beers, a young waitress made her way over to one of the tables in the back corner of the club. After serving her customers, she walked back to the bar, where she awaited another order for two shots of Patron tequila. As soon as she received the order, she quickly served the men at the counter.

"Damn, you are the sexiest waitress that I've ever seen, by far!" One of the men tried to make a pass at her.

The young waitress slightly blushed. "Thanks, I appreciate it," she said nicely.

"No problem. As a matter a fact, can I get yo number to call you tonight?"

Believing it to be a joke, the young woman laughed. "Um, I don't think I can do that," she replied quickly, much to the man's dismay.

His friends laughed upon her rejection of his offer, but the patron didn't find it funny.

"Why not? What's wrong—I ain't good enough for you or something?" the man asked, clearly upset that he was being denied in front of his friends.

"Nah, it ain't that. It's just that I'm already involved with someone," she was trying to quickly diffuse the situation, but the man persisted.

"Really? Where he at?" he asked, looking around.

"Actually, she ain't hea. She work at Club Spades downtown," she replied although it wasn't true.

But the revelation of her being a lesbian seemed to motivate, rather than discourage, him. "Okay, so lemme get her number too," the man said, before realizing he spoke too much.

The waitress rolled her eyes as she made her way back into the kitchen, unintentionally bumping into Sheila Lagares, another waitress. "My fault, Sheila," she apologized. "I just had to get away from the bar. I think these guys had way too much to drink."

Sheila raised her eyebrows. "Uh oh. What did you say to 'em this time, Valentina? Tell me you let him down softly," she said, laughing as Valentina Cruz shrugged her shoulders with a sheepish grin on her face.

Chapter 7

At the end of her shift, Valentina removed her work tag and walked back into the break room where she kept her purse and other belongings. The room was adjacent to the locker room, which was reserved for the dancers and other entertainers. Looking across at the locker room, Valentina saw the dancers making their way back with their earnings for the evening. Trash bags were used to gather the huge increments of single dollar bills that were scattered on the floor. Valentina chuckled to herself while watching the women divide the cash among themselves. She remembered how, when she applied for the Apple Kim Club, Stacy initially offered her a job as an exotic dancer. It definitely was not difficult to fathom.

Valentina stood about five-feet-seven with long black hair that she sometimes curled or colored with brown highlights. She also had an hourglass figure, and some would refer to her as being "slim-thick." Her soft brown eyes drew the attention of various men, including the inebriated man that she encountered earlier that evening. But she had turned down the dancer position and settled for waitress and part-time bartender. She had begun to take online courses in bartending and found it not only rewarding but also satisfying. People seemed to love her service, and the good looks were always a plus, aiding her in receiving big tips.

Another reason she didn't take up Stacy's offer in becoming a dancer was the fact that she didn't want her father to see her dancing on a stripper pole. That was a thought that often mortified her more times that not. Although she was 22 years old—technically old enough to make her own decisions—Valentina knew her father was very traditional and prided on working hard with his hands and building wealth without bodily exposure. This was the essence of hard work that was embedded in her family for generations. Both her mother and her father were immigrants from the Dominican Republic, and they came to search for a better life and opportunities in America, as so many others did before them.

After marrying in their native country, Luis and his wife Ana moved to Queens, New York, where they gave birth to Juan, Bruno, and Valentina. As the youngest child, Valentina was always the child that was most doted on, receiving more gifts during birthdays and holidays, which would make her brothers envious of her. But with that envy came harsh lessons. Her brothers taught Valentina to be tough and to not allow any boy to treat her has an object. They were also fiercely overprotective of their sister and were wary of anyone who dated her.

In later years, her father's once-successful moving company began to lose business. When the United States hit the recession period between 2007 and 2008, the company finally went bankrupt. Luis began working other jobs with other larger moving companies to keep their family fed. Juan and Bruno also worked part-time at Key Food grocery store in Jamaica, New York. But a larger threat loomed over the family as Juan and Bruno immersed themselves in underground gambling rings and gang activity. Although gentrification had all but eliminated the gangs that ran rampant in the area years earlier, there were still a few sects that were considered dangerous.

Juan and Bruno were affiliated with the 85th Street Serps, who were known for their huge investments garnered through fixes of tennis matches, horse races, competitive card games, and boxing. If they were ever crossed, the Serps would retaliate violently. Luis never picked up on the fact that his two older sons were gang members in training. In his mind, his sons were earning their money working at Key Food. Still, he never asked about their extra activities.

Eventually, Juan and Bruno moved out of their parents' home and rented their own apartment on Northern Boulevard. Valentina remained at home while she continued working. The tips she received from her night job as a waitress helped tremendously as she set an account aside to save money to attend a school for the fine arts.

That night she counted her tips and found out she had made over eighty dollars. Not a bad night.

"Aye, chica. What's up?"

Turning around, Valentina realized the voice greeting her from the door was Passion Jenkins, one of the exotic dancers in the club and one of the very few people she considered as a close friend. "What's up, Passion? I'm chillin' just countin' da green," Valentina boasted proudly, holding up the wad of cash.

"Go on wit' yo bad self, girl!" Passion exclaimed as she sat next to her friend.

"Thank you, thank you. You know I aim to please," Valentina said. "How much you made tonight?"

"Girl, I made ova three hunid bones. You know when they feel that passion, they can't help but drop dem bands," Passion laughed.

"You wildin', girl," Valentina said, laughing as well.

"I'm tryin' to tell you, girl. You need to drop dem bottles and get up on that pole one time. Hell, I'll play da tracks for you," Passion urged.

"Nah, I'm good, Passion," Valentina replied.

"Watch, one day I'mma get you up there, and you gonna make money for both of us. I'm still waitin' fo' that penthouse," Passion said.

"Don't worry, girl. We'll get that penthouse. Trust me," Valentina reassured Passion, referring back to the time that when they were both hired by Apple Kim, they bonded immediately and made a promise to get a penthouse in Florida one day.

"Anyway, we got $4 bottle night on Saturday, and you know we got da serious rollas comin' through that night," Passion reminded Valentina.

At the same time, another dancer came through the door. "What's up, Dream?" Passion greeted.

Dream came into the breakroom with a bouquet of flowers and a note. "Some guy dropped this off earlier today for Valentina," she said, handing the flowers over to its recipient, before exiting the room.

"Oh well, Ms Cruz. Those are beautiful. I wonder who dropped 'em off," Passion said.

But Valentina knew precisely who dropped the flowers off, and she wasn't too pleased that she received them. "Pedro," she said in exasperation.

Her ex-boyfriend never understood that it was over between them. They dated for more than two years, but when Valentina found out what activities Pedro was involved in, she worked for months to leave the relationship, even resorting to certain aspects of her early adulthood that she did not like to revisit. But Pedro had been consistent in trying to win her heart back, sending necklaces, flowers, candy, and gift cards despite her constant reminders that they would never be an item again, not to mention all the devious things he'd had her do.

"Damn, girl, he feenin' hard for you."

"I don't give a shit, Passion. He should've thought about that before messin' around wit them other bitches. Did you even see him tonight?"

"Nah, I ain't seen him. He must've had one of his homeboys drop that off. That's really a shame though. I thought ya'll were cute together. And judging the way you used to walk in hea all smilin' and what not, I know he'd be puttin' it down at night too," Passion said laughing.

"Yeah well, all that's history anyway. Besides, I got too much going on right now to be focused on any man."

"Girl, bye!" Passion dismissed her friend. "That's a reason why you need a man in yo life. Tell you what, I got a cousin of mine that stay off Bed-Stuy—real cute—and he ain't wit' nobody. Lemme hook you up."

Valentina wasn't in the mood for her friend's get-laid-quick scheme. "Nah, I'm good, and before you say anything else, you betta' not hook me up with anyone behind my back. I know how you get down, Passion," Valentina warned, laughing.

"Who, me? No, I would never do you like that, chica."

"Really? Well what about that one guy you tried to set me up wit' last week? D'Angelo?"

"Oh, well that was different. I was just helpin' a brotha out by hookin' him wit' my sista. Tell me that you wasn't feelin' D'Angelo though."

"Well, let's say it like this. He wasn't the neo soul D'Angelo. I'd rather see this copy with his shirt on."

"That's cold, Val."

"I'm fo' real. The guy looked like he was packin' a six-pack of beer cans under his shirt, and he smelled like he didn't know what Old Spice was."

Passion laughed.

"Quit laughin', girl. It ain't funny," Valentina added, but she was almost hollering too.

"Well, I ain't givin' up on you. Lemme' holla at my cousin, and tell him to drop by here tomorrow. You gon' like him. I promise." Passion quickly left the room, leaving Valentina to her thoughts before she had a chance to protest.

As the fight between Bokavic and Sylvio loomed closer, Wolf amped up his training, hitting the heavy bag, jumping rope, and jogging around Farmers Boulevard in the morning. Then he started sparring in the afternoon in Steel Glove Gym's Long Island location. Normally, depending on his next opponent, Sylvio's sparring partners varied in size and power. During this session, Sylvio was sparring Tom "Tank" Robinson, a man who stood about six-feet-three, weighing about one hundred and sixty pounds, which placed him around the same size as Bokavic. Tank, a longtime friend of Jim's, had blows that could break his opponents' ribs if they didn't protect themselves.

Jim was in Sylvio's corner during his sparring sessions, urging him on. "C'mon, Wolf, get inside him!"

Through a whirlwind flurry of fists, Sylvio was finally able to break through Tanks defense and managed to land some blows to the body.

"That's it, son. Kill the body, and the head will fall. Stay at it! Keep the pressure up," Jim urged as Sylvio continued pressing his opponent.

The electronic bell finally rang as Tank and Sylvio touched gloves at the center of the ring. Sylvio walked over to his corner as Jim took his headgear off.

"Great job getting into the body, but we still need to work on getting inside sooner than later," Jim said as he gave Sylvio a swig of water. "Bokavic will bide his time and drag the match out as much as he can. Our goal is to end it quickly, but if we can't, we gear up for a 12-round fight, so dig deep."

Sylvio sat in his stool, reflecting on his trainer's words. As he sat panting, he mentally placed himself in a dark place—the place where the media, the fans, and all the "Wolf" hysteria couldn't faze him. It was the very place where he remembered seeing his mother yell at his father for the final time before storming out of their house with his little sister at the tender age of four. It was the place where he endured his father's brutal beatings and his strict upbringing to fight for everything he had.

Sylvio had no time for hanging out with friends or relaxing, even cancelling the kickback at the club with Kyle and Omar because he wanted to think about nothing but the fight. It was no longer solely about the middleweight belt or improving his record. People didn't respect him. He saw the news articles and heard the naysayers on the sports networks: "Dominique doesn't have what it takes. He's overrated, and he's been fighting all easy fights. Bokavic will pose a new threat to Dominique, and he will be in for a rude awakening at the MGM Grand come May."

The talking heads had no idea what they had woken up. They aroused more than just the wolf. They woke up the beast, and he was ready to tear whoever got in his way.

Illuminating neon lights painted colors along the Las Vegas strip as travelers, gamblers, actors, athletes, and other on-screen personalities made their way to the MGM Grand. The air was abuzz with talk about the upcoming main event featuring the towering Croatian boxer versus the young upstart. From the beginning of the promotion tours, the fight was billed as a redemption for Rosjan Bokavic, who was heavily favored to win against Sylvio Dominique. As the slot machines churned in the casino halls for excited players and tourists, both boxers and their entourages treated this sporting event as a business trip.

There was no time for gambling, live shows, or impromptu marriage ceremonies with fake caricatures of Elvis Presley. It was serious business, and the fighters prepared for their upcoming bout. However, to the disappointment of spectators, boxing promotors, and rabid fans, there was no sign of animosity between the two. Bokavic, who was naturally a humble man by nature, did not provoke Sylvio, nor did he attempt any psychological games before the fight. Sylvio, in return, did not berate his opponent or predict any round in which he would win. Unlike Brown, Bokavic remained meek and calm, both in the press conferences and out in public. When asked about his upcoming bout with Sylvio, he praised his upcoming opponent's fierce aggressive style and quickness.

Sylvio took note of the interview and grew to respect Bokavic. In fact, he had so much respect for Bokavic that he nearly considered calling off the fight. He did not want to engage in battle with a man who had been nothing but respectful. However, backing away from it was not an option. Sylvio knew that Bokavic stood between him and his title shot, and he was not going to relinquish the opportunity. He had to give himself a reason to hate Bokavic.

He found that reason, which Jim was quick to remind him. "This man is the media's darling. Don't be fooled by his game. He's tryin' to psych you out before the fight," Jim said, while taping Sylvio's hands. "He's the white knight, and you're the black pawn, but tonight, you gon' teach 'em all that you can play chess too. We gon' go in thea and bust his ass."

Kyle walked into the locker room, returning from the restroom. "Look at this shit," he said, showing Sylvio his odds from the major sports networks.

But Sylvio never flinched, only tightened his eyes in concentration, staring ahead as if he was looking through the wall. So, he's favored to win in five rounds, huh? Okay, it's on now. Now Sylvio really had his motivation. He was resolved to stick it to all the sportswriters, pundits, and critics who doubted him.

"He's not ready for this challenge. I expect Bokavic to win easily. It's a man versus a boy, and we all know who wins that matchup. It won't go the full twelve rounds." Sylvio heard all those quotes from sports pundits and analysts, and he watched the sports shows on television.

Tonight, they'll see. They'll all see.

Finally, it was time. Sylvio and his team received the call from the venue official to proceed into the ring. Bokavic was already in the ring waiting for him. As Sylvio's entrance music played upon his ascent into the ring, the spectators had mixed reactions, some yelling and jeering, others cheering for him. Yet, it went unheard by Sylvio, who was focused on nothing but Bokavic. For the first time since entering the ring, through all the anger and rage at the media, Sylvio felt a twinge a fear.

Measuring at 6' 3" during the weigh-in, Bokavic appeared much taller with his trunks on. That secretly terrified Sylvio.

After the announcer introduced Bokavic and Sylvio to the crowd, both boxers approached center ring. Sylvio eyed Bokavic, glaring at the pretty boy, the white knight the media was rooting on to win the fight. The referee gave the rules, and as Sylvio walked back to his corner, Jim took the few brief minutes to address his fighter.

"Remember, it's about you, not him. This man is standing between you and your destiny—your birthright. Seize it tonight, and shut all they asses up," Jim said, gesturing to the crowd. "Remember the strategy. Straight to the body," he added, placing the mouthpiece in Sylvio's mouth as the bell rang.

The first round started very slow, with both fighters throwing light jabs, reminiscent of the Brown fight, with neither wanting to press the other. Sylvio worked his jabs to the body, using his speed and footwork to avoid the overhand jabs thrown by Bokavic. Toward the end of the first round, Sylvio stepped dangerously inside Bokavic's space and threw three quick crisp punches. But they had little to no impact. Bokavic continued to fight in his pace. After the first round ended, the fighters headed to their corners.

"Good way to end that round. This is how it's gonna be all night. Would be great to get a knockout if you could, but keep paddin' the points. Just remember, in this bout, pace is important," Jim reminded his young fighter.

After a few seconds, the bell rang for the second round.

Sylvio came back out and continued to throw light jabs at Bokavic while his opponent seemed to be unable to catch Sylvio because of his quick lateral movement. Towards the end of the round, Bokavic managed to regain the upper hand. Figuring out that Sylvio would try to press his attack at the one-minute mark of the round, he waited for Sylvio to approach his range. This time, he responded with a quick hook to the side of Sylvio's head. Sylvio did not block the blow in time as Bokavic connected on his left cheek.

Knocked off balance by the blow, Sylvio managed to remain standing, but Bokavic, sensing he had hurt his opponent, continued to press the attack with hooks that Sylvio blocked fervently. Finally, Sylvio tied his opponent up, and the referee separated them just as the bell rang. Walking back to his corner, Jim and cutman Harvey Delmond assessed Sylvio's face. There were a few red marks, and a lump had started to form on his left cheek. Harvey applied a steelwell to Sylvio's cheek to slow the swelling down.

"He got you in that round, kid. Keep your guard up. Remember, it ain't a crime to duck his hooks, Wolf. Stay on him," Jim instructed Sylvio.

The bell rang, signaling Round 3. As both fighters approached the center of the ring, many thoughts ran through Sylvio's mind. This guy punches hard. I gotta stay away from his right hooks. Bastard's droppin' bombs from the left and right. Come on, hands. Stay busy.

A left jab to the Croatian's head by The Wolf caught Bokavic off guard. In a quick second, he saw his opening and unleashed a jarring uppercut through Bokavic's defense. Sylvio continued to rain a flurry of blows towards the body, but Bokavic, although hurt, remained valiant and responded with a few left jabs of his own.

Sylvio backed away, his face as stoic as ever, but one thought burned in his mind. I threw my best combinations at this guy, and he's still standing. What's it gonna take to knock him out?

Bokavic advanced toward Sylvio. Although his face was red and puffy from Sylvio's jabs, he showed no signs of slowing down before the bell rang. The round was finally over.

"Okay, judging by the way this shit's goin', both of ya are just about even, which means it could come down to a decision. You gotta knock him out, Wolf. The last thing you want is for the fight to come down to another decision. They could pull a Chavez on you again," Jim warned Sylvio.

But the fight continued. By the end of Round 7, Sylvio realized that it was going to be a long night. Bokavic seemed to have reserve stored up somewhere in his body. It seemed after every round, he got stronger. By Round 10, Sylvio was panting heavily. Harvey poured water down his throat and wiped the perspiration from his face. Sylvio's head had a few bumps, and he even got a small cut just above his eyebrow that Harvey was applying an astringent gauze on to stem the blood flow.

In Round 11, both weary fighters came out swinging once again. Bokavic now seemed intent on knocking out his opponent, throwing a range of headshots, but none of them landed. Sylvio, taking Jim's advice, ducked the wide swinging blows and continued chopping away at Bokavic's body with right and left side hooks. He saw a red spot formed above Bokavic's chest where his glove had found a home. He continued pounding away while Bokavic threw uppercuts, trying to keep Sylvio at bay. The round ended, and judges were still scoring the fight even.

"Final round, Wolf," Jim said. "Everything is instinct right now. Breathe, breathe," he repeated, calming down his fighter. "You're tired, but so is he. He ain't got nothin' left. Now's your chance to go out there and tear into him. Don't give him an inch," he added as the bell rang for the final round.

Both fighters met at the center of the ring to touch gloves. After the gesture of sportsmanship, the battle was on. Bokavic continued to look for the knock-out blow by throwing more punches at Sylvio's head, but Sylvio noticed that Bokavic wasn't throwing the punches with the same effectiveness. They were coming like slow cannons. Sylvio, arms heavy and sweat pouring down in streams from his body, pushed himself to continue pressing Bokavic, but no matter what he did, he couldn't get Bokavic against the ropes.

Bokavic decided to switch tactics and threw two right hooks to the body that connected and caused Sylvio to double over in pain. In retaliation, Sylvio threw more stinging jabs at Bokavic's face, and they landed as the blood started dripping from Bokavic's nose. Bokavic clinched his pressing opponent, and both fighters were exhausted when the bell finally rang. The fight was over. Both fighters made their way back to their respective corners, and the announcer came back into the ring.

It's gonna happen again. It's the Chavez fight all over again. They're gonna give Bokavic the decision, and I'll never get my shot. Sylvio knew that he couldn't knock Bokavic out. He just hoped he scored enough points to win.

"Ladies and gentlemen, we have a split decision!" the announcer bellowed on the ring microphone, and the crowd yelled in response. Some of them were thinking Sylvio won the fight while others gave the fight to Bokavic. There were three judges ringside, and when they gave their cards to the announcer, both men waited for the outcome.

"Winning the scorecards two-to-one, the winner of today's middleweight bout..." the announcer began while Sylvio closed his eyes. He couldn't bear to hear the words that were going to come out of the announcer's mouth next.

Chapter 8

The locker room door burst open as Kyle, Gary, and Kevin ran inside, the adrenaline of victory ringing throughout the air.

"YEAH, BOY!" Kyle yelled ecstatically as he high-fived Gary and Kevin.

Before long, The Wolf entered the sanctuary of his locker room den. After it was announced that he had won a split-decision against top contender Rosjan Bokavic, the whole crowd went into bedlam. Many were fans of Sylvio, so they celebrated raucously while Bokavic's fans protested, stating their fighter had been robbed.

After embracing each other in the center of the ring as a sign of sportsmanship, Bokavic whispered briefly in Sylvio's ear, patted him on the back, and returned to his locker room with his trainers. Jim hugged Sylvio so hard that his fighter winced in pain. His excitement had him forgetting that Sylvio had just fought the hardest bout of his career.

At first, it hadn't sunk in for Sylvio that he had won. It was a bout that he had been favored to lose by all the Vegas oddsmakers and gamblers, but tonight they all paid the price for underestimating him. Jim taught him to channel the rage towards the ring, and he performed masterfully.

"Good shit, son!" Gary said while fist bumping Sylvio.

"Appreciate it, homie," Sylvio replied.

"Way to take the fight to him, Wolf. Now, you've proven yourself as a true boxer in this game. It's not just about technique. You showed endurance, perseverance, and stamina tonight, and those are the true characteristics of a fighter," Jim said. "There are still people who are gonna doubt you, but I believe in you, and your team believes in you. Now you've earned the chance to get a title shot."

"Thanks, Jim," Sylvio said. He was barely able to move. Every inch of his body was sore, and his left cheek had significant swelling, so he was icing it with a pack.

Stanley Givens, his public relations agent called him into the press room for interviews. After a few minutes, Sylvio, although in pain, managed to shower and dress up in a black Blair Underwood suit with designer frames. He stepped into the conference room at the MGM Grand with Jim and Frank by his side. As soon as they opened the floor for questioning, Jim looked at his fighter, hoping he would be able to answer without tempers flaring.

"Mr. Dominique, there are some people who believe that the fight was judged incorrectly. There are those who said that Bokavic was robbed and that he should have won the fight. What do you say to that?" an interviewer from NY1 News asked.

"It was a fight that could have gone either way. Bokavic has a lot of power in both fists, and he's one of the toughest guys I've faced in this division, so I understand why his fans may say that he won, but the judges have the final word," Sylvio replied, shrugging. Now they want me to apologize for winning? They better go sit down somewhere with these lame-ass questions.

"After the fight was over, Bokavic walked over to you, and we saw him whisper something in your ear. What did he say?" another interviewer asked.

"He just said that it was a good fight, and he wished me good luck in my next fight. He also said that we'll meet again, so I know it's not over between us," Sylvio answered.

"Mr. Dominique, there are indications now that you've defeated Bokavic that you are now ready to contend for the middleweight belt, currently held by Felipe Maximo, who is undefeated. Do you think you have what it takes to challenge a seasoned fighter such as Maximo?" a third interviewer asked.

Sylvio mulled over the question for a minute. Although in the past, he was known to berate his upcoming opponents before a match, this time he was aided by Jim's advice and instinct, which told him not to brag about the next opponent.

"At this time, I don't know who my next opponent is gonna be, so I'm just gonna celebrate this win today, then head back to New York to rest and recuperate. Then it's back to the gym to prepare for the next challenge," he replied. "But if it is Felipe Maximo, I know that I got my work cut out for me. He's an excellent fighter and tactician in the ring, but I believe I can hold my own against anyone."

The answer seemed to satisfy the interviewers because they grew silent. Nobody had another question, which caused Sylvio to smile, remembering what Jim told him about the press. "All they want is another story, Sylvio. The press, while very informative, is also a very dangerous entity. Their job is to mainly stir up controversy, and they do so by twisting your words or by underestimating you. If you show them up, they ain't got nothing to say," he would say.

As soon as the interviews were over, Sylvio walked back to the locker room to grab his sports duffel bag. Kyle and Gary joined him within minutes. "Ight, Wolf, level wit' me hea man. What's it gon' take to bring you out into this nightlife man?" Gary asked.

"Right, you da champion, bruh. You in Vegas. They got Rehab pool party out hea, and they got casinos. If I thought Atlantic City got casinos, this is the king right hea, dawg," Kyle chimed in.

"Nah, man, I'm sore as hell right now. Ya go ahead, and do ya thing. If you win some cash at the casino, break me off a lil' somethin'," Sylvio replied, laughing.

"Yo, you buggin' right now, dawg. You just made $12 million dollars tonight. I know you ain't gon' need no damn money from me," Kyle said laughing.

"Nah, I'm just playin," Sylvio said. "Go have fun. I'mma just lounge in my hotel room tonight. "Damn, I'm definitely gonna need a massage too," he added rubbing his sore shoulder. "Where's Tiffany when you need her?" he asked the members of the pack.

"Man, forget that bitch. I could go to the nightclub on da strip and bring you five Tiffanys," Kyle said, laughing.

"Yeah, true that," Sylvio replied. "Yo, but on the real though, what about that spot in New York? Apple Kim or something like that? You said they had some bad females up in there."

"Oh no doubt, man. These women are A1, but we can check it out when we get back to New York," Kyle said.

"Aight bet. Next Saturday we'll go there so I can see what the hype's all about," Sylvio said as he went back to his hotel room for the evening.

Apple Kim's Adult Entertainment Club flashed red, gold, and blue lights for most of the evening as young adults made their way into the club. As the line stretched beyond a block, the bouncers were busy at work, checking identification and opening an express line that was separated by a velvet rope and was reserved for celebrities and athletes making their way into the club.

At about 10 p.m., a black Escalade stopped directly in front of the club doors. Kyle was the first to step out, followed by Gary and Harry Delmond. Then two other men in black polo shirts, black pants, and army-fatigue style Timberland boots stepped out. Finally, Sylvio appeared from the Escalade, causing the crowd to yell itself hoarse. Several fans even pressed the line to get a glimpse of him or a chance to get his autograph. But Sylvio was closely surrounded by the two bodyguards who rounded out the Pack: LaTravion Anders and Simeon Bronson.

As Sylvio approached the door, the bouncer turned to greet him. "What up, champ?" he said, dapping Sylvio.

"Wassup, big homie? Packed house tonight," Sylvio replied, glancing at the crowd.

"Hell yeah, we got all da' high rollas comin' through tonight, playa. VIP's ready fo' you, dawg," the bouncer confirmed, opening the brass-handle red doors.

"Good lookin' out, B.," Sylvio said as he and the rest of the Wolf Pack made their way inside the packed club.

Exotic dancers were already putting on shows for their clients. The air was full of music, lust and opportunity with women prancing around in their lingerie. Some wore only a bra with no panties underneath the thin layer of cloth that partially covered them. One woman that walked past the Wolf Pack was stark naked, unabashed with her breasts and vagina exposed. Sylvio wondered if the girl was aware that she was even naked. But that didn't bother him one bit.

"Oh, yeah. This shit's bout be lit!" Gary said as they walked towards the right end of the club to the VIP rooms. As the Pack made themselves comfortable, an older black woman emerged from a back room and walked toward them.

"Wassup, Mr. Dominique! Welcome to Apple Kim Adult Entertainment. It's a huge pleasure having you hea. I'm the owner, Kim Simmons, and I hope you enjoy your evening. If you have any concerns, feel free to approach me. And I do mean any concerns," Kim gushed seductively, passing Sylvio's bodyguard a card before retreating to her office.

"No doubt, Kim. Thanks," Sylvio said as the bodyguard handed him the card.

Kyle scowled at his friend. "Must be nice, huh?"

"What you talkin' bout, man?" Sylvio smiled sheepishly.

"To have pussy thrown in yo face twenty-fo' seven, dawg," Kyle replied, laughing.

Sylvio shrugged. He couldn't help it if the ladies couldn't keep their hands away from him. "Yo, I know you ain't hatin', dawg. Don't even sweat that. There's plenty of coochie out there. I gotta share the wealth, man. Can't have 'em all to myself."

"Whateva, man. Lemme get us a drink real fast. Yo, waitress!" Kyle called to one of the waitresses at the bar. "Lemme get four bottles of Moet and some Patron," he said, and she went to the kitchen to get their orders.

"Yo, what up, champ?" a loud voice yelled from Sylvio's right side.

Turning around, he saw that it was Omar.

"What up, son?" he greeted as Omar tried to make his way over to the VIP section before he was stopped by Latravion and Simeon.

"Yo, fellas, he straight. You can let him through," Sylvio said, and the two bodyguards stepped a few inches apart to let Omar into the room.

"Damn, man. I thought fo' a minute, you weren't gon' call off your foot soldiers, dawg," Omar said.

"I know, man, but it's necessary nowadays. Cats out hea be tryin' to stick you fo' your paper. Can't take no chances," Sylvio said seriously.

"Yeah, but you finna be world champion soon, anyway. Ain't nobody gon' be fuckin' wit' you when that happens," Omar reminded Sylvio.

"If that happens..."

"What you mean?"

"I don't even know if they gon' give me a title shot. It's funny how hard I be goin' in the gym, and I still gets no respect in this fightin' game, man."

"So, what? Forget all da haters. That's the same shit they'd be tellin' me when I was ballin," Omar said. "Everybody was tellin' me how I suck, I ain't goin' nowhere, I ain't gon' be nothin...all that. So, I went up to Iona, averaged a triple-dub and dumped on all they asses. Of course, I ain't go pro yet, but I ain't givin' up on that. My time's coming, and soon your time will come."

"Appreciate it, man. Yo, when I get to the top, I ain't eva' gon' forget who really ridin' wit' me. You one of da' real ones, man," Sylvio said, dapping Omar.

"Real talk, B.," Kyle chimed in.

"You already know," Omar replied. "Aight, aight, ya done got me all sentimental and shit. I'm tryna get lit tonight, you feel me. Matta fact, lemme get ya a private lap dance real quick," he added as he walked to request a few dancers for their VIP room.

"Aye, good lookin' out, man, and if that NBA thing don't work out, there's always room for you in da Pack!" Sylvio shouted as Omar jokingly flipped him the bird.

Aye Dios mio. It's busy as as hell today. Valentina and the other waitresses ran orders from table to table and to and from the kitchen for their customers. As she approached the kitchen for her next order, she was pulled aside by her manager, Kim.

"Aye, Valentina, I need you to run these two bottles over to VIP," she said, handing her the bottles.

"Yeah, sure no problem. Who's the order for?" Normally, when she was asked to deliver bottles to VIP, they were ordered by a movie star or a famous athlete. She was hoping for the latter because she didn't follow sports very often, except when it came to her ex-boyfriend, who was an avid boxing fan. His brother also happened to be a middleweight boxer, so he took the sport very seriously, often more serious than their relationship.

"Order's for middleweight boxer Sylvio Dominique," she replied before walking back into the kitchen.

What a weird name. But he sounds familiar. I've heard that name in the past, but where do I remember it from? Valentina made her way to the VIP section. With those thoughts still lingering, she approached the suite where two bodyguards were standing in front of the room. She saw that two strippers were already at work, dancing and gyrating seductively for the boxer and his friends. As she walked closer to the scene, the bodyguards began to create a barrier, blocking her entrance.

"Two bottles for Mr. Dominique," she said. The bodyguards stepped aside, allowing her access inside the room. Valentina walked into a madhouse, where two men were throwing dollar bills at one of the strippers, who

Valentina recognized as Kandilicious. The other stripper, nicknamed Tangerine, was already in her birthday suit, her garments spread all over the floor, except for the black tape strap she had around her waist that allowed men to slip dollar bills around her.

All the men appeared to be having a ball, and Valentina expected no less than a wild scene before she even entered the room. However, she couldn't take her eyes off one of the guys sitting between his rowdy friends. Holding a bottle of Moet in one hand, his shirt partially torn off his shoulders, he was hypnotized by her two co-workers, not realizing she had walked in. Once he finally caught Valentina's eye with his dark brown skin and muscular physique, she noticed he was in peak shape. She knew right away she was staring at Sylvio Dominique. One look at his piercing eyes, chiseled cheekbones, and lips took her back fourteen years. She could almost hear his voice as if they were nine again.

I gotta get my muscles up. I'm gonna be a boxer one day.

She remembered how skeptical she was that day as her family was helping him and his father move out of their apartment. Now, here he was in the club, not only a well-established boxer, but a good-looking one at that.

"Order for Mr. Dominique," she said, but to her dismay, it was one of his friends who answered her.

"Oh damn. Appreciate that, baby. You come hea to shake yo ass, too?" one of the other men asked.

"No, I'm just a waitress. That's all," Valentina replied.

"Come on, stop frontin," the man said. "You ain't even a naughty waitress?"

A quick glance at the man's eyes told Valentina that he was already drunk. "No, I'm not. You ain't heard me the first time?" she asked, and the other men fell silent after hearing the quick reply from the waitress.

"You talkin' to me, shorty?" he asked.

Instead of satisfying him with an answer, Valentina turned to walk away when she felt a violent tug on her arm.

"Hold up. I asked you a question, bitch. I ain't feelin' your customer service," he slurred.

Hell no! Now this guy's walking on thin ice. "Get yo hands off me," Valentina warned.

"Aye, aye, Gary. What's up wit' you, man? Always tryin' to start something. You don't grab no lady like that," Sylvio said.

Gary released his hold on Valentina. "My bad, boss man. She walkin' up hea wit' an attitude. I was just lettin' her know wassup."

Shaking his head, Sylvio turned to Valentina. "Yo, excuse my homeboy ova there. He be playin' too much. Thanks for the extra bottles," he said, reaching into his pocket to pay Valentina.

She waved it off. "Don't worry 'bout it. It's on da house."

Sylvio still handed her the money. "Nah baby, this is a tip. Just to show my appreciation,"

Valentina could tell by his hazed eyes that he was slightly inebriated as well. "Thanks, Sylvio. I appreciate it. I'm a huge fan by the way," she lied, knowing full well she hadn't watched any of his fights.

"Um, it's Mr. Dominique to you," another member of his crew interjected.

"Yo, shut up, Kyle. Ain't nobody tryin' to hea all dat," Sylvio replied before turning to Valentina. "Please call me Sylvio."

"Okay." As she started to walk out of the room, she didn't know what made her do so, but she blurted out: "Sylvio, I know this is kinda random, but we actually met before. A long time ago, we were talking when you were moving out of the old apartment when we was kids. Sounds weird, I know, but I was wondering if you remembered me?" she asked, before she realized she may have made a fool of herself.

Sylvio absentmindedly looked at her while the members of his entourage laughed. "Yo, what is this chick on? Must be that good kush cuz she outta her her damn mind," Kyle said, laughing.

Valentina could feel herself blushing. Maybe she should have kept her mouth shut.

"Nah, it's been a minute. I mean I moved a few times as a kid, but nah, I don't remember you cuz I definitely wouldn't forget that beautiful smile," Sylvio replied.

Valentina hung her head a little. Of course, he wouldn't remember me. Who was I kidding? He's a big-time athlete, and I'm just a regular person. He probably met hundreds of girls after me.

"Whoa, whoa, hold up. What's yo name though?" Sylvio asked.

"Don't worry about it," Valentina walked out the room, disappearing among the throng of dancers in the club.

After the waitress left, Sylvio got up to follow her, leaving his temporary carnal entertainment to his entourage.

"Yo, Wolf, where you goin', dawg?" he heard Kyle yell behind him, but the rest of his words went unheard as Sylvio disappeared into the crowd.

He initially waved his security detail off because he didn't want them to follow him everywhere throughout the club, but he found it difficult to walk the length without being stopped by excited fans or other strippers.

In the maze, Sylvio saw a woman's brown hair, tied in a ponytail, disappearing behind a back door of the club. He followed a few feet behind her, making sure he was silent so she wouldn't hear him coming. She walked out and took a deep breath of the warm New York air.

Damn, what am I gonna say to her? I wasted all that time walking out here, and I'm out here scrambling to find something to talk about. Come on, Wolf, man up. Sylvio approached the waittress. "Hey, you neva told me your name," he said before laughing when he realized he'd frightened her.

"Oh my God, you scared the shit out of me," she said, clearly flustered.

"My fault, B. I ain't mean to scare you. I was just tryin' to figure out somethin' to say."

"What's wrong? Did the cat bite the wolf's tongue?" she joked.

Damn this girl is feisty as hell. She remind me of this other girl I met years back. Then the sudden realization of who she was hit him. "Hold up. I remember you now. Gigapet girl, right?"

That caused the young woman to laugh. "Really? 'Gigapet girl?' That's all you remember about me?"

"I mean, I ain't really too good with names, and to be honest, I'm a lil' tipsy right now. You can help a brotha out wit' some hints."

The waitress looked at him intently, her brown eyes scanning him as if she was trying to process him. "Okay, if you want a hint about my name, it starts with a V, and that's all I'm telling you." She didn't know why, but she enjoyed making him work for her attention. She quickly realized that Sylvio was not as obnoxious as most TV personalities were.

"Okay, don't tell me. I got this. It's Victoria, right?"

"Nah," she replied, laughing.

"No, no, no wait. It was Val-something. Val---erie?" He was hoping his answer was correct, but it wasn't. "Okay, stay wit' me, girl. I ain't thrown in da towel yet. Is it Valentine, like da holiday?"

"Close, but no dice."

"Well, your name should be Sexy, cuz you definitely got it goin' on," Sylvio said, throwing away all pretense. When the joke didn't amuse her, he suddenly became serious.

"Nah, I'm just playin'. You're Valentina, right?" By the way she smiled, he knew he guessed correctly.

"How'd you figure it out?"

"Cuz, I remember thinking back then that your name's spelled the same way as Valentine, only with an 'a' at the end, and I thought that was because you was an angel."

Ater he said those words, Valentina couldn't help but to blush for moment before getting herself together. "So, how many women did you use that lame-ass line on?"

"It wasn't a line. I'm fo' real. It was so messed up cuz of the way things went down between me and my dad. Meeting you that day was really the only positive thing that happened at that time," Sylvio confessed.

To his surprise, Valentina laughed. "Oh, break out the violins! You gettin' soft on me, Sylvio?"

Sylvio suddenly realized that Valentina was a street-smart young woman. "I'm anything but soft. You could see that in the ring, right?"

Valentina didn't reply for a few minutes, and her eyes began shifting. "Yo, can I keep it real wit' you?"

"Yeah, what's up?"

"I lied when I said I was a huge fan of yours. Honestly, I ain't a boxing fan, and I ain't neva seen none of your fights," she confessed.

Sylvio's mouth dropped open. "What? You ain't watch me rumble against Brown, Hernandez, and Bokavic?"

"Nah, I'm sorry. I don't even recognize them names you just mentioned. My bad," she apologized.

Sylvio waved it off. "It's all good. I don't expect everybody to know me like that. To be honest, the whole 'Wolf' thing is a persona that I put on before each fight. It's like self-promotion, you feel me?"

"Yeah, I got you," Valentina smiled. "Oh, and by the way, I don't have that Gigapet anymore."

"Well, in this day and age, who does? Did yours eventually die on you?"

"For your information, no. I took care of my kitty till my batteries ran out, unlike the way you treated your poor fish, Mr. Boxer."

As the night rolled on, Sylvio and Valentina continued talking, disregarding the club scene behind them.

Never thought I'd find a girl that's chill like this chick.

Chapter 9

Neighborhood kids and young adults from every borough filled the bleacher seats at Dyckman Park the following Saturday as the annual Summer Basketball Tournament kicked off with the Red squad facing off against the Gray squad. A tradition that has been held for decades, the Dyckman Summer Basketball tournament featured some of the best young talent in the tri-state area, ranging from high school phenoms to professional basketball players. Among those watching in the stands was none other than Sylvio, accompanied by the Pack. He was fortunate enough to get a courtside view of the action. While he was always grateful when people approached him to sign autographs, he was also thankful that the attention wasn't placed solely on him this day. It was about the talented pool of basketball players that were participating in the event.

Omar was the captain of the Gray team. He felt confident that his squad would win the game because he had two other All-American players on his team, and of course, he wasn't new to the streetball scene. But the Red team boasted talent of its own, led by a player who stood over six-feet-six and had skills to match Omar.

Sylvio sat down and ate some pretzels while he watched the two teams go head-to-head. Although he was a boxer by profession, Sylvio always loved the sweet artistry and fluid movements of basketball. He played the sport when he was younger but quickly found out that basketball wasn't for him. He figured if one shot about five brick shots and two airballs each game that he participated in, that God was telling him to stick to boxing.

As soon as the game started, Omar began to demonstrate why he had been a standout player at Iona, using fancy dribbling and crossover moves to finish with smooth layups at the basket.

Both teams had the word "Dyckman" printed on their jerseys, so the announcers followed by their jersey colors. There were four quarters in each game, but instead of 12-minute quarters, each quarter was only seven minutes. With the same standard rules as college basketball and the NBA, each player strived to perform with maximum effort, not only to impress the predominantly African-American crowd that enjoyed seeing highlight plays, which included several rim rattling dunks and consistent three-point shooting, but also to impress professional scouts from the NBA. International professional teams would watch these games too, and if they were impressed with a player, they would give him or her an offer for a try-out.

Sylvio knew that Omar waited for this moment to prove that he was underrated and that he could play the game.

One aspect that made the games interesting was the trash talking that took place between players on the court, but it seemed that nobody talked more trash than Omar. When he was in his zone, he would let his opponent know about it. During one play, he stutter-stepped his defender, freezing him in an isolation, before draining a three.

"That's automatic, B.!" he yelled at the six-foot-six player who guarded him.

But that player didn't back down. When he came across the floor, he took a few dribbles and stepped into his own shot, which was a long two. "Right back at ya," he said, winking at Omar.

Sylvio, being courtside, was able to hear the conversation between Omar and the extremely talented player from the Red team. In the third quarter, with the Red team holding a slim 40-36 lead over the Gray team, Omar used his wingspan and quickness to knock the ball away from his defender. With nobody able to catch up to him, he finished with a ferocious two-handed dunk that excited the crowd. Omar prematurely celebrated the play by dapping fans in the stand, including Sylvio.

"They can't hold me!" he yelled confidently to the crowd.

But Omar would quickly realize that he spoke too soon because while the Gray team-built momentum off the play, the Red team started to expand the lead. The captain of the Red team began to show his dominance. He started by dishing off a couple of no-look passes that excited the crowd and ended up being dunks for his teammates. He continued to abuse Omar on the offensive end, driving past him for layups, and in one play, Omar had to guard him. But Omar left too much room along the baseline, and the captain was able to drive past him and throw down a vicious two-handed reverse dunk, hanging onto the rim for emphasis. The crowd went into a complete frenzy.

Even Sylvio took a couple of breaths, shaking his head. How was Omar going to top that play?

As the action continued, Kyle asked Sylvio, "So what was up between you that waitress at Apple Kim's the other night? Ya hooked up, or what?"

"Nah, man, it wasn't like that. I just remembered her from years ago when we were kids. We were just catchin' up. It wasn't nothin."

"Right, so you were just catching up for ova two hours. Whateva you say, Wolf. The club was almost empty by the time you got back. L.A. and Simeon were lookin' all ova the club, thinkin' you got held up."

"Well, I got back, right? So, we can squash all that noise, man. I ain't tryin' to talk about it now. I gotta watch my boy battle. He gettin' worked by dude from the Red squad right now." Sylvio turned his attention back to the game.

By the three-minute mark of the fourth quarter, most of the crowd was standing up, expecting a close finish. The score was 83-81 as the Gray team stormed back to take a two-point lead. People were waiting to see what would happen between Omar and the captain of the Red team who appeared to have his number throughout the game. While he was on offense, the Red captain took three dribbles and pulled up for a long three beyond twenty-six feet.

Swish. The Red team was back up by one. Omar had the ball in his hands, but looking at his opponent clapping his hands in front of his face taunted him. Omar used a quick first step to get past him and pulled up for a mid-range jump shot. It rattled home, and the score was 85-84. The captain wanted the ball back, and Omar began to play defense more aggressively, swiping at the ball to get a steal. The other eight players on both teams appeared to be part of the onlookers as the game became a man-to-man showdown.

With Omar overplaying his opponent on defense, the Red captain said, "Why you reachin', dawg? Betta' back off before I put another one in yo eye." Then he proceeded to step back and knock down a three over Omar's outstretched hand.

87-85. With less than a minute left, Omar had the ball and gestured for one of his teammates to set a pick to block his defender, but the Red captain saw the signal and fought over the pick easily to remain on Omar. Now only thirty seconds were left on the clock.

Omar knew he had to make his move. But he unwisely exposed his dribble directly in front of the Red captain. Sensing that Omar was going to go for the crossover, the captain cleanly stripped the ball away from him. Within a few seconds, he was at the other end, throwing down a windmill dunk before coming down with a primal yell. The buzzer sounded, ending the game with a final score of 89-85.

Omar's head bowed in defeat. Sylvio couldn't help but feel bad for his friend. He knew how badly he wanted to show out for his neighborhood.

The Red captain was awarded MVP of the game. When he walked over to Omar, he dapped him up in a show of sportsmanship. "Good game, man. But you shouldn't have tried that weak crossover in front of me at the final minute. It ain't worked when we were kids, and it don't work now."

Omar managed a laugh. "Whateva, man. I got you next year. Watch," Then he called Sylvio over along with his pack.

"That was a helluva game, yo. Both of ya were goin' at it," Sylvio said.

"Yeah, but this man kicked my ass again," Omar replied, gesturing to the Red captain. "But yo, where my manners at? Sylvio, you remember my boy Jamal Samuels from I.S. 139? We grew up on Richmond Hill together, and he's still bustin' ass and takin' names. Jamal, this my dude Sylvio Dominique," Omar said, introducing the two young men as they dapped each other.

"What up, B.? Yeah, I peeped some of yo fight highlights. You doin' work in that ring," Jamal complimented.

"Appreciate it, homie," Sylvio said. "We came a long way since them Richmond Hill High days. Omar always be talkin' 'bout one of his homies that left during freshman year."

"Yeah, it's a long story, but let's just say I left it to Omar to run Richmond Hill in my place," Jamal laughed.

"Yo, I still think it's a damn travesty you ain't stay all four years there. We could've had that one-two punch like T-Mac and Vince, but you had to dip," Omar said.

"Why we bringin' that up again?" Jamal replied, laughing.

Sylvio looked down at his watch. He realized he was late to the gym for afternoon training. "Yo, I'm 'bout to be out. I gotta get some of that work in."

"Yo, so are you gon' be fightin' Maximo for that belt soon?" Jamal asked.

"Shit, I don't even know right now. Kevin's still out there trying to set up a card for me, but Maximo's people still ain't replied yet," Sylvio said, shrugging.

"Probably tryin' to dodge you cuz he know you finn' whup his salsa-bean-burrito ass," Omar said, laughing.

"Whatever it is, I'm still gon' stay ready," Sylvio replied as he left the park to go to the Steel Glove Gym location in Queens.

Later that afternoon, after twenty minutes of cardiovascular movements, including jumping jacks and jump roping, Sylvio got into the ring to spar with Terry Patterson, who had been training in the gym for a few months. With Jim Shaw watching the sparring session, Sylvio worked on keeping his jabs busy and his hooks sharp.

"Snap it fast!" Jim ordered as Sylvio continued working away at Terry.

Terry was proving to be a difficult sparring partner for Sylvio. He defended by shielding his head and chest with his arms. According to Jim, Terry was using the boxing technique of legendary light heavyweight champion Archie Moore, and his unique fighting style allowed him to absorb more contact. It was a style that frustrated many fighters because it would prove difficult to punch with a direct jab, uppercut, or hooks. Sylvio found out the hard way when Terry began gaining the upper hand in the sparring session. But Sylvio still had superior speed and managed to rock Terry in the head a few times before he got in his defensive position.

"Time!" Jim yelled as the bell rang.

Sylvio and Terry went to their corners. Several of the other boxers who were training at the gym had stopped to watch the sparring session, marveling at Sylvio's incredible hand speed and footwork.

But it didn't satisfy Jim. "Sylvio, you've got to keep your hands busy. There can be no lapses in your offense. A few seconds can be the difference in a fight," he advised Sylvio.

"It's hard to get through his defense, man!" Sylvio said, frustrated by the fight.

"That's why we're here to learn. If you're gonna go against a boxer like Maximo, you gotta keep pressuring him. If he gets you off balance, he will knock you out with either hand. He ain't no joke."

"He's right, homie," Terry said from the other side of the ring. "I spoke to a couple guys at a gym in Jersey where Maximo trains, and he already broke jaws of his sparring partners. And they were wearing headgears."

Sylvio showed no reaction outwardly, but inside he felt the familiar churn in his stomach, which invited doubt and fear. What if he wasn't ready for the challenge?

"It's alright, son," Jim said, sensing his fighter had lost confidence. "That's why we're here. We gon' win that belt, whether they believe us or not."

As soon as the bell rang for the next round in the sparring session, Sylvio got up from his stool and prepared to touch gloves with Terry when he suddenly looked past him as if in awe.

"Yo, who that?" Terry asked.

Sylvio turned around. A young black woman, about nineteen or twenty, entered the gym. She was wearing sweatpants, which was expected, but what wasn't expected was the thin athletic sports bra she had on. For the average flat-chested woman, it was ideal, but this young woman was clearly well-endowed in the chest area, sporting huge cleavage that would've put many Hollywood actresses to shame. She seemed to be asking information at the desk, and Sylvio noticed that the receptionist pointed in his direction.

She gotta be at least a 32G.

Terry noticed it as well. "Yo, dawg, you know her?"

"Gentlemen, the bell rang over two minutes ago! Ya'll sparrin' or ya drooling?" Jim yelled at the fighters.

"Nah," Sylvio replied as they prepared to fight.

The woman made her way over to their ring, walking through dozens of young men, whistling and staring in her direction. "Excuse me, is Sylvio Dominique here?" she asked.

"Okay, Wolf, do ya thing!" one of the other young boxers yelled out.

Sylvio smiled at the young woman. "And who wants to know?"

The woman didn't reply for a moment. Instead, she just stared Sylvio up and down as if he was a disease. "Can we talk for a minute?"

"Oh yeah. I got plenty of time for you. You need to get fitted for some gear? We got gloves and pads, but it seems like you got enough padding to go around," Sylvio joked.

The woman never showed any sign of being amused. It was strange for Sylvio because, besides Angie and Valentina, he couldn't remember the last time a woman spoke to him without being flattered or going into fan mode. This woman didn't appear to be fazed by his celebrity status at all.

"Is that what you tell all yo groupies?" she asked.

"First of all, I ain't got no groupies, so I'd appreciate if you chill wit' that, and secondly, you still ain't told me what yo name is," Sylvio replied.

The young woman raised an eyebrow, shaking her head. "You mean, you don't remember me?"

Here we go again. Didn't I go through this at the club? My mind been trippin' the last few years. Maybe this is what it's like to be punch-drunk.

"Hey, baby don't sweat him. He just don't know how to appreciate true beauty, but I definitely can. Lemme take you out sometime," Terry said.

"Shut up, fool!" Sylvio replied, but thankfully the woman wasn't interested in Terry either.

But it was her response that floored the whole gym. "Nah I don't think so. Sylvio wouldn't like anyone fuckin' wit' his lil' sister, would he?"

The gym suddenly went silent. Even Jim was speechless at that moment as all eyes turned to the little sister confronting her older brother.

Sylvio's jaw dropped. This can't be real. She can't be serious. Tell me this crazy chick is not here sayin' she my sister. I haven't seen my sister for over seventeen years. "What did you say?" he said slowly.

"Yeah, you heard me right. My name's Rebecca Dominique," the woman replied.

"Yo, why you ain't tell me she was yo sista, man?" Terry asked Sylvio.

"What? Yo, she ain't my sister, B. This bitch buggin' foreal," Sylvio replied.

"I know Momma ain't raised you to call no woman a bitch," Rebecca said.

"My momma ain't raised me at all!" Sylvio yelled. "She left without so much as a goodbye and never even bothered to visit or nothin'. So, she dead to me right now."

"Sylvio, I think you and Rebecca need to talk in the office," Jim said.

Sylvio stepped out of the ring while Jim took off his headgear and gloves. Rebecca walked into Jim's office, and Sylvio followed her inside. As soon as the door was closed, Sylvio turned to the mysterious young woman who claimed to be his sister. "Okay, real talk, who the hell are you?" he asked.

"I already told you. I'm your sister," Rebecca insisted, but what should have been an easy answer became complicated for Sylvio.

He had questions, and he intended to test her immediately. "Okay, so if you my sister, then prove it," Sylvio challenged.

"Okay, fine," Rebecca replied. "I know that you had a Stretch Armstrong action figure when you were four. I took it when Momma walked out on Daddy. I know that you have a birthmark on the left side of your hip that looks like a crescent moon. I know that you loved Reading Rainbow because you liked to read books, especially sports books. Finally, I know your middle name, Yvens," she finished, laughing.

Damn, she is my sister. I've been looking for that Stretch Armstrong toy for years and never found it. I'm sure nobody knows about that birthmark but my mother, and she was living with my mother. And only my mother knew how much I loved reading, especially when I was younger.

Realizing that Sylvio was still processing the information, Rebecca walked over to pat her brother's shoulder as he couldn't stop the tears from flowing once he realized that Rebecca's revelation to him was true.

"Only Mom would know all that stuff," he said quietly. "But where had ya been? Why haven't you ever come back to visit my father?"

"Momma and I moved to Philadelphia after the argument with Daddy. She was living with her sister for a few years. Then she eventually remarried. I wasn't feelin' him too much though. He never respected Momma. He was always playin' her, messing around with other women, but she still stayed with him. I couldn't understand why she stayed with him, but she didn't give Daddy another chance. So, I made it a mission to try to find you. Then I saw you blowing up in the sports world, and everyone's talking about The Wolf—how great of a fighter you were. When I later found out that it was you, I wanted to try to reconnect," Rebecca confessed.

"There were ways you could've gotten to me though. I mean, with social media and all," Sylvio said, but Rebecca gave him an incredulous look.

"Are you serious? You damn-near millionaire status now. Anybody coulda said they were related to you to try to get to yo bag. I didn't wanna make it seem like I needed a handout. I just wanted to check up on my big brother."

Sylvio paced around the office in silence. For years, he felt the sting of his mother's neglect and was constantly reminded in his younger years that she wasn't there to bandage his first cut, and she wasn't around to watch him excel in school and in the boxing world. Whenever he had questions about her, his father would forcefully change the subject or sternly warn him not to mention her name again.

Most of all, Sylvio blamed his mother for his father's abuse upon him. Maybe if she was there to soothe him or talk to him, he wouldn't take out his frustrations on me. For years, Sylvio thought that.

Although he commended his little sister for tracking him down after nearly two decades, he still didn't know how she pulled it off. "How'd you even know I was here?"

"Daddy told me you might be here."

"Figures," Sylvio rolled his eyes.

"Sylvio, I know what happened between you and Daddy that night when ya fell out and you left the apartment because he didn't support your dream. Please don't hold that grudge against him or Momma," Rebecca urged Sylvio, but he was still pacing the office, his back still bearing the scars of past beatings.

"Holding a grudge got me this far. You don't know what it's like, waking up only to keep fighting battles, or going into that ring and looking across from you is the dude that wanna knock yo ass out," he replied, eyeing Rebecca intensely. "You know, there were times when I would look across that ring, and I wouldn't even be fighting my next opponent. I would be fighting Dad, paying him back for all them beatings I took from him ova the years. No, these scars are my war marks—a reminder for me to keep fighting. I don't owe him nothin'."

"Well, Daddy's sick. He has diabetes, Sylvio."

"What?"

"Yeah, that's right. Daddy's been taking insulin to regulate his blood sugar, but he's been in and out of the hospital for months."

The news hit Sylvio like a ton of concrete bricks. Why was his father sick, and yet, he never took the time to tell his son? "Where is he? Is he still at the house?" Sylvio asked his sister.

"Yeah, he still there, but he can't get around the way he used to. He really wants to see you."

"So, he sent you here to ask me to go visit him. What about Mom?"

"I'll keep tryin' to talk to Momma, but I don't know if she'll wanna come back hea."

"Of course not," Sylvio replied sarcastically. Why would his mother suddenly pop up in his life? He certainly didn't owe her anything. "I'll visit Dad when I have a chance." Sylvio was unsure because the anger gave him the edge he needed in the ring. Without it, he would lose the essence of his "Wolf" persona. But with his father reportedly in failing health, he had to see him after four years.

"Thanks for stoppin' by, sis," he said to Rebecca as she got up and prepared to leave the gym.

"Ain't no thang. We family at the end of the day."

"Right, and by the way, I want my Stretch Armstrong action doll back."

"Um, yeah about that. I lost that thing a long time ago," Rebecca replied, laughing as they exited the office.

Chapter 10

A few days later, Jim Shaw found himself pacing the grounds of Public School 11 in Brooklyn. Normally, a location such as an elementary public school would bear no significance to a middle-aged man, but it bore significance to Jim. It was in Flatbush where he was born and had attended school. He learned to fight in the streets after his father was thrown in jail for burglarizing homes in the area.

Raised by his mother, who worked day and night to provide for him and Kevin, Jim had to survive and become the main breadwinner of his family. In junior high school, he began his boxing training at a local gym called Flatbush Fists. There, he won many sparring sessions and bouts at the gym. Jim's old boxing coach, Flip Timothy, always believed he was a natural and felt he had a chance to be a professional prizefighter. Unbeknownst to his mother and Kevin at the time, Jim had begun fighting for small change at school.

Growing up in an apartment in the Flatbush projects, young Jim was often teased and bullied and learned very quickly that kids would try to test his mettle. He figured that if they were going to force him to fight, he may as well make money out of it. So as a result, he began to fight kids who were perceived to be bullies in the area, often placing bets with them. If they beat him, he would give them his weekly allowance, which was around three to five dollars. But if Jim won, they had to pay him twice the amount. At the end of one year, Jim had already earned over fifty dollars from impromptu fights, but he had also begun to gain a reputation as a neighborhood bully.

One day, Jim savagely beat a boy named Grant Butler, who had been bragging to the neighborhood that he was going to kill him. Jim tore into him, and during the fight, an ominous event occurred. Grant, who was born with a brain condition, began to convulse on the ground, suffering from an epileptic seizure. Fortunately, he survived, but the ordeal frightened Jim so that he stopped fighting in the streets once he realized that he could have ended the young boy's life.

Flip took Jim to the gym and began to help him channel his aggression in the ring. The strategy worked, and Jim began honing his craft through high school and fighting in the Golden Gloves as a lightweight. Between 1986 and 1992, Jim was climbing the ranks as a lightweight boxer. Fortunately, during the early stages of his career, another life-altering event occurred: the birth of his son, Dante Shaw. His mother, Natalie, was a childhood friend of Jim's. Throughout the years, they grew closer and took the relationship to the next level.

After Dante was born, Jim wanted to close to his son during the stages of his early development, so he made the painful decision to retire from boxing. He took a job as a boxing instructor and physical fitness trainer at Flatbush Fists, where he trained young upstarts. With those jobs, he was able to remain at home with his son and his girlfriend, who would later become his wife.

As Dante grew up, he attended Public School 11 and was showing signs of academic brilliance. His teachers felt the current curriculum wasn't challenging enough and suggested that he skip a grade so that he could further develop his academic abilities.

Instead of elevating to the fourth grade with his friends, Dante was a nine-year-old fifth grader. There was some resentment—not from kids Dante's age—but from his fifth-grade classmates. Dante was often ridiculed and bullied for his intelligence, and he was often goaded into fights at the schoolyard.

One fifth grader by the name of Lawrence Kirkwood became Dante's worst nightmare. He was often outshined by Dante in class, so in retaliation, he would bully Danta by tripping or pushing him unexpectedly. Dante couldn't tell the teachers because he knew that "snitches," which was the label put on folks who blew the whistle against other people, would be in danger.

One day, before school, Jim was shaving his beard in the bathroom, and Dante walked in. "Dad, can you teach me how to box?"

Jim laughed as he washed the remaining shaving cream off his face. "Why, what's goin' on?"

"It's this kid—Lawrence—he keeps beatin' me up before and after school. I'm tired of it,"

"Son, I want you to listen to me very carefully," Jim said, bending down so he could look at his son face to face. "The fight life is a hard life, and it's not the kind of life I want for you. You're a smart kid, and other kids are gonna see that, and they're gonna be jealous. But it's only out of insecurity. Just ignore him, and don't hesitate to tell the teacher if he's bothering you. As a matter of fact, why don't I drop you to school tomorrow morning, and I'll talk to this Lawrence for you," he offered.

But Dante quickly declined. "No, please, Dad. I don't want you to be there. It's already embarrassing enough being the only small kid in fifth grade. I don't want kids to see me with my dad around."

"No, I insist. Tomorrow morning, I'm gonna drop you off at school, and I'll wait around for Lawrence," Jim said, despite Dante's protests. He felt he had given his son the best advice as a father. But he was unaware that it would be the final advice he would give his son.

That very next morning, Jim drove Dante to school. It was busy that morning, and all the parking spots were full, so Jim had to park across the street nearly a block away. Dante nervously examined the car, checking the passenger seat as if he expected Lawrence to pop out from the side of the car.

"Do you see him, yet?"

"No," Dante replied.

"Let's go."

Dante stopped him. "No Dad, please! Look, you drove me here, so please can I walk to school? I got this."

Jim shook his head. These kids don't appreciate nothing anymore. But he wants to be a man, so I guess I'll watch him walk to school.

Dante said goodbye and walked out of the car.

Watching his son walk to school, Jim couldn't help but to shake his head, smiling. My boy walkin' outchea thinkin' he grown.

But the smile was wiped away as he saw a boy, almost six feet tall, hiding behind a vehicle. He seemed to be eyeing the throng of kids walking into the school. Jim thought the scene seemed odd, but he didn't think anything of it at first. Then Jim saw the boy's eyes widen and his lips curl into a smile when he saw Dante walking to school. Sensing trouble, Jim took the keys out the ignition and opened his car door to get to his son, after finally realizing it had to be Lawrence eyeing Dante. The bully approached Dante as swiftly as a predator approached its prey. The young genius never saw his attacker coming.

"Hey, loser," Lawrence said, pushing Dante with extreme force from behind.

Before he realized what happened, Dante's small frame was pushed about five feet into the Flatbush Street. Unable to catch his footing, Dante fell face-forward into the busy intersection, just as a Honda Accord approached, driving at speeds of forty-five miles per hour. The driver was talking on his cell phone and wasn't paying attention to the road until Dante fell in front of him. He pumped his breaks as fast as he could, but he couldn't stop the car in time.

Jim witnessed the impact as the car hit Dante with a loud, sickening thud. "DANTE!" Jim yelled as he ran to his son, lying motionless on the road. "God, no please! God no! Somebody call 9-1-1! Hurry!" Jim yelled to the bystanders in the streets.

The driver stepped out of his vehicle and ran to Jim, who was applying CPR, trying to revive his son. The scene was grisly as Dante's blood ran from his mouth and nose. The brilliant fifth-grader was in critical condition. Jim held his son in his arms, weeping loudly. During the commotion, Lawrence stood back, but after realizing what he had done, he fled the premises, leaving Jim on the curb, holding Dante.

A few hours later, Dante Shaw was pronounced dead. From that point on, life as Jim knew it turned sideways. Nothing made sense anymore for him. It didn't matter that the driver was charged with vehicular manslaughter and that Lawrence was placed in juvenile hall for his part in Dante's death. Jim's life began to unravel.

His marriage with Natalie ended in divorce a couple of months later in the aftermath of the tragedy, and not too long after, Jim left Brooklyn and moved to Queens for a fresh start. Although the grief from his son's death still lingered, Jim began a personal quest to equip young men and women in defending themselves, mainly by using boxing tactics. With Kevin's help, the Steel Glove Gym was Jim's legacy to Dante's memory, and he was happy to be a part of a new community that invited him in and supported the gym.

But there were days when Jim's depression and mood swings took him to various places. He would often walk by schools, playgrounds, and basketball courts, determined not to let others suffer the same fate that Dante suffered. It was an odyssey that landed him near P.S. 55, where he encountered the boy who very much resembled Dante—the boy who became one of the best middleweight boxers in the world.

As Jim stood over the curb where he'd watched his son die sixteen years earlier, he was joined by his brother, Kevin. "Something told me I'd find you hea today," Kevin said.

Still hunched over the curb, Jim didn't respond to his brother for a while. "Yeah, I ain't 'bout to stick around too long. Can't stay in a place where everything fell apart," he finally replied.

Kevin stood next to Jim. "Look bro, I lost my nephew that day, and for a moment I thought I lost you too. But you can't keep coming back over here reliving that moment. That was a dark time for the family, and now we gotta let go," he said, clearly unaware how deeply the tragedy cut Jim.

If he had taught his son to be more assertive, maybe if he taught him how to defend himself, Dante would've grown into adulthood. "You know, I can't even bring myself to go visit him at his resting place," Jim said, as a tear rolled down his eye. "I wanna believe that he's still here and that he knows how deeply sorry I am for not getting there in time."

Kevin patted his brother on his shoulder. "I'm sure wherever Dante is, he knows that you still love him and what happened that day wasn't yo fault."

"You know what I've realized?" Jim asked Kevin rhetorically. "It doesn't matter who's the aggressor. Whether it's Lawrence or Brandon, they're all the same. Kids out there who ain't got nothin' for themselves, so they gotta take from other people, by any means. There's gotta be a way to put a stop to it all."

Kevin suddenly realized what Jim was pointing out in his statement, and it wasn't just about his dead son. "Listen bro, you can't save 'em all, and you can't live Dante's life through Sylvio. I know how much he reminds you of your son, especially when ya first met. But he doesn't know about Dante."

"He doesn't know that's why you're so hard on him and why you're overprotective of him. But you're not doing him any favors by coddling him. You have to let Sylvio be a man."

"What if he ain't ready?" Jim asked Kevin. "I've seen Felipe Maximo, and he's gonna pose a bigger threat to The Wolf than anyone we've ever faced. If I rush to take the fight, I'm essentially doing the same thing I did to Dante years ago, leaving him on his own to fight a battle that he can't win. I don't wanna be in that situation again."

"Jim, you've trained Sylvio to be one of the fiercest fighters in the game. When he steps into that ring, there's a look in his eyes that I see from him, and it's telling me that he won't be denied. He'll be ready to face off against Maximo."

Mulling it over the location where his son took his last breath, Jim realized that Kevin was right. All these years, he'd been replacing Dante with Sylvio. He had to come to grips that Sylvio wasn't Dante and maybe, just maybe, Sylvio has what it takes to fight the undefeated champion.

"Come on. I'll give you a ride to the gym. We got a busy day today," Kevin said, helping his brother to his feet before reaching into his pockets and pulling out a small pack of Twizzlers cherry licorice candy. "Remember these, man?" he said, showing them to Jim, who started laughing.

"Come on, dawg. We finna go the gym, and you out here eatin' candy? Yeah, these Twizzlers, man. Dante used to tear these up back in da day, lemme tell you," he laughed.

"Especially them peel-off joints," Kevin said, and he broke a piece of Twizzlers candy off to his brother on the way to the gym.

Walking up the subway stairs after taking the F-train, Valentina went three blocks to Apple Kim's when she heard a car honking behind her.

"Hey chiquita, como estas?" a voice called out from behind a blue Ford Mustang.

Oh my God, I recognize that voice anywhere. Valentina's worst fears were confirmed as her ex-boyfriend Pedro drove up next to a parking meter and stopped his car before stepping out to talk to her.

"Dejame en paz!" she replied, asking Pedro to leave her alone while she walked to her job.

"Aw, come on, Valentina. Why you gotta be like that?" Pedro attempted to grab Valentina by her shoulders, but she ducked out of his grasp.

"Don't make me act a fool outchea cuz I will, Pedro. We're done. Can't you understand that?"

"Yeah, I understand, but I don't think you mean it," Pedro said, which angered Valentina even more.

She hated when he told her how she should feel. It was a contributing factor that led to the end of their relationship, along with the fact that Pedro kept his bed full of other women at night.

"Well, I do mean it, Pedro. I mean, what do you take me for? You can't play me like your other hoes anymore. I ain't the one."

"Oh, really?" Pedro asked in false amazement. "Ain't I the one that helped you get up out of yo parents house when they kicked you out for working for me? I ain't the one that bought you rocks, bands, and dem fancy North Face jackets with the mink hoods? I got you everything. You're a princess, but I helped make you a princess," he bragged confidently.

Okay, now he's outta pocket. "Yeah, you helped get all that stuff with money that you stole. Or didn't anybody know about you gamblin'?" Judging by the way Pedro looked around nervously, she knew she struck a nerve.

"Damn, can't you keep mouth shut about that? You gotta put all my business out in public?"

Pedro was nervous because he knew Valentina was right. He was a part of a secret underground gambling ring that was run by his organization, along with drugdealers and secret Vegas connections. They would bet on basketball games, baseball games, football games, and even put stakes on horse-racing and golf. But the largest sum of money that Pedro earned came from bets placed on boxing matches. Although mixed martial arts made its inception in the fight world, boxing still drew millions of fans and billions of dollars. Pedro and his friends would look up information from Vegas oddsmakers and were able to make the correct predictions about ninety percent of the time, so their predictions normally ended up in huge returns.

In Pedro's defense, gambling wasn't illegal in Atlantic City, so he felt that since there was plenty of money to go around, he wasn't breaking any laws. But Valentina knew that Pedro had an ace up his sleeve. He knew some of the boxers in the heavyweight, welterweight, and middleweight division. Some of his connections included a few of the judges that would score the fight, and Valentina was sure that the judges would sway fights to help Pedro's group win money. But while she never complained about the gifts he bought her while they were still an item, she was not intrigued about the lifestyle that he garnered from his winnings. Pedro turned from the nice boy next door to a gambling womanizer, and after he was caught more than once with other women at the end of his king mattress, Valentina decided to call it quits. It had become less about her and more about the money.

"Whateva, Pedro. I just don't care anymore, okay? So, you can stop sending me flowers at work because at this point, it's getting annoying."

"Why? Look, is it because of Gabrielle? Come on, Val, she was nothing but a one-night stand. You actin' like you ain't eva fucked any other dudes."

"Not while I was in a relationship."

"You know what? It's just like a self-entitled bitch to act brand new when she got a lil' bit of money. You ain't no different than them other hoes that you work with," Pedro said, before turning around to head back to his car.

"Yeah, you better go back to that Mustang of yours before you get a parking meter ticket," Valentina said, and she continued walking to work, thankful that Pedro was finally leaving.

Maybe now he gets the picture that I'm not interested in him. There are plenty of other men out there who care more about women than their pockets...down-to-earth guys who are chill, laid back, and someone I can talk to for hours. Guys like Sylvio Dominique. Whoa, where did that come from?

She had to admit that after that night when they talked for over two hours, she felt a connection to him. But she was certain that she probably wouldn't see him again. After all, he was a famous boxer who traveled around the world, and she was just a waitress.

If Pedro could have ten women at once, Sylvio might have fifty women at once. He might not be any better than Pedro, or any other guy.

Later that afternoon, Sylvio decided to visit his father in the apartment that he had left over three years earlier. He decided not to go with his bodyguard detail because he did not want to cause a huge commotion, but no sooner did he step out his car, a group of kids recognized him Immediately and ran over to use their phones to snap a few pictures with him. Sylvio was happy to oblige, even signing autographs for some.

"Are you finished yet, superstar? Took you long enough to get hea," Rebecca said to her brother from the entrance of the apartment.

"Shut up. I wonder if you ever keep a man more than a month with that smart mouth."

"That's for me to know and for you to mind yo own business. Stick to punching bags," Rebecca answered slyly.

Sylvio was tempted to throw a clever, vulgar comeback at his sister but decided that it wasn't worth it. They both entered the apartment building and pressed the buzzer under the corresponding apartment number.

"Yes?" a deep gravelly voice answered.

"It's me, Dad. I got Sylvio with me."

The hallway was silent for a few seconds until they heard another buzzing sound. Jacques unlocked the door.

"So, since you've stayed over with Dad, how's he been holding up with his condition?" Sylvio asked as they made their way to their father's apartment door.

"He ain't been too bad, but his sugar level's been dangerously high these last couple weeks. I've had to give him his insulin shots. It's been keeping him up pretty good, but he's got his next checkup coming up tomorrow."

Sylvio felt a wave of gratitude toward his sister. "Yo, Rebecca, for the record, I think it's dope that you came down and took care of him. I wish I knew earlier. Maybe I would've helped out sooner."

"But you were busy with your career and couldn't be bothered, right?" Rebecca asked.

"Look, I did what I had to do, okay? I couldn't stay hea foreva. I had my own goals to accomplish. I had to get mine," Sylvio insisted, feeling less gratitude and more irritated by the second.

"Yeah, but while you were out there chasing the dream, you could've given your own father a phone call. Maybe he was worried about you. Did you ever think about that?"

Sylvio hated receiving the guilt trip that was being administered to him by his own sister, but he knew she was right. Still, it didn't absolve her from not checking up on them either. "Is Mom coming?"

"She'll come at her own time, I guess," Rebecca replied, as they reached their father's door.

After a couple of knocks, Jacques opened, letting them inside. Closing the door behind them, Sylvio looked at his father. He was barely recognizable. His eyes were sunken in, and he had dark circles as if he hadn't slept in days. The skin around his face and neck had begun to sag, and he had gained some pounds since the last time they had faced each other. Sylvio suddenly felt remorse for the man he once feared and thought to be abusive.

Surprisingly, Jacques was thrilled to see Sylvio. "Hello, son. How are you?" he asked in his strong Creole accent.

Sylvio extended his hand to shake his father's hand. Instead of shaking it, Jacques took an extra step and hugged Sylvio as if he hadn't seen him in decades.

"I missed you," he whispered quietly.

Sylvio rarely showed any emotion outside the ring, but today tears were streaming down his face as he hugged his father. He didn't remember the last time he'd done that. In fact, he didn't remember the last time his father expressed any type of love to him...

"Dad, I'm so sorry that I stayed away all those years. I was wrong to run away and not keep in touch."

"No, I owe you an apology, Sylvio," Jacques said. "My arrogance and my stubbornness drove you away like it drove Rebecca and your mother away from us years ago. I would sit and think that if I controlled my anger, I would have saved my marriage, and maybe we would've stayed together."

"I was scared of you, Dad. Sometimes I thought you hated me," Sylvio said as he and Rebecca helped Jacques sit on his couch as he had difficulty sitting on his own.

"Pa di sa non," his father said, encouraging Sylvio not to let those thoughts run his mind. "I just wanted the best upbringing for you. I was strict, just like my parents were strict. I thought I was doing the best for you. I was preparing you to face life."

While he sat listening to his father's confession, Sylvio realized that maybe he hadn't lost his father after all. Maybe his father needed time to find himself.

Chapter 11

In Brooklyn, Roberto Maldonado, a novice boxer and sparring partner for various middleweight contenders, stepped into the ring at the Crown Heights Boxing Gym. Maldonado had not fought any professional bouts in his young career, so he decided to build his reputation by sparring his contemporaries. He had sparred with Victor Hernandez, Rosjan Bokavic, and Jose Chavez, but it was only the week before this very day when he was warned about his next sparring partner who was a legend in the Hispanic community and was known to inflict serious injury upon his opponents.

Such warning would have discouraged many boxers from sparring with the fearsome man, but Maldonado felt he could hold his own against any boxer. Therefore, he was eager to find out about the man everybody called "Manos de Muerte" or "hands of death." Maldonado laughed at the name, thinking this man had to have balls to give himself such a name.

I guess we'll see what the hype's all about. Maldonado looked as his opponent finally made his way into the ring.

With more than two dozen tattoos covering his shoulders, chest and back, the boxer climbed under the ropes to get into the ring. His large muscles rippled as he banged his gloves together in anticipation of the sparring match. Felipe Maximo towered over the smaller Maldonado, as he had about four inches on his opponent.

Finally, the bell rang, signaling the start of the sparring session. Both fighters circled the ring, throwing jabs, looking for an opening. Roberto managed to stay away from Felipe for half of the first round, but he could see Felipe's eyes narrowing in anger and concentration as he chased him through the ring.

"Why, you runnin' away, homes?" Felipe asked, slightly taunting Roberto, who realized that Felipe was testing his nerve and goading him to press the attack.

Roberto swung hooks at the defending middleweight champion, but with unmatched dexterity and speed for his size, Felipe slipped and ducked all of them. Then with a deadly combination of strength and speed, Felipe responded with three hard hooks to Roberto's head. The young man never knew what hit him. The first two hooks knocked Roberto off balance, and while he was still teetering, the third hook came in with enough force to knock down a small shack. Roberto crumpled to the canvas.

"Get up, homes! You ain't hurt!" Felipe yelled as the assisting trainer in the gym assumed the role of the fight official and counted Roberto out.

After the ten count, Roberto made the effort to stand up on his own but fell back down. As the other trainers in the gym ran to check on Roberto, Felipe retreated to his corner, smiling broadly.

His trainer, Marcos Paz was none too impressed. "Felipe, how many times do I have to tell you to take it easy on our sparring partners? It's not a real fight."

"Every fight's real to me," Felipe replied in Spanish. "If he didn't want no smoke, he shouldn't have tried to put out the fire."

Marcos poured water in his mouth. "That's the third sparring partner this month, Felipe. You broke the ribs of one a month ago, and before your fight with Bokavic, you dislocated another sparring partner's jaw."

"They're the ones that came to fight me. What do you expect me to do? Dance with him?" Felipe asked rhetorically. "The moment anyone is in a ring with me, they instantly become an enemy that needs to be destroyed. How do you think I'm still undefeated? Did I do that by giving love taps to my opponents?"

Marcos stopped arguing. Who was he to stop the rabid aggression of his fighter? "I guess not. Good fight," Marcos said as they both laughed.

Marcos had known Felipe for about fourteen years, meeting him when Felipe was fifteen. He was locked up in juvenile hall for savagely attacking his social studies teacher in high school. The teacher required over thirty stitches after the brutal beating, and Felipe faced time in juvenile hall until he reached eighteen so the teacher's family could then try him as an adult.

However, Marcos came along as a boxing instructor at newly-formed Crown Heights Boxing Gym. He had seen the punching power Felipe possessed firsthand when he'd visited a relative at the juvenile hall facility. That day a fight had broken out between Felipe and another boy in the sleeping quarters. It was an unfortunate ordeal for the boy. Thanks to Felipe, he had a couple teeth knocked out and was bleeding profusely from his face.

Marcos was amazed by the brute strength of the teen, so he took it upon himself and asked Felipe's judge to lessen the sentence and to grant Felipe an early release from the facility. Soon, Felipe was out of juvey and in the care of Marcos Paz, who taught him fight techniques and combos.

Turning pro at age nineteen, Felipe proved to be a devastating fighter with a track record of knocking his opponents out eighty percent of the time. He was a big draw in Atlantic City and Las Vegas. People would place bets on Felipe and would cash out immediately. Until his previous match with Bokavic, Felipe had never allowed an opponent to reach the twelfth round. He would knock them out early and often, but through Bokavic, Marcos wanted Felipe to realize that many boxers were not simply going to back down, not even to Felipe's intimidating stare that usually psyched his opponents out hours before they entered the ring with him.

With a record of twenty-seven wins and zero losses, Felipe stood atop the perch where he remained champion. He was beginning to realize that no other boxer was at his level.

Felipe was drinking water when his brother walked in the gym. "Que pasa, mi hermano?" Pedro asked as he approached Felipe at his corner.

"You already know. Kickin' shit, as usual. Dominating these clowns," Felipe wiped his forehead although he'd barely broken a sweat.

"That's how you gotta be wit' these pretenders. What happened to homie?" Pedro was watching the small group of trainers surrounding Roberto.

"Aye, he knew what he signed up for. I don't play, homes." Felipe could care less about what he'd done to Roberto.

"I know. Soon we gonna have to start gettin' new protective headgear," Pedro joked as he sat next to his brother.

"So, what's up with you and Valentina?" Felipe asked, drinking more water.

"Man, that chick is on some otha' shit, homes. I'm through with that broad. She don't even want me to bring her flowers, candy, nothin' like that. I'm out of options, bro."

"What you need to do is stop messin' around with that puta, homes. She ain't even worth your time."

"I mean, what did I do wrong? I slept with one, okay, maybe two women in our relationship, but she ain't innocent either. I mean she's working at that whorehouse with these other hoes, and she act like we didn't elevate her to that status. She's using that gig to become an actress or some shit like that," Pedro said, disdainfully.

"Yeah, and I wanna be the champion of the world! Oh, wait. That already happened!" Felipe added as they both laughed. "But for real, all jokes aside, who else is out there, man? Feels like I've beaten everybody."

"I don't even know. Bokavic was the best fighter you faced in the division, and it took you the full twelve to drop him. You scared me for a minute there, homes. I was about to lose twelve mill."

Felipe glared at his brother. "The only reason you bet on me is because you know I'mma win. Would you still back me if I fought someone who actually posed a threat?" Felipe asked, and he got his answer when Pedro didn't answer immediately.

"Of course, I would. We still brothers at the end of the day. I'd put you up against anybody."

"Really? Like who?"

Pedro pulled out his phone and logged into his ESPN app on his phone. After a couple of minutes, he showed his brother an image on his phone. "This guy right hea." Pedro showed Felipe the image of Sylvio Dominique.

"What? You want me to fight this perdedor negro? Nigga's darker than me," Felipe chuckled.

"He's been makin' noise in the division. He fought Bokavic right after you, and that fight came down to a split decision. That dude barely pulled it off."

"What's his record, anyway?"

"He's eleven and two right now."

Felipe confidently shook his head. "He ain't ready yet. I'mma wipe the floor wit' his black ass."

"Well, word on the street is that his team is looking to schedule a title fight,"

Felipe shook his head again. "Nah, not until he gets another fight under his belt, and he gotta convince me that he's ready for this."

Pedro couldn't believe his brother was starting to show a streak of arrogance in this stage of his career. He knew his brother was dominant, but he also knew people loved to watch the downfall of greatness and knew his brother's career and legacy was on the line each time he stepped into the ring. "Can we at least talk to his team?"

"Yeah, I don't care. Find his team, and let 'em know that their lil' darkie gotta fight one more opponent, then we can talk," Felipe said as Pedro left his side to allow him to continue training.

A few nights later before the end of her shift at Apple Kim's, Valentina completed her last bottle order and was heading to the employee's room when she saw a small crowd of people near the back of the club. Must be another celebrity. She began to make her way past the throng, desiring nothing more than to make it to the back room so she could punch out and catch the late F subway train to Lexington Avenue, where she would take two other trains home. She wanted to rush by whoever was in the vicinity because she was not going to deliver any more bottles for the evening.

"Yo, Valentina!" a familiar voice shouted to her.

Turning around, she saw it was none other than Sylvio Dominique. What is he doing back here? Maybe he came to order a drink. Good luck finding someone else to deliver it cuz I am out.

Then she realized he was beckoning her to walk over to him. She saw that he didn't have his usual posse around him, just one bodyguard who stood a few feet behind him. Most of his fans and admirers were female, which didn't surprise Valentina. Even she had to admit that Sylvio was not bad on the eyes at all. And with his dark skin complexion and muscles, he resembled an early Wesley Snipes. She always found dark-skinned men to be debonair and attractive, and Sylvio was definitely no exception. Then there were the fantasies that she would have about him, his sweat glistening from his broad shoulders and bulging muscles, not to mention she hadn't helped but noticed that he was bulging in other places.

"So, back again, huh? We must be your favorite club," Valentina said.

"Oh yeah, the club's definitely dope, but I like the waitresses that work hea," Sylvio replied, giving Valentina the smug confident look that turned her off to other men, but whenever Sylvio gave her the same look, it was a turn-on.

"What about the exotic dancers? You don't think they fly?"

"They aight, but I ain't scopin' out no dancers tonight." Sylvio was sending undeniable hints to Valentina. The other girls that surrounded him suddenly got the sense that he wasn't paying them any attention, and two began eyeing Valentina enviously.

"So, what can I get you? I was finna get off, but I guess I'll serve one more drink," she said.

Sylvio waved his hand dismissively. "Nah, don't even worry 'bout that. I just came back to see you again. It was just great choppin' it up wit' you last time." With a slight hand gesture, he called his bodyguard over. Sure enough, he came and guided the other women away from Sylvio. Mistakenly, the bodyguard also began to motion to Valentina, but Sylvio stopped him at the last minute.

"Yo, Sim, chill. She wit' me," he said, and Simeon stepped out of Valentina's way. "So, how much longer you gotta work?" he asked Valentina.

"I'm actually getting off now," Valentina answered.

"You got a ride back to yo crib?"

"Nah, I ain't got a car yet. I normally take the subway back home."

"Lemme give you a ride," Sylvio offered.

"Nah, it's okay. I'm fine with taking the subway."

"Aw, come on. This late? You know what kinda crazy shit go down in the subway at this time?"

"It's okay. I'll be cool. I've been taking the subway for almost my whole life, and ain't nothin' happened to me yet," Valentina replied, but she realized that Sylvio was not going to give up easily.

"Come on, Valentina. I'll drop you home. Maybe we can catch up some more," he said, but he saw the stern expression cross Valentina's face.

She was determined not to fall for any mind games. "What are you doin'?" she suddenly asked.

"What you mean?"

"I mean, why are you wasting your time with me? You're Sylvio Dominique, middleweight boxer, rollin' in Escalades with God knows how much money and can have any woman you want. Hell, even my manager's tryin' to do you, so what you doin'?

At first, she was met with silence from Sylvio.

"I don't know. I guess I just wanna get to know you betta'," he finally replied. "Look, I ain't askin' you to marry me or nothin' like that. I just wanna give you a ride home, and if it's all good, ask you if you wanna kick it some time—no obligation, no commitment," he admitted, suddenly wishing he hadn't.

The last image that Sylvio wanted to paint in Valentina's mind was a desperate simpleton who wasn't eloquent with words.

Valentina looked at Sylvio. *For a big boxer, he sure knows how to put on the puppy dog eyes.* She wasn't looking to rush into another relationship very soon. Pedro had broken her heart too many times, and she wasn't ready to enter another situation. But she soon realized she was drawn to Sylvio and couldn't explain it although she would be the first to admit that a large part of her attraction to him was his body. *Abusive jerks have nice bodies too. But Sylvio was a different kind of man.* "Okay, bet. You can drop me home. Just lemme go back and get my work gear off."

"Need help?" Sylvio said, smiling slyly.

"Uh no, you can keep yo horny ass out hea, and wait till I get back out." Valentina headed back to change out of her work attire.

Valentina, what are you getting yourself into? No sooner did you break it off with Pedro, here you go, falling for another smooth Don Juan figure again.

As soon as she came out of the employee room, Valentina saw that Sylvio was alone. He explained that he had sent Simeon home for the evening.

"Ain't you afraid someone gonna come at you if your bodyguard ain't wit' us?"

"Nah, I ain't scared. Besides, I only break out the bodyguards if I need to do any regulatin', you feel me?" he replied, noticing the look of doubt that crossed her face. "I'm just playin. But nah, he just wanted to check to make sure I got here okay. Besides, if anyone comes at you wrong, I got bodyguard skills," Sylvio boasted.

"Yeah right, whatever," Valentina laughed. "You got boxing skills. I bet your bodyguard got some martial arts skills or military skills. Boxing ain't gonna help you much if all you got is yo fists."

"That's all I need, though," Sylvio said.

"Not if somebody's comin' at you wit' a piece though," Valentina countered.

"I don't see that happening. I'm a public icon," Sylvio boasted as they walked out of the club to his Escalade.

While driving Valentina home, they talked about their childhood and the difference in discipline and culture in Dominican and Haitian households, when the topic suddenly arrived at food.

"Oh, did I mention that my favorite dish is fried plantains?" Valentina said to Sylvio as he got off the interstate through a Queens exit.

"Get outta hea! Yo, I love fried plantains too!"

"Word? We used to eat that with some arroz con pollo. You can't go wrong wit' that combination."

"Hell nah. It's been a minute since I cooked much of anything. I ain't got time like that anyway. If I'm not fighting on TV, I'm sparring or workin' out at da gym."

"That's good cuz I doubt if yo ass know how to cook anyway," Valentina joked.

"Oh, you tryna play me? light bet, I'mma bring you a dope-ass dish one of dem days, and you gon' wish I was yo chef after a couple bites, believe that."

"So, the nickname "Wolf," where did that come from?" Valentina asked, changing the subject.

"To be honest, it was my trainer Jim that gave me the name," Sylvio said, shrugging. "He gave that name to me back in high school when I was winning amateurs. I would box all over the tri-state area, building my rep, and one day, I was going against this kid named Rodney Goddard, and this fool nicknamed himself 'Rod the god,' so you knew this dude had an ego."

"Rod the god?" Valentina asked, laughing.

"Hell yeah, but he wasn't no god. Matter fact, I doubted if he was even a man, I cleaned his clock inside of three rounds. After that fight, Jim said, 'Damn son, you like a wolf, the way you aggressively attack your opponents, relentlessly. Dogs can be tamed, but wolves are wild. You can't train a wolf house dog tricks,'" Sylvio said.

"That's dope," Valentina said.

At last they arrived at Valentina's place, a small house with two front windows, and a slanted roof that was slightly bent on the right.

"Nice spot. You stay here by yourself?"

"Nah, I live with my two brothers, Juan and Bruno."

"You mean the brothers that could whup my ass? Those brothers?" Sylvio was referring to the conversation they had as kids.

"Yeah, them guys," Valentina rolled her eyes. As she started to open the car door, Sylvio shifted into park before exiting the driver's side and rushing around to promptly open the passenger door for Valentina to step down.

Oh my God, what a gentleman. Not too many men would have offered to open the car door for their women. Pedro certainly didn't.

"I can walk you to yo door," Sylvio offered.

"That's so sweet. Thank you, but I think I'll be okay," she said.

"Okay, but you never know. A burglar can run up and snatch you right before you reach that doorknob. Can't be too careful these days," Sylvio laughed.

"Right, but I thought yo fists was supposed to handle all that," Valentina replied, laughing.

As Valentina fumbled for her keys, Sylvio decided to take his shot. "Yo, there's a new movie spot downtown. I know you probably have to work, so if you ain't too busy next Saturday, maybe I can take you out?"

He had never been that nervous whenever he entered a ring against an opponent or with other girls when he was playing the "Wolf" character in the media. But Valentina had a chance to be the selected few people who got to see who he really was behind the camera, gloves, or mean-mug.

"Yeah, I'd love to go."

"That's what's up."

Not too long after, they exchanged phone numbers, and for a moment there was a split second when Sylvio and Valentina just stared at each other.

Damn, she fine. I would love to kiss her, but maybe that would be moving too fast.

For a moment, Sylvio felt that the same thought ran across Valentina's mind, and she took a step towards Sylvio, and their lips were only a few inches away before her cell phone rang.

Damn, I was mad close.

Valentina answered her phone. He couldn't tell who was on the other line, but whoever it was, Valentina clearly wasn't in the mood to talk to them.

"Yeah, I told you I got a ride home today. No, it wasn't a dancer from the club. It's an old friend," she explained, while Sylvio watched her. "Okay, I'm going inside now. I'll see you when I see you," she said before hanging up. "That was Bruno. He just checks periodically to make sure I got back," Valentina said, rolling her eyes.

"Gotcha. So, I'll catch you next Saturday," Sylvio said as he walked back to his car.

Chapter 12

The next day at Steel Glove Gym, Sylvio worked out as usual, starting out with his normal forty-five minutes on the treadmill and elliptical machine. After hydrating, one of the trainers wrapped his hands so he could finally put his gloves on to work on the speed bag. After thirty minutes on it, he climbed into the ring to work on combinations with Jim.

Holding two glove pads, Jim helped Sylvio work on his slips, jabs, hooks, and overhand shots when Shareef walked in. He had been scheduled to meet with Sylvio's team the day before, but he missed the meeting, and for good reason. He was busy communicating with Felipe Maximo's team, attempting to negotiate a title match between Sylvio and Felipe. The talks went nowhere, and Shareef was handed the brutal task of informing Sylvio that their bid for a title bout had been denied yet again.

"Lookin' good, man!" Shareef said, as he watched Sylvio work on his double jab and hook combination.

Jim took off his glove pads, motioning to his fighter that he could take a breather. "What's goin' on, Shareef? Tell me you got some good news."

Sylvio sat next to him, drinking from his gallon of water.

"Well, I spoke to Henry Santiago, the fight manager for Felipe Maximo, and in essence, they informed me that Maximo does not want to give Sylvio a title shot at this time."

"What?" Sylvio asked in disbelief, although Jim already knew the answer to the question. There were two reasons why a current champion refused a title defense of a fight: if the champion felt the challenger had not earned the shot or if the champion was merely dodging him out of fear. Jim felt it was the latter, but his protégé felt otherwise.

"He's scared," Sylvio said. "He's duckin' me. He don't want none of this. That's what it is."

"Actually, it's the opposite. He feels that you haven't earned the title shot. He wants you to fight another high-profile bout. Depending on the results, he'll consider it."

Sylvio looked at Jim as if he was expecting him to argue and insist upon the title bout, but Jim sat in silence. It spoke volumes, especially to Sylvio. "So, what do you say? You don't think I'm ready either?"

"Look, Wolf, it ain't a question of whether I think you're ready or not. It's obvious that he's toyin' with you. If you want that shot, you gotta show him why you deserve it," Jim replied.

"I ain't gotta show him shit! I don't fight for Maximo. I fight for me!"

"There's one thing that we can do. He wasn't convinced by the last-minute decision with Bokavic. He probably thought you got lucky as hell. What you need to do is get a fight with another contender. Then we gotta get to work cuz if you want any chance of fighting Maximo, you gotta win convincingly in your next match," Jim advised.

Sylvio thought about what his trainer said, and it made sense. But who was out there that he could fight? "Who's ranked behind Maximo?" he asked Shareef.

"I think you already know who," Shareef replied.

Right away Sylvio felt the familiar anger stemming from the last bout that he lost controversially. "Okay, fine. I want Jose Chavez again. Talk to his team, and set up a fight. Immediately," Sylvio told Shareef, who quickly agreed.

Later that afternoon, Sylvio met up with Omar and Jamal at Brookville Public Park in Rosedale, Queens. After a full day of work, they opted to shoot some hoops at the park. They didn't play any competitive games. They just talked while shooting hoops in a basket that had no net.

Sylvio, who never thought of himself as a basketball player, grunted in disgust as his free-throw midrange shot hit the side of the rim. "Man, I was never good at this," he laughed as Omar grabbed the rebound off the missed shot.

It also didn't help that both Omar and Jamal were five feet taller than Sylvio. Because of that fact, Sylvio's only chance of getting the ball to shoot again was if a long rebound came his way, but it didn't matter. He loved the environment. He loved getting away from life in the ring, so the park was the perfect outlet for him.

"True that. Good thing yo ass stuck to boxing. That's yo callin' card right there," Omar replied as he took a shot from the three-point line that went straight through the rim.

"Damn, yo, you'd think after all they did to change the neighborhood, they would at least hang some nets on these rims. I wanna hear my shot when it's money," he complained as Sylvio threw him the ball so he could shoot until he missed.

"Always complaining about something. What you need to do, is fix that weak-ass crossover of yours," Jamal said.

"Whateva, dawg. You know I gets mine," Omar replied as he shot another long-range shot.

This time it missed, and Jamal out-hustled Sylvio for the rebound. Dribbling past the three-point line, Jamal took a shot from beyond thirty-five feet. Without grazing the rim, the ball went right through. Omar shook his head. Jamal was too good. It was a wonder that he was still in the professional development league, trying to get into the NBA.

"Man, you shot that from almost half-court. You sho' nobody ain't called you up yet?" Sylvio asked.

"Man, the NBA's a tough game to get into. You could be ballin' out yo mind, but when they don't got a roster spot for you out there, you gotta grind and make them notice you," Jamal replied.

"That's crazy, son. You got range for days though. There gotta be a squad in the league that needs shooting like that," Sylvio said.

"Tell the league that," Jamal laughed as he drove to the basket and put down an easy two-handed jam. "Man, you know who I was thinking about just now? Remember the janitor game?" he asked Omar.

Sylvio, who attended Richmond Hill at the same time they did, but had not been in the same social circles with them, looked blankly at Omar.

"Janitor game?" Omar also stared at Jamal questioningly, until finally remembering the event. He burst out laughing. "Oh, you mean when Nate Plummer embarrassed yo boy Alex that day? Hell yeah, I remember that!"

Jamal decided to recount the story with Sylvio. "This happened when I was still in Richmond Hill during freshman year. We were both tryin'out for the freshman team, and we playin' these big-mouth sophomores, and there was this one kid named Alex who was talkin' crap all day. So, he thought he could beat everyone one-on-one. Then Nate came by. Mind you, this dude was still a janitor at the school, mopping up floors and cleaning up the cafeteria or whateva. Anyway, Alex thought he could beat Nate, and Nate smoked that dude in the game. Left Alex scoreless."

"Yo, I thought that dude was gon' cry. Nate got him all in his feelings that day," Omar chuckled.

"Wait, ya'll talking about Coach Nate? The one used to coach varsity at Richmond Hill?" Sylvio asked.

"Yup, but this happened before he became a coach. I think that one-on-one game helped him get that coaching position. You know our school sucked at ball when the best players get beat by the school janitor," Omar said, while Sylvio and Jamal laughed.

Suddenly, Omar's cell phone rang and vibrated from within his Adidas sports bag. "Hold up." He ran back to answer the phone. "Yo, what's up?" he greeted to the caller.

Jamal continued putting up more shots, but Sylvio continued to stare at Omar, whose body expressions seemed to have flipped like a switch.

Omar hung his head, stunned in disbelief. "You sure about that?" he asked the caller after a few minutes.

Sylvio watched his friend shift uncomfortably. Whoever's calling Omar is not giving him any good news right now. He watched Omar for a few more seconds.

Finally, Omar ended the call and headed back over to his boys, but with a sick look on his face. "Yo, I'mma holla at ya'll. I gotta bounce," he said as he picked up his sports bag.

"You good?" Jamal asked.

"Yeah, man, something just came up," Omar replied.

"Who was that on the phone?" Sylvio asked.

Omar hesitated for a moment but said, "That was my girl, Ashley. Shorty and I been chillin' for about a year now," he explained.

"Is she okay?" Jamal asked.

"Yeah, she's good. She called because she…she uh, took a pregnancy test, and it came out positive."

Sylvio and Jamal eyed each other. Could Omar really have gotten his girlfriend of one year pregnant? "Wow, uh, congratulations," Sylvio said, but he couldn't help that the accolade came out of his mouth awkwardly. He was certain that Omar never expected to receive the news, and he knew that his friend's mind had to be racing.

Omar was only 22 years old with aspirations of playing pro-basketball. It seemed that his dream would now be put on hold to support his girlfriend and unborn child. "I gotta go, son. I'm still tryin' to process this shit," he said as he turned to leave.

"Go handle yo business, B. If you need anything, let me know," Sylvio said, going over to Omar and dapping him.

Omar dapped Jamal then left the park.

A few days later, Sylvio and Valentina walked out of Sunshine Cinema in Manhattan. He decided not to bring his security detail with him because he wanted to give Valentina an actual exclusive dating experience. He'd observed that other people didn't go around on dates with security following them everywhere.

Sylvio had also decided not to inform Jim of the decision, for he knew Jim would swiftly disapprove and would insist that his bodyguards followed him.

"You can't do what you did before you became a prizefighter. You're an expendable commodity to some of these people, especially in New York. People gon' stop at nothing to take what you got," Jim would say, but Sylvio didn't want to give off the image of being a big shot.

The Wolf was already doing a fine job of playing his role. Whenever he kept the "Wolf" persona on the media, it allowed him to show others, including Valentina, his more personal side. They just finished watching Fast Five and were walking out of the movie theater. It was the first date Valentina had been on in a few years, and she was impressed by Sylvio, more so since Pedro rarely took her out on dates. It wasn't because he couldn't date her, but he found it cumbersome and a waste of his time.

Sylvio cleared his calendar that Saturday afternoon and evening so they could go out. It was an interesting location in Manhattan, and Valentina began to realize why he chose it. Hollywood stars, TV personalities, and athletes walked around the city frequently. Although a few would be recognized, many of them were able to blend into the crowd without having to worry about two hundred fans asking for autographs. Sylvio dealt with that enough in Queens, and he wanted to escape.

"Yo, deadass, Paul Walker and Vin Diesel are the top two action movie stars today, 'nuff said," Sylvio said excitedly as they walked toward his Escalade.

"What? Get outta hea! They ain't betta than Arnold Schwarzaneggar or Sylvester Stallone," Valentina said as they hopped in the car.

"What? You crazy. Can them dudes even run anymore?"

"Whateva, they still kick ass. You just don't wanna own up to that."

"So, you like action flicks, huh? I would've neva guessed that." Sylvio started the car and began driving away from the movie theater.

"Why? Is it cuz I'm a female?"

"I ain't gonna front, but I thought that you was into some chick flicks, like Love and Basketball or something."

"What's wrong with Love and Basketball? That was my shit."

"I mean, there ain't nothin' wrong wit' it except that it ain't true. I mean where in sports do you see a brotha' and a woman get back together, and they both have pro careers? In real life, that relationship's doomed to die."

"What makes you say that?"

"Come on, that 'happily ever after' shit don't work today. If a man and a woman both playin' professional sports, they ain't gon' have time for each other cuz they always out of town on road trips, and who knows what happens on the road these days?"

"No, please tell me what happens on the road, Mr. Professional Athlete," Valentina egged on, raising one eyebrow.

Sylvio knew he walked into a trap, insinuating that all professional athletes cheated with their significant other. "Nah, hold up. I ain't mean all that now. Don't be twistin' my words," he laughed and glanced over at Valentina.

"You twisted yourself, loco."

"Loco? I'm crazy now?" Sylvio asked. "Well, maybe I am crazy cuz I'm takin' you out."

"Ay, you knew what you signed up for. Don't ask for milk when you ain't prepared to put a down payment on the cow."

Yo, I'm having a great time with this chick. She's mad chill, and she don't care about my status or me being a boxer. "So, are you workin' today, or am I droppin' you back home?"

"I got someone coverin' my shift at the club tonight, so I'm free. I know you ain't ready to go home yet. It's still early."

From the corner of his eye, Sylvio could tell that she was eyeing him. When he glanced over, she was batting her eyelashes. It was clear she didn't want the night to end.

"Well, we went to dinner and a movie. I took our dating concept back to the fifties. I think our great grandparents were going to dinner and movie dates," he said, attempting to make a weak attempt at a joke, but it didn't register with Valentina.

She was still staring at him. "So, what was your ex like? I mean, did you have a girlfriend?"

"Yeah, I had an ex. Her name was Jasmine. She was pretty dope. She was chill, real smart, had big brains and big…hmm something else," he said, gesturing his eyes toward Valentina's chest, attempting to be discreet, but nothing got past her.

"You mean she had some tig ole' bitties?" she asked, causing Sylvio to stare at her incredulously.

They both burst out laughing.

"Yeah, she did. Anyway, we kicked it for about eight months. I thought she was down for me."

"What happened?"

"Turns out, all she was interested in was my status. She loved who I was in the ring because I was makin' money. She was feelin' The Wolf, but she wasn't feelin' Sylvio. So, once I found out what she was on, I dropped her ass. I ain't been in no serious relationship since then cuz I never knew if a girl would like me for me or if she likes me cuz I'm a name."

Valentina listened and secretly felt bad for Sylvio, partly because she had just left a toxic relationship herself. "My ex was like that too, except his vice was other women. He had a lot of money, most of it through gambling. He never really worked a day in his life. He was a spoiled prima donna who thought he could have everyone and everything he wanted because of his money, but I was just sick of him playin' me, so I left."

"It's hard out hea tryin' to find someone with real intentions. That's why I go twice as hard in boxing. I can't trust nobody." Suddenly he felt Valentina's hand rub his own hand in a sympathetic gesture.

"You can trust me," she said softly.

With her hand caressing the back of his hand, Sylvio felt electricity as his hair stood up on the back of his neck. Perhaps, Valentina knew she was getting to him because her hand moved from his hand to the center of his legs. Sylvio wasn't sure if she'd planned it or not, but she was in no hurry to displace her hand, and the adrenaline rush that Sylvio felt a few seconds ago, went into overdrive. It was as if he was entering the ring with another opponent, but while he was able to stem the flow of adrenaline at times in the ring, he found himself unable to stop himself from getting aroused when Valentina touched him. Yo, she need to stop doing that cuz I'm starting to get hard as a rock down here.

But she didn't stop. Before he knew it, her hand was on his manhood. "Oh, so that's how you feel?" she asked seductively.

For the first time, Sylvio was at a loss for words. "Umm…well, I…" he started, before realizing he was swerving two lanes, causing the driver behind him to honk, before pulling up next to him. He rudely flipped his middle finger at Sylvio before driving off. Valentina laughed.

This girl's a freak. She ain't no closet freak either. She goes for it. He took a moment to glance at Valentina. It didn't help that she was wearing an extremely short skirt with flip flops and a blue halter top. Valentina wasn't what most people described as voluptuous, but she had big breasts, and by looking at them, he knew she was getting excited as well.

"Come on, girl, you know I'm drivin'. What you doin' is killin' me."

"Then maybe we should hurry up and get to your place," Valentina said, without removing her hand from his pelvic area.

"Shit, you ain't gotta ask me twice," Sylvio accelerated the car over twenty miles so that he could get home faster. He didn't know what to expect when he got there, but if Valentina's trick in the car was an opening act, he couldn't wait to enjoy the rest of her show.

No sooner did they arrive at Sylvio's house in Jamaica Estates, he walked her upstairs to the hallway outside his bedroom, kissing her every step of the way. His roaming hands found their way under her skirt and caressed her jewels. She was already wet. Oh, she ready to get some.

"So, this is my place. What you think?" he asked after kissing for what seemed like minutes.

Looking around, Valentina appeared impressed. "Wow, this is dope. You live in this big house by yourself?"

"Yeah, pretty much," he replied, secretly hoping that they were not going to stop the lovemaking session for an impromptu tour of his home.

"Whateva. You probably have groupies in and out of your house all day," she said sarcastically.

"Why you always thinkin' that I'm some type of playa?" Sylvio asked, raising his eyebrow.

"I mean, they call you 'The Wolf,' for God's sake. What woman wouldn't wanna get with a beast?" she asked seductively.

"Well, you ain't eva' lied," Sylvio replied, laughing.

This girl's strokin' my ego as much as she was strokin' away in the car. "But I don't just let anybody up in hea. You gotta be a special jawn if I let you in this spot."

Valentina smiled, unable to hide the red tinge coloring her cheeks and neck. "Am I really special?"

"No doubt," he answered, before picking her up and carrying her into his bedroom. "Enough talkin'," he added, placing her softly on his bed before taking off his T-shirt, revealing his chiseled abs and muscular physique.

He started to unbutton Valentina's blouse and softly slipped her bra off. Reaching into his pockets, he pulled out a condom. He kissed her breasts gently, and Valentina closed her eyes in pleasure as her nipples became erect, but they were hardly alone. Sylvio's underwear were stretched out about six inches and still growing. Their body heat radiated off each other as Valentina kissed his bare chest, licking her way down to his throbbing member.

"Lemme show you something, papi," she said, removing his underwear while getting down on her knees, and as she pulled her hair to the side, she revealed a unique tattoo in the center of her back that resembled two long snakes or ropes that Sylvio glimpsed, but paid no mind.

A few seconds later, Sylvio felt a rush of euphoric pleasure. Oh my God, this girl is a fuckin' freak. Come on Sylvio, you betta hold yo shit and not bust quick. He gritted his teeth in concentration.

It felt so refreshing to hold someone so soft, so sensual, yet aggressive. He found out quickly that Valentina was not afraid to be spontaneous in the bedroom. After her oral performance, he applied the rubber accordingly, and Valentina mounted on top of him. For the next fifteen minutes, they exchanged energy and bodily fluids.

After both bodies climaxed, Valentina laid under Sylvio's arms, looking at him in a light that she never thought she would see him in. "Round 1 goes to Miss Cruz," she said, seductively kissing his chin.

"Hell yeah, girl. Straight knockout too. I'm done."

"Yo, I know it's kind random and shit, but since we did the do, I guess you my girl now?" he asked sheepishly.

"You know it." Whispering in his ear, she revealed, "What I did for you tonight, I didn't even do that with my ex. So, you're real special to me too," she said as they both drifted off into sensual sleep.

Early the next morning, Sylvio's cell phone rang and vibrated. He woke up, and realizing that Valentina was still sleeping under him, he reached over her to answer his phone that was ringing on the lampstand.

"Hello?" he answered, with his back turned on his consummated mate on the other side of the bed.

"Wolf, where the hell were you at, son?" Jim's voice blared out from the other end, causing Sylvio to turn back around nervously, hoping he didn't wake Valentina up. "You ain't check yo voicemail? I called you at least five times last night."

Sylvio checked his call log, where he saw Jim's number appear five times within a two-hour period. "My bad, Jim. I was busy last night. Something came up," he concocted wildly.

"It's okay. Listen, we spoke with Chavez and his trainer, and they agreed to the rematch. We only got one month's time to train. So, we need to start ASAP."

This was exactly the news that Sylvio wanted to hear. "Word? Aight bet. I'm on my way. I'll be there in a couple hours," Sylvio replied before hanging up. Looking at Valentina, his head flashed back to when he thought she was an angel. There was an air of innocence about her, especially when she slept so peacefully, but she was anything but innocent the previous night. But Sylvio knew he had to tread softly in the new relationship. The rematch with Chavez was fast approaching, and he needed to stay prepared for the rematch against the fighter whom he'd previously lost to.

Chapter 13

After an unexpected first night together, Valentina woke up to find the left side of the bed empty. Sylvio was in the bathroom, taking a shower and brushing his teeth.

Although certain areas of her body were sore, Valentina had to admit that Sylvio lived up to his name, at least in the bedroom. She couldn't remember the last time she reached her pleasure peaks in sex. Pedro was incapable of giving her the same pleasure. In fact, none of her ex-boyfriends had the same stamina Sylvio had. As she sat in bed, reflecting on the previous night, Sylvio walked back in the room.

"Hey, baby, good morning," he said, kissing her on the forehead.

That's so sweet. "Good morning, Wolf," she greeted back, smiling.

Sylvio rubbed the back of his head nervously. "Look, about last night...if I did anything wrong—"

Valentina interrupted him. "Nah, you ain't done nothing wrong at all. Everything was right. For the first time in a long time, this feels right. So, who was that on the phone?"

"Oh, don't worry. It was just my trainer, Jim Shaw. He was discussing our next fight. I gotta head to the gym right now to train."

"Oh okay, but why would I be worried?"

"Well, I know how ya'll get when a man get a phone call from someone other than his mama."

"I ain't like these other chicks, Sylvio. I get it. You're a celebrity. You're in demand. That's how it is." Valentina shrugged.

"Yeah, but even in my busy life, I ain't gonna be too busy for you though. I just gotta focus on this next fight, so if I'm preoccupied over the next month, I ain't ignoring you. I'm just gettin' ready for war."

"I know, and when that day comes, I'll be right there cheering you on." Valentina got up to kiss Sylvio again before heading to the bathroom. "Mind if I use your shower?"

"Yeah, go ahead."

"Can you bring me my clothes, please?" she asked as she turned on the water.

Sylvio took her clothes to her, and after Valentina showered got dressed, he said, "I can drop you by yo crib."

Valentina's eyes widened with sudden realization. Her brothers would certainly be home at this time, and she did not want them finding out about her relationship with Sylvio, at least not yet.

"Actually, you can drop me off at the Q9 bus stop. I'll take the bus home. It's all good."

"What? Nah, I'll drop you home. I know where you stay at anyway."

"Yeah, but I'm expecting company at home this morning. The last thing I wanna do is get you stirred up in public controversy that you don't need, especially with your upcoming fight and all."

Sylvio was still confused but didn't question her any further as he packed his training duffel bag. Valentina followed him downstairs and outside to his car.

After the bus dropped her nearly a block away from where she lived, Valentina's mind flashed back to the last night's activities with Sylvio. What a man. I haven't felt this way in a long time. I mean, last night had to be just a good time, right? Or could it be much more than a good time?

Is it too early to fall in love with a man I just slept with? Ugh, so many questions and very few answers. It's driving me crazy.

As she walked up to her house, she sighed when she saw the old red Mazda parked on the small driveway. Her brothers were home, and they would no doubt ask about her whereabouts the previous night. Since she moved out of her parents' house a few years earlier, she had been living with her brothers until she made enough money to stay on her own.

Bruno and Juan were both about five and six years older than her and were fiercely overprotective. Bruno was tall and lanky with black wavy hair that he often combed to the side. He would cut the sideburns and shave the hair off the sides so it looked like a fade. Juan was more heavy-set than Bruno. Weighing over two hundred and ten pounds and standing at about six feet three, Juan was intimidating with his shaved head, small mustache, and goatee.

Valentina loved her brothers, but she had often questioned their life's choices. During the daytime, they worked as contractors and construction foremen in Manhattan, but at night, they were both involved in the underground gambling ring. In fact, both were sponsored by Pedro's group, earning extra winnings when all gambling bets have been returned. If anyone outside of their circle failed to pay a lost bet, Juan and Bruno were considered enforcers, often threatening people with violence and death. Valentina had always attempted to convince them to leave the underground gambling world, but the extra money they generated was too good, and leaving the operation wasn't an option.

Determined to slowly unlock the door and tiptoe to her room, her hopes were dashed when her two brothers saw her sneaking in.

"Valentina! Donde estabas?" Juan asked as they saw Valentina through the kitchen door. The brothers were eating breakfast.

"Don't worry about it. It ain't none of your business," she said as she attempted to walk to her room.

Juan snatched her arm. "What you say? Everything you do is my business. You're my little sister, and if you ain't been home last night, I got a right to ask where the hell you been."

"Why do you always have to know? It's not like ya came in last night either," Valentina replied angrily.

"It ain't about us though. It's about you. You're barely twenty-two years old. You ain't supposed to be out on these streets," Bruno said.

"What are you now—my mother and father? Yeah, I am twenty-two, and guess what? It makes me a grown-ass woman who can make her own decisions," Valentina countered.

"Not as long as you stayin' with us. When you stay under this house, you live by our rules, comprendes?" Juan asked.

Valentina rolled her eyes. "Okay, whatever. I was off work yesterday, so I went out with Passion and some of the girls. It was late, so we went to her house, and I crashed for the night. No big deal," she lied. She couldn't tell her brothers about her rendezvous with Sylvio. She wasn't sure how they would take the news.

"Yeah okay, whateva. I bet you she was with some dude last night. Did you get back with Pedro?" Bruno asked.

"That fool? Hell nah, I told you I was done with Pedro, and if ya'll knew what was good for you, ya would leave him alone too," Valentina replied.

"What? You buggin', sis. All the money he done made us? I think you the fool for droppin' him. You need to find a way to fix up whateva beef ya got between each other," Bruno said.

"It's over, Bruno. I'm done being that boy's hoe. Save the speech for all the bitches that he sleeps with," Valentina said.

The warm feelings she felt after leaving Sylvio's home were being replaced with anger at her brothers for their hypocrisy. So they could stay out all night as much as they can, betting on sports teams and sleeping around, meanwhile I gotta be the good Catholic school girl all the time. "Look, I gotta be at work later on, so if you're done giving me the third degree, can I go now?" she asked.

"Yeah, get outta hea. Make sure you come back tonight though," Juan said.

Whatever. They really believe they are my parents now. At times, she couldn't stand her brothers. Brushing the ordeal off, Valentina headed over to her room and checked the mail from the day before. One of the letters was one from YAA, or the Young Actors of America acting agency. Valentina had been searching for talent and acting agencies for years as she still clung to the hope of being an actress in Hollywood. Opening the letter, she read the contents. Within moments, she was grinning from ear to ear. She was invited to the agency, where she would provide a headshot and await representation.

Later that day, Sylvio was sparring with Terry. From the onset of the session, Jim realized that his fighter appeared distracted. His reflexes were slower, and Terry was popping him with quick blows from jabs and hooks to the body.

"Yo, Wolf, what's wrong with you, man? Wake up!" Jim yelled as the two fighters exchanged punches.

But although Sylvio tried to stay focused, all he could think about was her touch, her scent, and her delicateness. The way she methodically worked on his body last night was wondrous, but it was costing him his reaction time in the ring. Sylvio saw Terry's right hook coming, but he slipped one second too late, and Terry's hook caught him in his temple, causing Sylvio to bend over slightly.

"Ring the damn bell already!" Jim told Jersey Jack, another trainer.

Sure enough, Jersey sounded the bell, ending the round.

As Sylvio approached the corner, Jim grabbed Sylvio by his sweat-soaked tank top. "What's wrong wit' you, son? Where your head at today? Forget about Maximo. If you keep exposing yourself like this, Chavez will knock the shit outta you inside of five rounds!" Jim bellowed, clearly upset that Sylvio was not focused.

"Okay, I got you, man. I'm good!" Sylvio argued back.

"You sure?" Jim said. "If you ain't feelin' up to it, you best go home and sleep it out, and come back hea when you're actually ready to start boxing!"

"I said, 'I'm good!'" Sylvio yelled.

"Well then, go out there and prove it then! The way that you fightin' right now, my grandmother could probably whup yo ass," Jim said.

That was all it took for Sylvio to glare at Jim. "Don't push me, Jim. I ain't yo robot or yo slave. You gon' show me the same damn respect I show you, or I'm gone," he replied, getting up from the stool to walk back towards the center of the ring.

"Is she worth it?" Jim yelled.

Sylvio looked at him in amazement.

"That's right, son. I was a boxer long before you was even thought of. You think I don't know that you whipped right now?" Jim asked, before he stepped closer to Sylvio. "Listen," he said in a hushed tone. "I don't know who you messin' wit' right now, and maybe, it's none of my business, but this is your best shot at getting a chance at the middleweight crown. You have a chance to be the best in the world, and you can't allow a girl to let you miss the opportunity. Beat Chavez, and let's get Maximo. The moment you become champion, then you can enjoy the fruit. But now, we gotta focus, okay?"

Sylvio nodded his head to indicate that he heard his trainer as the bell rang for the next round. Sylvio's timing improved, and he used his anger that was previously aimed toward Jim and refocused it back onto the ring. Terry partially blocked his blows but was still able to land a few shots himself.

After the round was over, Terry spoke to Sylvio, who was leaning forward against the rope. "You good, man?"

"Yeah, I'm straight," Sylvio replied.

"I don't know what it is. Either I'm having a really good day or you're having a really bad one," Terry said.

Sylvio looked at Terry, raising his eyebrow. "Go wit' that second theory B. cuz you couldn't hold a candle to me on a good day." Sylvio wiped his face with a towel.

Jim stepped away from the ring to check on the other gym attendees, which Sylvio was extremely grateful for because he didn't have to hear his trainer's mouth run.

"So, what you get into last night, man? Is what Jim said true?" Terry asked.

"Come on, dawg, you tryin' to be all up in my business too?" Sylvio asked rhetorically.

"You primetime, brotha. Spotlight's on you every day, man. Better me than the public media anyway," Terry replied.

He does have a point. If the media ever caught me with Valentina, they would have a field day with me. Plus, Valentina would be getting all this unwanted attention and dragged into my world. "Okay, I'll level wit' you, but you can't tell nobody 'bout this, iight?" he said to Terry.

"I got you," Terry confirmed.

"Okay, so I ran into this girl that I knew from childhood, right. She works at Apple Kim's in Astoria as a waitress, and we reconnected. Dawg, this chick got me goin' crazy, man. I mean, I don't got problems talkin' wit' other females or nothin' like that, but she's different, man," Sylvio said.

Suddenly, Terry smiled a wide, toothy grin. "You hit it, didn't you?"

Sylvio did not wish to tell anyone about his relationship, but since the cat was out of the bag, he confirmed Terry's theory. "Bruh, when I tell you that girl had body for days, and she knew how to work that too."

"She black or white?"

"She's Dominican," Sylvio replied. Terry seemed to understand and continued listening. "Yo deadass, it just started as a simple movie, then it turned into something else."

"I feel you, man. And believe me, I'm all for it, dude. I already knew you hit, not just cuz of your reaction time, but you got that glazed look in yo eye."

"What you talkin about, 'glazed look'? Man, we came back to my place last night, but not soon after, she started suckin' my dick, B."

"What is she, a nymphomaniac or something?"

"I don't even know, bro. First minute, we going back to my spot, and the next thing I know, she's on top of me, and I'm pumpin' and pumpin'. I don't know what the deal is, man, but I'm feelin' this chick."

"Just be careful, man. Trust and believe when I say that these women make you weak in heart, mind, and soul, bro."

"I know, but I gotta train, and then I got to find out where I stand with her. All we did was dinner, followed by a movie, followed by intense sex."

"Was she A1?"

"You know she was, man. Her man wasn't treating that right, so I had to unleash the wolf on her," Sylvio bragged.

"Man, you wild, Wolf," Terry replied, laughing. "But on the real though, Jim's right. We gotta get right for this next fight against Chavez. Word on the street is that after he accepted the fight, he started talkin' greasy, tellin' people how he was gon' beat you like last time."

"Dude barely beat me last time. The judges saved him. This time I won't leave it up to them judges. I'm knockin' his ass out," Sylvio said firmly.

"That's what I'm talkin' about!" Terry said as they put on their gear to resume sparring.

Back in his house after a long, hard day at the gym, Sylvio was flipping TV channels. It was three minutes to midnight when he heard his cell phone ring. It was Valentina.

"Hey, baby, what's up?" he asked.

"Hey, Sylvio, I'm sorry to bother you like this. I know you're getting ready for the fight and stuff, and I don't want to distract you, but my shift ended early and I don't have enough money in my Metrocard to take the bus or train. I gotta reload tomorrow morning. You mind giving me a ride home, please?"

Internally, Sylvio debated on if he should give Valentina a ride. If he got caught up again, he was looking at another sluggish performance at the gym the following day. But Sylvio was not known to abandon people who needed help.

"Okay, I'll be there in like forty minutes. Hang tight," he said. Valentina agreed and Sylvio hung up.

Come on, Sylvio. What are you doing? This girl is beautiful, but is she worth throwing away everything you worked hard for? Jim's words rang through his head like alarm bells. If Sylvio could possibly balance his career and his new relationship, one wouldn't interfere over the other.

After fifty minutes, the last ten being because of unexpected rush hour traffic on the interstate, Sylvio arrived at Apple Kim's. Unfortunately, there was no parking in the front of the club, and the valet service appeared to be off-duty. As a result, Sylvio had to drive around the block to find a spot. Parking in an empty lot, he decided to enter the club through the back door, which was two stair levels above ground. His phone rang again.

"Did you arrive yet?" Valentina asked.

"Yeah, I'm in the back," Sylvio replied before hanging up.

After two minutes, the back door opened, and Valentina stepped out and looked around for a moment. Sylvio knew she couldn't see him yet. The street lights were dim as Valentina's figure was shadowed by the moonlight.

Yo, she looks beautiful in the moonlight. Sylvio stared up at the backdoor. "Looking for me?" He shouted just loud enough for Valentina to hear him.

Looking down, Valentina finally saw Sylvio. "Oh good, you're here. I thought you would've blown me off or not come because of your boxing thing."

"Technically, I shouldn't have come. But you were worth it."

"That's so sweet," Valentina said. "Give me a sec. Let me grab my things, and I'll be right down," she added, running back inside.

Fifteen minutes later, Valentina walked back out and down the stairs, embracing Sylvio in a long kiss.

"Yo, let me get you home. You bout to get me caught up again out hea," Sylvio said, but Valentina was flirting heavily with him.

"Maybe I wanna get caught up," Valentina cooed, batting her eyelashes.

"So are you gon' let me drop you home this time and not just the bus stop?"

Valentina laughed. "Yeah, you could drop me at my place. I had you drop me at the bus stop in the morning because I knew my brothers were home, and if they saw a man bringing me home…" Her voice trailed off. "Let's just say they don't play well with others."

"Why, are they gangbangers or something?"

"Nah, they don't roll wit' no set. But they just got dangerous associations."

"Oh, you mean they know some gangstas."

"Something like that."

"I don't know what's the big deal. They don't want you datin' rich, tall, dark, and handsome brothas or something?"

"It ain't nothing like that. They just don't like me rollin' with anyone that they don't know," she answered.

"Who doesn't know me at this point though? They probably peeped me on ESPN or something. If they don't know, they betta' ask somebody," Sylvio bragged.

Valentina let out a fake sigh. "This is what I get for dating another big head."

"Yeah, whateva. You know you like my big head," Sylvio said, laughing.

"Well, I like your lil' head, too," Valentina replied, gazing between Sylvio's legs and just like before, her hand went to work on him again.

"Val, look, at any other time, believe me, I'd be down for this. But I'm training, and I gotta be focused for the next fight."

Valentina stopped her foreplay immediately with a look of rejection on her face.

"But I promise, once the fight's over, it's on," he said, winking slightly.

Then, Valentina's cell rang. "Hello?"

"Girl, where you at? I'm askin' all around for you, and everyone told me that you left already. Why'd you dip out on me like that? I thought I was yo girl," Passion said in her typical loud, shrilling voice.

Overhearing her loud friend, Sylvio began to chuckle.

Valentina tapped Sylvio hard on his arm before replying to her friend. "My bad, Passion. I had an early night tonight, and my man came to pick me up, so I'm on my way home now."

"Your man?" Passion asked, astounded. "Wait, wait, hold up. Since when were you gon' tell me that you was givin' it to another nigga? Who is it? Anybody I know?"

Valentina instantly regretted opening her mouth to Passion. If there was one characteristic that she knew about Passion, it was the fact that she could never keep a secret from anybody. Once she found fresh gossip, she would turn on and couldn't be turned off.

"I know. I'm sorry, Passion. I kept it on the low-low for a while, but I just started seeing this new guy, so we just chillin' right now," she replied, smiling at Sylvio.

"Okay, well excuse me, mamacita. Chill away. But you know I'mma stay on you till you give me da 4-1-1 on Mr. New Man," Passion said, still oblivious to the fact that Sylvio was listening to their conversation.

"Okay, I'll holla at you lata," Valentina said.

"Okay. Later," Passion replied, and Valentina hung up.

Sheepishly, she stared at Sylvio. "Passion is a hot mess."

"Hmm, which one was Passion? Was she the brownskin one with a ton of ass? Bootius Maximus?" he joked.

"Aye, don't diss my girl now, Sylvio," she laughed. "Besides, all the dancers at Apple Kim's got a big ass. You should know, since you was holdin' a whole lotta ass when I saw you in VIP that day."

"Touche," Sylvio replied laughing as he continued to drive Valentina home for the evening.

Chapter 14

Training intensified at the Steel Glove Gym as Sylvio focused on his upcoming rematch with Jose Chavez. Sylvio ran around the block where the gym was located some days while on other days, he worked on increasing his punching power over at the heavy bag.

Aside from sparring with different fighters, Jim was also breaking down films of Chavez's previous fights, including his first bout with the Mexican brawler. Chavez was a rangy middleweight who was considered a top-heavy contender. He wasn't quick, nor was he very strong, but what Jim feared the most about Chavez was that he was one of the craftiest fighters Sylvio had ever faced.

As they dove in deeper into film work, Jim and Sylvio were finally able to break down Chavez's habits and expose his weakness: an open left flank. Chavez would always fight with his hands up, defending his arms and his face, but Sylvio realized that if he could get close enough, he would be able to strike Chavez just enough to do internal damage and sway the decision of the judges.

"Remember, Jim, the goal ain't to leave it up to the judges. I underestimated this man last time, but this time, my goal is to knock him out," Sylvio said, as they continued watching tape.

"That's right. Make it so convincing that Maximo will have no choice but to give you a title shot."

The hype machine went into overdrive as Sylvio and Chavez traveled with their training teams all over the tri-city area to promote their bout. Sylvio was never a fan of promoting fights with his opponents. He felt the moments were wasting his time, and he longed to get back to the gym.

Sylvio also realized that Chavez did not have the same meekness or humility that Bokavic had.

Chavez was a talker, and he was known for berating his opponents at the promotional events. At one such event in Philadephia, Chavez, his trainer, and other members of his entourage arrived at a venue for the fight promo. After five minutes, Sylvio showed up with his team, but as he walked in, Chavez started the trash talk.

"Yo, Wolf, why you always late to every event? Oh wait, I forgot. Haitians are always late to everything. I see that you got yo peeps behind you. What you call 'em again, Wolf Pack? They look more like pound puppies to me," Chavez said, expecting Sylvio to overreact, even attempt to charge him. But his tactics were unsuccessful.

"Chavez, I know what you doin' dawg, and it ain't workin'. You need to take them washed up jokes, and do exactly what I'mma do to you on fight night: drop 'em," Sylvio replied as he sat down on the opposite table from Chavez before taking or answering any questions from the media.

"Remember, it's about quickness. Chavez starts off every round on the offensive. He does this to rack up points before the midway point of the round. What we need to work on is countering his attack as he moves forward," Jim said at the gym the next day.

While Sylvio resumed training, Valentina walked into the gym. Sylvio turned around, saw Valentina, and smiled. "Aye what's up, baby? You hea to watch me work?"

"You already know!" Valentina replied excitedly.

"That's what's up. Hold up, lemme introduce you to the rest of the crew here," Sylvio said as Valentina looked around. It was her first day at the Steel Glove Gym, and she felt out of place. "First off, this hea's my trainer, Jim Shaw. Jim, this is my girl, Valentina," Sylvio introduced.

Jim shook Valentina's hand. "So, you the woman that my fighter's been talking non-stop about."

"Yeah, he told me about you too. He said you were like a father to him," Valentina answered.

Jim flashed a quick grin at Sylvio, but it was only for a split second before it was replaced with his usual stoic face.

"I promise I won't get in the way. I'm just here to support and watch his training," Valentina said.

"See, Jim, I told you my girl's a hundred," Sylvio said, and from that point on, Jim allowed Valentina to remain in the gym during training.

During his workout breaks, Sylvio introduced Valentina to the other members of the Wolf Pack. Of course, Gary and Kyle recognized her immediately from Apple Kim's.

During the sparring session with Terry, Sylvio focused on pin-pointing his shots to the lower left flank, which proved to be the weakest point for Terry, so much so that Terry had to remove his sparring gear and ice his sore hips and sides.

The next day, Sylvio arrived at the gym, but upon leaving the parking lot, he saw something unusual. Jim's car wasn't parked outside.

He's probably gonna arrive late. Sylvio entered the gym. Valentina picked up an earlier shift at Apple Kim's and had informed him she wasn't going to make it to see him. That was expected, but Jim's absence wasn't.

"Yo, what up? Any of ya see Jim?" Sylvio asked the other members of the gym.

"Nah, we ain't seen him all day," one member said.

Sylvio walked into the gym office, where he saw Kevin Shaw working at his desk. "What's up, Kevin?"

"What's goin' on, champ?"

"I'm good, man. Yo, have you seen Jim?"

"No. Why? He ain't out there?"

"Nah, he ain't there. It ain't like Jim to be late, man. He's normally on point. He ain't sick or nothin' like that, right?"

"Well, I spoke to him last night, and he never told me he wasn't coming." But at that very moment, his eyes widened. "Unless he went to go visit him."

"Visit who?"

"His son, Dante."

Instantly, Sylvio was floored. Jim Shaw has a son, and he never told me? "How do you know he went to visit his son?"

"Today is August 10th. Dante was born August 10, 1986," Kevin answered, still deep in thought.

"Damn. I ain't even knew he had a son. I never met him."

"You wouldn't have met him. Dante passed away in 1995. A bully pushed Dante into the street outside his school. He was struck by a car right in front of Jim's eyes. He always blamed himself for the incident. The only place I could see him being today is at Liberty Street Memorial."

Sylvio walked back outside, determined to find his trainer.

Arriving at Liberty Street Memorial Funeral Home later that afternoon, Sylvio walked by countless headstones, and he couldn't help but to feel a wave of depression. Although he knew it was a part of life, Sylvio hated death and every aspect that came along with it, from watching a person draw their final breath, to the actual funeral and watching their final resting place. Walking through the cemetery wasn't helping, and Sylvio began feeling a sense of dread and fear. The cemetery stretched over five hundred yards.

Where the hell is Jim? He buggin' if he think I'm gonna walk through all this death. He looked around but saw no sign of Jim.

Finally, Sylvio looked inside the funeral home and walked through a hallway where marble tablets of the deceased ascended, row by row. It was in this hallway that he finally saw Jim hunched over, unaware of anyone or anything. As he slowly approached his trainer, Sylvio saw the inscription on the marble tablet that read DANTE SHAW in large block letters. Below the words, he saw an image of a young angel suspended in the clouds.

"Shouldn't you be training right now?" Jim asked when he saw Sylvio's reflection through the clear marble stone.

"How come you never told me you had a son?"

"I try to keep my life as private as possible. He would want it that way."

It was only a second later that Sylvio found out that he was referring to his son. "Kevin told me how he passed away. I'm sorry, man," Sylvio said, kneeling down beside Jim.

"Appreciate it, Wolf," Jim replied as he brushed away a tear. "You know, as a young boxer, I had so many fans in the game, but there was no bigger fan than Dante. He wasn't planned or nothing, but when my girl at the time gave birth to him, I knew that I had to man up to take on the biggest fight of my life: fatherhood. I was there for his first bike ride, his first loose tooth, and his first day of school. When it was time, I sacrificed the back end of my career to raise him. Boxing was lucrative, but raising a child is priceless. However, the very thing that he looked up to me for became the very thing that cost him his life. It's been hard bouncing back."

"Jim, it wasn't your fault. Some punk kid ended Dante's life. You tried to stop it from happening. But maybe, just maybe, Dante is somewhere watching you, and he's still your son. He never really left cuz he's still in there," Sylvio said, pointing at Jim's chest.

"Yeah, you right. You know, I never got the chance to tell you this, but you reminded me of Dante when we met outside P.S. 55."

Sylvio nodded his head in realization. Now he understood why Jim had his back from the very beginning. Watching Brandon torment Sylvio was reminiscent of Dante being bullied in Jim's eyes, and he did not want to see another child become a victim.

"It makes sense now. Remember that night when my father saw you, and he didn't want me coming into the gym, and you mentioned that being suspended because of a fight was better than a death certificate? I get it now."

"You know, when I said that to your father, I saw how protective he was of you. He wanted to keep you on the straight and narrow, and for that I commend him. Listen to me, brother. If you got any beef wit' your pops, now's the time to end it cuz you never know if your next conversation with him could be your last."

Sylvio thought about his father, who was home battling diabetes. Jim, no doubt, knew the history between Sylvio and his father, dating back to the night Sylvio packed and left home.

"I visited him again this past week. He's hangin' in there. He's still a tough man," Sylvio said. "But for the years when my father and I never saw eye-to-eye, you took his place. You were the better father to me than he was."

"I wasn't the better father for Dante. I should've listened to him. I should've equipped him, the same way I equipped you," Jim admitted, looking at his son's grave.

"So, when you met me, you saw Dante in me?"

Jim looked at Sylvio. "I know that it wasn't the right way of thinkin', but I'd be lyin' if I said that I never saw Dante in you. Not to mention, at that time, when he tried on his first boxing gloves as a youngin, it was hard for him to get em on too. Remember when you first tried them joints?" he laughed.

"Hell yeah, Them jawns were hard to put on! But you helped me, and I got nothin' but appreciation for what you've done."

"Thanks, Sylvio. For long time, I couldn't bring myself to come back here because it was just too painful. Training you and other boxers was therapy for me. Watching you from the age of nine until today...ain't nothin' like it."

"Appreciate it," Sylvio replied. "As a matter of fact, I'm gonna give it all to you and Dante. As God's my witness, I'mma do it for Dante. We gon' get this title belt for him and make him proud."

To Sylvio's relief, a smile broke out on Jim's face. "Okay, let's go for it," Jim replied, as Sylvio helped him to his feet. They both walked out of the funeral home.

Finally, after three weeks of training, television, radio, and Internet promotions, it was fight night. More than twenty thousand people filled the Staples Center Arena in Los Angeles to watch the middleweight fight between Jose Chavez and Sylvio Dominique. The judges were already seated behind their designated tables, and the official was in the ring after going into the locker rooms to make final checks on each boxer. The fight was aired on Showtime, and subscribers from all over the world were tuned in.

The time finally came as Sylvio's team walked out of the locker room and towards the ring. Sylvio wore his usual stoic expression as he climbed into the ring, flanked by Jim and Kevin. Kyle and Gary rounded out the rest of the Wolf Pack. Jim nervously wiped a tear from his eye, having just experienced an emotional moment a few minutes before entering the ring. While still in the locker room, Antoine Parham, the cut-man and doctor, wrapped Sylvio hands with a special, customized wrap before putting his gloves on.

"Yo, Jim, check this out," Sylvio had called to his trainer.

Jim was staring outside the visitor's locker room door down the long corridor. He walked back to his fighter, and Sylvio showed him his glove wrap.

A few days earlier, with Kevin's help, Sylvio had his wrap customized to display a photo of Dante Shaw. The designer deftly took the photo and created a detailed image of Dante through the glove wrap. Jim was stunned when he saw the wrap in Sylvio's hand. Once Antoine finished wrapping Sylvio's hand, Sylvio closed his fists, and Jim saw his son once again.

"Like I said, I'm doin' it for him. Wherever I go, he goes wit' me," Sylvio said.

"Thanks, son," Jim said, unable to stop the tears from flowing. It was a thoughtful gesture and one that Jim did not expect to receive from Sylvio.

Now in the ring, Jim and Sylvio waited for their opponent, and sure enough, Jose Chavez walked out of the corridor to the sound of loud cheers and applause. Chavez was in his hometown, and he felt confident that if he lured Sylvio away from the confines of New York, he would be able to psyche his opponent out mentally. But Sylvio had already made up his mind that he didn't care where he fought Chavez, and although the people booed him as he entered the ring, it just provided him more fuel.

It's me against the world again. Just how I like it.

Jim took Sylvio's robe off and approached the center of the ring where Chavez was waiting for him. While the official gave instruction to both fighters, Chavez continued taunting Sylvio.

"You ready to take another L? You in my hood now, homes. Come get some," he said.

Sylvio shook his head, smiling outwardly, but he internalized the insults, planning to load them into every punch he would throw that evening. Let's see if he keeps talking after I break his freakin' jaw. Never responding, Sylvio went back to his corner.

The fight was entering the fifth round. Chavez found out very quickly and brutally that the advantage he held at home made no difference. Bleeding, battered, and bruised, he had taken significant punishment from Sylvio, who fought smart, yet aggressive. Chavez's reaction time was delayed as Sylvio landed over eighty percent of his jabs and hooks. The cunning hometown kid was out of tricks as Sylvio capitalized on the errors he made in their first bout and continued to chop away at Chavez's body.

"I don't hear you talkin' now, cholo," Sylvio taunted as he rocked Chavez's chin with a bone-crushing uppercut, stunning his opponent.

He followed it with a deadly left hook to the temple that floored Chavez. With the blood pouring down the side of his eye, nose, and mouth, Chavez struggled to get to his feet as the official began the ten-count. Chavez looked at Sylvio's eyes and saw that his opponent would not be denied again. Valiently he tried to rise back up, but he had nothing left.

"Get up! You wanna talk like you mafioso. Back that shit up!" Sylvio yelled over his prostrate opponent as the official yelled at him to get into a neutral corner.

At the count of nine, Chavez managed to get to his feet but was still groggy, but once he stood, the fight ended with a knockout. The crowd booed as Sylvio raised his hands in victory, almost in defiance.

A Showtime reporter finally managed to pull him aside for an interview. "Great fight, Wolf! You had people that doubted your punching power and many others that felt you lost the Bokavic fight, but you came out against Chavez and executed to perfection. What do you think made the difference from the first fight?"

"I just stayed persistent, continued to work, and with the help of my trainer, Jim, we just followed the game plan, and it resulted in victory. Chavez is a good fighter, but I had something for him tonight," Sylvio replied.

"Thank you," the reporter said, but Sylvio, still high off the win, requested to talk to the reporter again.

This time he sent a defiant message to the defending champion, live on-air. "Yo, Felipe, I know you watching this right now. Is this good enough for you? What more do you need? I'm right hea, boy. I ain't goin' nowhere. Quit runnin', and come see me. I want a shot now, you hear me?" he yelled at the camera furiously, before turning back and making his way into the locker room.

Chapter 15

Back in New York, Alex Rojas, an Astoria resident and close family friend to Juan and Bruno Cruz, was hosting a small party at his small two-story house. The bachata music blared inside the house where a huge contingent of Queens' Hispanic population gathered. Drinks were flowing, and many dishes, prepared by his wife, Maria, were laid in aluminum platters across the table. Out on the patio, the old men were playing cards while drinking beer and smoking cigars.

Bruno and Juan were inside one of the bedrooms, counting the cash winnings they had accumulated when their soccer game scores matched their predictions. Oddsmakers grudgingly paid their losses, and the Cruz brothers were there to pick up the spoils. Since being hired by Pedro to manage the cashflow, Juan and Bruno didn't take their jobs or positions lightly, knowing that any stolen or mismanaged funds would be met with extreme force, administered by Pedro's shady associates.

"Yo, Pedro, we hit the motherload, homes! I told you that squad had that game all day, son!" Bruno gloated proudly.

"Word, but for real, when's yo brotha gonna step back in dat ring? I'm lookin' to count them millions instead of just thousands, you feel me?" Juan asked.

Pedro, who was also counting the money, gave Juan a stern look. "He'll fight when there's someone out there worth fighting."

Before they could continue, Felipe Maximo walked out of the opposite room, flanked by three Hispanic women.

"Well, if it ain't el mujeriego walkin' up in this piece," Pedro joked as Felipe joined his brother and the Cruz brothers.

"Aye, I can't help it. I can't choose just one sexy chica. I gotta have all three flavas. Neopolitan shit, you feel me?" Felipe answered, laughing.

"Like that, homes? Yo, save one fo' me, man," Juan said, eyeing one of the girls, who responded by winking at him.

"Nah, you gon' have to drop me first before I give her fine ass up," Felipe replied, his expression suddenly turning serious.

The room was silent for a moment and Juan felt beads of perspiration fall down his face. The last thing he wanted to do was to upset or agitate the defending middleweight champion. But Felipe broke out laughing, drawing a sigh of relief from Juan.

"I'm just fuckin' wit' you, B. Damn, you looked like you was about to lose yo shit. You good, bro?" Felipe asked.

Alex, who had been in the living room, watching television, emerged from the bottom of the staircase. "Yo Max, get down hea, man! Did you catch the middleweight fight tonight?"

"No, because if it ain't me fightin', I don't give a damn who else is fightin'. They all just linin' up to get their shit rocked," Felipe replied.

"Well, you might wanna come down here cuz you might wanna fight this guy next," Alex said, before going back into the living room.

Curiosity finally got the better of Felipe as he walked to the living room with his three female companions. The television was flipped to the sports channel, and the two sportscasters, Lenny Highwater and Rob Rendman, were discussing other topics before they discussed the middleweight fight that aired just a couple hours earlier.

"And in other sports, it looks like the formidable Jose Chavez was brought down by young phenom Sylvio Dominique. Dominique managed to knock him out in five rounds," Rob said.

"Whoever started the rumor that this guy was a pushover with no knockout power is certainly delusional. Dominique entered the fight as a three-to-two underdog but wasted no time dispatching the older, more experienced Chavez," Lenny replied, and the highlights recapped the fight.

Felipe stared on as the man that he'd ridiculed for his dark complexion, knock Chavez senseless on the canvas.

"Ooooooh," Alex reacted as he saw the replay of the knockout blow that felled Chavez. Felipe rolled his eyes.

"And he wasn't done either. Right after the fight, it seems as if Sylvio had something to say to current champion Felipe Maximo," Rob said, before they replayed the interview after the fight.

"Yo, Felipe, I know you watching this right now. Is this good enough for you? What more do you need? I'm right hea, boy. I ain't goin' nowhere. Quit runnin', and come see me. I want a shot now, you hear me?"

"That's right, Maximo, you heard it here correctly. Dominique is calling you out, and now the boxing world holds its breath, awaiting the response of the defending champion," Lenny said.

"Boy, I tell ya, what a fight that would be. Maximo is methodical in the ring, but he may be in for a wakeup call when he faces young Dominique. He's hungry, aggressive, and he wants that title shot. So wherever Maximo is, if you can hear this, you need to send a message back to him, and it needs to start with, 'Yes, I will take this matchup. I will shut down this hype job to remind him who the real champion is,'" Rob said.

Felipe watched the show and saw the brash interview. Turning to Alex he asked, "What you think, man? Should I take the fight?"

"Max, all he's doin' is gettin' under yo skin. He was probably told to say that by his trainer. You ain't gotta do it on his terms," Alex countered.

But Felipe was bothered. Who does this guy think he is, calling me out on national TV? Kid must have a death wish. "Get Shareef on the line right away. Tell him that I accept his challenge, and I wanna fight this Haitian pretty boy so I can put him in his place," Felipe said, among cheers from the partygoers.

"Kid's stupid. You ain't undefeated for nothin' bro. Show him what's up," Alex said.

"If he wants the boom, he's gonna get it. Someone should tell the kid to back out now while he still can," Felipe said, as Shareef's number was dialed.

After his rematch against Chavez, Sylvio returned to New York and was taken aback when he walked out of the plane at JFK International Airport. More than a thousand fans and supporters were there to greet him. If there was a cloud higher than nine, it would describe the way Sylvio felt at that moment. There was no better feeling than a fighter's hometown showing love to their favorite son after a fight.

Sylvio's bodyguards worked overtime to maneuver Sylvio to a limo and waiting for him in the backseat was none other than his girlfriend, dressed in a dazzling blue mini-dress with blue heels.

Turning to Kyle and Gary, Sylvio said, "Yo, ya ride wit' Jim, aight? My ride ova hea," he said gesturing to the limo.

Gary and Kyle retreated to Jim's car, both smiling devilishly at Sylvio.

"Thought I'd stop by and surprise you, baby," Valentina said seductively.

Yo, this life got Val dressing like J-Lo. Sylvio climbed into the backseat. "Damn, baby it's been too long," he said, kissing her nonstop. Gesturing to Simeon to start driving, he rolled the window partition up.

As soon as Simeon's head was out of view, Sylvio turned to Valentina with a devilish grin, and they both gave in to their passion. Heels, sneakers, and his shirt were flying in all directions as Sylvio removed his warmup pants, and Valentina slipped off her panties from under the dress. Mounting on top of the victorious boxer, she let out a moan as Sylvio entered her.

Thank God for tinted windows. The ride back to Sylvio's house took twenty-five minutes, but it felt like it might have been twenty seconds as the limo pulled up in front of Sylvio's front door.

"We've arrived, sir," Simeon said, rolling the partition down, slightly.

"Aight, Sim, cool. Give us a minute, bro!" Sylvio yelled from the backseat, his face buried under Valentina's hair as Simeon, taking the hint, rolled the partition back up.

For three minutes, neither Valentina nor Sylvio moved. Finally, Sylvio pulled out and Valentina sat down beside him, laughing mischievously. "Thanks, baby, I needed that," Sylvio laughed as he scrambled to put his pants back on.

"God, me too. You don't know how good that felt. How good you feel..." Valentina pulled her panties back on.

Sylvio wasn't one to fall in love, but he had to admit that she had him sprung, and the feeling was mutual. "I ain't eva' met anyone like you before. It's like you down for anything," he said, putting his shirt back on.

"Anything that involves you," Valentina finished, kissing Sylvio on his lips. He was wearing his favorite sports cologne, and it was driving her crazy. Nothing turned her on more than a man that smelled good.

"Hey baby, can I ask you something?" Valentina asked, as she snuggled up next to Sylvio.

"Yeah, you can ask me anything. What's up?"

"One of my friends from Apple Kim's is celebrating her birthday tonight at the club, and she wanted me to help host the event. She also invited you to come. Is that cool wit' you?"

"Oh yeah, no doubt. The Wolf's definitely gon' make an appearance tonight. But I did promise to hang wit' a couple of my dudes today, so since you planned over me, you mind if they come too?"

"That's a silly question, of course they could come!" Valentina said as Sylvio stepped out of the car and walked over to the other side to open the car for Valentina. She still appreciated the way he held the car door for her or pulled her seat out whenever they ate at a restaurant. She always admired how much of a gentleman he was. "Thank you," she said as he closed the door behind her.

"So, you sure you'll be up for this hosting thing?"

"Yeah, I've done it before. Ain't no thang wit' me."

"Okay, just makin' sure cuz I thought you might wanna rest after a brother handled his business," Sylvio said, laughing while looking back at his car.

"Boy, stop it. You didn't wear me out in there. I could go ten rounds and then some. I never get tired. Matter fact, I think I wear yo ass out."

"Nah, neva that," Sylvio replied as they both walked into his house.

Later that evening at Apple Kim's, Sylvio was accompanied by Kyle, Gary, and Simeon in the VIP lounge. Valentina was not working, but she was hosting the event for her friend, Honey Peaches, who was celebrating her twenty-third birthday. Bottle service was available all night, and many R&B artists as well as rappers were in attendance. Some performed that evening.

In between hosting and introducing the acts, Valentina spent time with Sylvio in VIP. She wore a long, sexy green dress with side slits that showed off her legs. Sylvio was wearing a white blazer with a T-shirt emblazoned with a photo of him in the ring. He topped it off with fitted jeans and white Tom Ford shoes.

As they were talking, a knock came on the VIP door. Simeon opened the door. "Yo, Wolf, got two brothas out hea sayin' you reserved 'em."

Behind him stood Jamal and Omar.

"Oh snap! Yeah, Sim, let 'em through. What's good?" Sylvio said as he dapped Omar and Jamal.

"Chillin, man. Yo, so this is how we livin' now, my G?" Omar laughed.

"Yeah, you know, man. Just showin' some love to my girl's friend and celebrating knockin' out Chavez," Sylvio replied.

"Oh, I already know, homie. I had five G's on you. I was tellin' niggas on da block that you was gon' knock that bum out," Omar said.

"So you makin' extra money off me now, dawg?" Sylvio asked, slightly rasing an eyebrow.

"Come on, man, it ain't like that. You a sure bet all day, Wolf. I knew you was gonna keep my lights on and my water runnin'," Omar replied, laughing.

"Aight, I feel you dawg, but chill with them bets, man. Remember, you in da Mecca, and you don't wanna end up on the losing side of the bet," Sylvio warned.

"Man, I got this. Ask Jamal," Omar countered.

"Nah, don't put me in this, I ain't got nothin' to do wit' it," Jamal replied.

"He stay schemin', right?" Sylvio asked Jamal with Omar listening.

"All damn day," Jamal asked, laughing.

"Whateva, B. If I ain't won, our asses definitely wouldn't have been up in hea tonight," Omar said.

Sylvio laughed before his eyes glanced at Valentina. Her look seemed to say, "Yo, you see me sittin' here. Am I invisible?"

"Yo, lemme introduce ya' to my jawn. Valentina Cruz, these are my boys Jamal and Omar. We been tight since junior high," Sylvio said.

Omar politely shook Valentina's hand.

Jamal oddly hesitated for a quick second, before shaking her hand as well. "Nice to meet you, Valentina."

"Likewise," Valentina said before another brief awkward moment of silence.

"Yo, where the bottles at? I'm tryin to get lit!" Omar shouted excitedly, breaking the silence.

"Got some in ice on the side. You thirsty, Jamal?" Sylvio asked his boy.

"Nah, I'm good, but lemme run to the restroom right quick," Jamal replied, before stepping out of the room as four exotic dancers walked in.

"You know what, baby. I'm gonna use the bathroom too. I'll be back," Valentina said.

"Really? So, you ain't tryin to be entertained wit' me tonight?" Sylvio asked.

"Nah I'm coming back. But I probably seen their routine over a thousand times. Remember, I do work hea," Valentina reminded Sylvio as she walked out of the room.

Instead of making his way to the restroom, Jamal made a beeline toward the club's exit doors, no longer in a festive or celebratory move. He could feel her body against his own and her heavy breathing after a night of wild sex. Out of all the women he could've chosen, he had to choose her. Finally making his way through the crowd, he pushed open the doors and headed to the intersection, intending on catching a bus.

"Leaving so soon, Jamal?" a familiar voice said behind him.

Before Jamal even turned around, he knew who addressed him. "What's it to you?"

"I don't know. It just seems messed up that you dippin' out on yo boys during the party," Valentina said.

Jamal rolled his eyes. She got some nerve coming to me passing judgement, acting like she gives a damn about my boys.

"Yeah, whateva. I just don't feel like partying tonight. Besides, the strip club scene—" he started.

"Ain't yo thang. Yeah, I remember that about you," Valentina said, finishing Jamal's sentence.

"Okay, so since you seem to know what the hell I'm thinking all of a sudden, what's runnin' through my mind right now?" Jamal was getting furious by the second.

"Damn, boy, slow yo roll. You ova hea raisin yo voice before we can even catch up."

"Ain't nothin' to catch up on," Jamal replied firmly, avoiding eye contact with Valentina.

"Oh, so it's like that?" Valentina asked as she approached Jamal. "You gon' act like nothin' went down between us, and you ain't jealous of what me and Sylvio got goin' on?"

"What you and Sylvio got goin' on?" Jamal repeated incredulously. "You doin' da same crap you did to me two years ago when I came up with da squad. Seduce, fuck, toy around, dump, and move on to da next one. Ain't that yo M-O?"

Jamal could still see her undressing herself in front of him, taking off his team jacket, his collar shirt, and his pants at the Residence Inn Motel two years ago when he was a junior star basketball player at Syracuse University. His team had just finished playing a holiday tournament, and he and some of his teammates headed over to the Players Bar, a small bar and grill in College Point, Queens. Valentina and a few other girls were working as escorts, or as Jamal saw them, prostitutes. She seduced Jamal, and like a foolish young college man, he fell head over heels for her. They had sex in the hotel room later that evening. He still felt her soft skin on his own, her mouth and tongue serenading his muscles.

"So, Rico Suave wasn't getting' it done, so you fallin' back to Plan B: find another black athlete who makin' some noise, and stick to him like glue so you can get some clout. Then when someone else comes by, you drop him like he ain't shit. It's like a broken record."

"Well, this time's different, okay? I'm really feelin' Sylvio, and he's feelin' me. I care about him."

"Yo, stop it aight? You don't give a damn about nobody but yourself. If you cared about Sylvio like you say you do, did you tell him about what your two brothers are involved in? The gambling, shipment of illegal guns— running them wit' the gangs here? Better yet, since yo man is a boxer, did you tell him that he might be goin' up against the brother of your ex-boyfriend?"

"It ain't none of yo damn business what I tell Sylvio in our relationship. Besides, Sylvio ain't stupid enough to challenge Maximo to a fight. He ain't got no chance against him."

"Oh really? I hate to break it to you, but did you see end of Sylvio's last fight? Lemme refresh yo memory," Jamal said, pulling out his phone. With a few keystrokes on his keypad, he replayed a clip of the video where Sylvio issued the bold challenge to Maximo.

Valentina put her hands on her mouth. She had been working, and although the TV was tuned into the fight, she'd never watched Sylvio's public challenge. "Oh, Sylvio, what'd you do?" she asked herself, wishing that Sylvio did not say anything after the fight.

If there was anything she knew about boxing as a sport, she knew Maximo had never been defeated in the ring, and he would be the overwhelming favorite. It was not going to be a regular opponent for Sylvio. On top of that, Maximo had been known to break bones inside the ring.

"You betta go warn Sylvio, and while you at it, tell him about the other stuff too cuz if you ain't gonna tell him, I will."

"So you're sayin' you would snitch and dime me out without thinkin' twice?"

"All day," Jamal replied. "I just don't wanna see my boy hurt or played with, like you did to me."

"I won't hurt him, Jamal, okay? I made a lot of mistakes the past few years, but with Sylvio, it's different. He don't care what social ladder I came from, what country, or language. None of that matters with him. He's real chill, and I like being with him."

"At what cost? You and I both know that he's gonna fight Maximo, and we both know that he's the underdog going into the fight, but do we know if he's still gonna be in one piece when he gets out the ring?"

"Which is why I need your help in keeping Sylvio away from Maximo. You have no idea what he's like. Before he was a boxer, Maximo used to be a bodyguard for his brother. Anyone who owed them money or got mixed up in these shady ass deals got dealt with by Maximo. He's a machine, Jamal."

"I know. I've seen some of his fights. But I also believe that Sylvio got what it takes to knock that man out."

"No, that's impossible. Maximo has never been knocked out in a single boxing match."

"First time for everything."

"Yeah, whateva," Valentina said, dismissively.

"But you ain't off da hook yet. You better tell Sylvio what you involved in, and keep him out of yo dealings."

"Yeah, but those are my brothers that you talkin' about!" Valentina said. "They could be looking at 20-30 years in Rikers."

"That doesn't move me one bit. I ain't gon' hesitate to make sure your crooked-ass brothers and yo ex get locked up if anything happens to Sylvio outside the ring. You got that?" Jamal asked, before walking to the next bus stop.

Valentina watched him walk, then turned to go back in.

Chapter 16

The next morning, Sylvio was awakened, not by the alarm clock, but by his cell phone ringing next to him. As disciplined as he was with his lifestyle and his training, Sylvio always set his clock to wake up at seven in the morning. That allowed him to prepare for his morning workout. But his phone vibrated at 6:53, awakening the groggy champ.

"Hello?"

"Wolf? You awake, man?" Shareef asked on the other end.

Sylvio rubbed his eyes. Dude's timing sucks, but he's good for updates on boxing. "I am now," he replied smartly.

Shareef continued as though he had no clue that he just woke his client up. "It's on, brotha," Shareef said in low tones.

"What you talkin' bout, man? Another tune-up fight?" Sylvio asked, wiping his eyes.

"Not this time."

Sylvio stopped wiping his eyes. Could this mean what he thought it meant?

"No more tune-ups and no scrubs this time, dawg. I just received a call from Felipe Maximo's team. It looks like your public challenge did the trick. Felipe Maximo has accepted and agreed to give you a title shot."

Sylvio stood up from his bed. "Are you serious?"

"Serious as a heart attack, man. We're holding a conference at the Marriott Lobby in Broadway this Saturday, where you'll be signing on to fight for the world middleweight title."

Sylvio couldn't bring himself to respond. He was finally going to have his shot. His mind was in a haze. It was all developing too quickly. At last he would have the opportunity to fulfill the goal he had sought after and to complete Jim's dream.

Not one day passed by where Jim didn't regret winning a title belt during his boxing days. He had been fueling Sylvio, preparing him for a showdown with the only man who stood between him and the title. Felipe Maximo was undefeated after thirty fights, and he not only had more experience in the ring than Sylvio, but he also had the stamina, rage, and power that was unmatched by any other fighter in the division. Although Sylvio was initially elated that he would have a chance to fight Maximo, he couldn't block the wave of doubt that crossed his mind.

What if he wasn't prepared for the fight? Maximo had a menacing presence in the ring to where he would simply glare at an opponent, a look that many of the sportswriters and boxing pundits nicknamed "The Death Stare." One look from him, and the fight was over before both men would enter the ring. Sylvio had not seen the stare, but he made up in his mind that he would not allow himself to be intimidated by Maximo although he knew the odds were already stacked up against him.

It also didn't help that Valentina spent most of the previous night trying to talk him out of fighting Maximo. Sylvio noted that her mood soured noticeably after her brief restroom break. Then he became more suspicious when Jamal left the club and never returned. Omar dismissed Jamal's departure by explaining that Jamal was a Christian, and he was not into the adult club scene, so he merely attended the party to support Sylvio. Omar even explained that Jamal planned to leave early that evening.

During the party, the subject was brought up about Sylvio's challenge to Maximo live after the fight, and Valentina didn't hide the fact that she was uncomfortable about the subject. When Sylvio prepared to leave the club with Valentina, they argued over the idea of Sylvio accepting any offers to fight Maximo. It was their first spat as a couple, and it couldn't have arrived at the worst time for Sylvio.

"Why does this fight with Maximo bother you so much?" Sylvio asked as they walked out the club.

"It bothers me because Maximo's a dangerous man, okay? You're just better off not fighting him at all. Can't you take another fight?"

"Take another fight? To what end? It don't work that way, Val. I'm a fighter, okay? I ain't runnin' away from this," Sylvio protested as Simeon walked them over to his Escalade.

"Ain't nobody said nothin' about runnin'. I'm just askin' you, why can't you take another fight? You don't have to fight him," Valentina pleaded.

"What's up with you?" Sylvio was starting to feel angry. "If you wit' me, you supposed to have my back. I thought we was a team, and now you tellin' me to back off? I made the challenge on TV, Val. How's it gonna look if I punk out now?"

"Who gives a shit how it looks? Please, Sylvio, if you care about me, don't fight Maximo. Please."

"He's got what I want!" Sylvio yelled, startling predestrians passing through the busy causeway.

"And what does he have that you want so badly? You're gonna risk your life going into the ring with a man who nearly killed other boxers in the same ring?"

"That ain't gonna happen. Besides you talkin' like he's gon' accept my challenge. He ain't responded yet, so it might not even happen. But I'm gonna do what it takes to get my shot with him. I ain't work this hard to stop now."

A few moments of silence passed between them. Valentina was about to tell Sylvio that Maximo had accepted the challenge, but she decided against it. "Um, listen, I'm gonna catch a ride with one of my friends from the club. I'll holla at you tomorrow." Valentina turned around and headed back inside the club.

Sylvio walked to his car that was parked at an intersection. He wondered why Valentina couldn't see that he needed to fight Maximo. It was more than just two men going blow for blow in the ring. It was about legacy. Maximo had built a reputation in the ring, but Sylvio wanted to build a legacy. His family came from poverty, and he wanted to make a name that would endure through the years. Valentina would not understand it right away, but he was confident that she would see why Sylvio was adamant about his decision.

While thinking back to the previous night, Sylvio heard his phone vibrate again. This time it was Valentina.

"Hey," she said, when he picked up.

"What's up?" he replied as he walked inside his closet to get his workout gear.

"I wanted to apologize about last night. I've heard stories about Maximo, and I get worried every time you get into the ring. I was trying to protect you."

"I figured that, Val. But check this out. I don't need protection. I got this. Anyway, I got a call from the boxing promoter, and he said Maximo accepted the challenge, so I gotta get ready to handle my business."

"What?!" The news horrified Valentina. "Sylvio, are you sure? You don't have to do this."

"Look, Val, I know how you feel about this, but I ain't goin' down this road again. I'm fightin' Maximo, whether you like it or not."

No sooner did he finish the sentence; he heard a click on the other end. Valentina had hung up.

Shaking his head, Sylvio decided not to call her back. She's too much in her feelings. She doesn't understand why I gotta do this, but one day she will.

"Mr. Dominique, how excited are you that you finally have the opportunity to fight for the middleweight belt?" a reporter named Abel Farouq asked.

"It's a long time coming, and personally, I feel that it is overdue. I worked very hard to get this opportunity, and I plan to make the most of it," Sylvio answered. He was sitting at the Marriott Lobby in Broadway, facing over one hundred reporters and photographers in the room.

A long conference table with cordless microphones were set up, and Sylvio, along with Jim, Kevin, Kyle, and Gary, sat on one end while the defending middleweight champion and his entourage sat on the other end. It was the first time Sylvio had sat in the same room as Felipe Maximo. Maximo was calm, almost smug in the face when he saw his challenger.

Sylvio realized very quickly that his sparring partners and trainers were not lying about Maximo's size and strength. It made Sylvio wonder why the boxing commission didn't place Maximo in a different weight class. But as he recalled, Rosjan Bokavic was a bit taller in stature and about fifteen pounds heavier. Yet, for all his power, he lacked the speed and footwork that Maximo possessed.

Every few minutes, Maximo would throw glances Sylvio's way. And every time he looked at Sylvio, he had a smirk on his face.

He probably thinks I'm not on his level. Sylvio knew otherwise and just watched as the reporters continued to reel off questions.

"Maximo, you haven't fought in three months, and in your last fight, you outlasted Bokavic in the twelfth round. Is there any concern that rust might be a factor in this fight?" another reporter asked.

"No, I don't think rust will be an issue at all," Maximo replied in a strong Spanish accent. "I've been staying in shape, working on my speed and combinations, and my sparring partners make sure I stay ready," he said, as photographers were busy at work, flashing the scenery around them.

"Did the public challenge that Mr. Dominique issued after the Chavez fight convince you to finally give him a title shot?" a third reporter asked.

"Well, I would be lying if I said that it didn't factor in my decision, but I felt that I've dominated all other fighters in the ring, and no one else stands between me and the belt, except for the man across from me," Maximo replied, as everyone's eyes followed his gaze at Sylvio.

I know what he's doing. He's trying to put the pressure on me to psyche me out. I know his game, and I ain't playin' it. Sylvio also thought he heard a sly snicker coming from Maximo as he answered the question.

"Mr. Dominique, Maximo sounds like he's pretty confident about this fight. How does it feel to go into the ring as an underdog?" a Latino reporter asked.

"Since I started boxing, I've always been the underdog. The media's always underestimated me before each fight, and each time, I've proved them wrong. You'd think by this time, things would swing my way, but I know it comes with the territory. Truth be told, I don't feel like an underdog in this fight. I have just about the same chances of winning as he does," Sylvio replied.

"We'll see about that, homes," Maximo said, dismissively. "Just be thankful that you got this shot, cuz on any other day, you wouldn't even smell a title shot."

Before he could reply, Jim, who sat next to Sylvio, whispered in his ear. "Don't get caught up in his mind game. He's tryin' to rattle you, Wolf."

Sylvio knew what he was doing before Jim spoke with him, but it didn't keep him from seething inside. What he wouldn't give to be in a room with Maximo, no cameras and no reporters.

"So, Maximo, what's next after this fight?" an ESPN reporter asked.

"Eh, I'm not too sure. Retirement hasn't crossed my mind yet, but I feel I have enough for maybe three or four more fights before walkin' off into the sunset," Maximo said.

"Mr. Dominique, there has been a lot of questions about your punching power, or lack thereof. Will you be compensating for that with your speed?" a Fox Sports reporter asked.

Sylvio chuckled and looked at Jim, who was laughing as well. "No punching power? I'm not sure where this information's coming from, but I'm sure Chavez thinks differently. Do you think he was knocked out because I slapped him hard?" he asked sarcastically. He was fed up with the media making Felipe their exclusive story while treating him as a formality.

"My guy packs as much power as the next middleweight, and as long as he's contending, he's gonna fight hard for the respect that you continue to deny him," Jim answered.

As the line of questioning continued, Sylvio found himself wondering what it was going to take to earn his respect in the ring. I gotta beat their show pony. Maximo must go down.

After a week of intense training, public promotional appearances, and interviews, Sylvio felt exhausted and decided to take the following Saturday off. He went to Omar's apartment in Hollis, Queens, to relax and play video games since Omar had the latest NBA Live 2012 game on his XBox, and he had the day off from his job at Horowitz Warehouse Inc.

When Sylvio arrived at the apartment, Omar's girlfriend, Ashley, a second shift RN at Mount Bethel Medical Center in Brooklyn, opened the door for Sylvio and was genuinely surprised by her famous guest. "Come on in!" she said excitedly as she opened the door.

"Thanks, Ashley. It's nice meetin' you," Sylvio said politely.

"Nice meeting you too. I mean, I seen you on TV and stuff, but it's crazy that you hea right now."

Clearly, Sylvio knew her mind was scrambling for words. She was nervous, but to Sylvio it was a normal reaction that he was accustomed to at this point in his career.

Ashley was very short and petite, with long brown hair that she tied in a ponytail and a mini-bump. "So, how far along are you?" Sylvio asked, staring at her belly.

"About three months now. It's a wonderful experience, besides all the morning sickness and mood swings."

"Well, congratulations. I know that kid's gonna be the same type of athlete Omar is."

"Hopefully, if it's a boy, he will be. But he'll be less of an A-hole than Omar," Ashley said, just loud enough for Omar to hear her.

"Oh, you got jokes this morning, Ash?" Omar asked, laughing.

"I'm just playin', baby. He or she is gon' be amazing when the time comes," Ashley said, as she went back to her room to answer a phone call from one of her friends.

Sylvio walked to the living room, which Omar had re-designed as an entertainment area. The only parts of the living room that were traditional were the couches and coffee table, but everything else was pretty unconventional. Omar had a 43-inch LCD flatscreen mounted on his wall, along with a neon blue sign that read TRUE BALLA next to it. He also had a small fridge plugged into the corner, which made very little sense to Sylvio because the couple already had a large fridge.

When Sylvio addressed the observation to Omar, he simply laughed. "Man, look, don't judge me, aight? If I need a drink or something to eat while I'm watching a game or gaming on Live, it takes too much effort walking to the fridge in the kitchen. So the solution? Cop you a small fridge for small things. Make life simple."

"Whatever man," Sylvio said, making his way to the couch.

Jamal was already there, picking his team.

"Yo, hand me that other remote. I got you in this game," Sylvio bragged as Jamal handed him the remote, which Omar temporarily vacated. "Yo, why do you always choose the New York Knicks?" Sylvio asked Jamal as he chose the Miami Heat.

"I always rep the orange and blue all day, playa. Meanwhile, you ova hea jockin' Miami's strap like everybody else just cuz they got LeBron James," Jamal replied.

"That's cuz LeBron's the truth. Ain't no argument about the best player in da game dawg," Sylvio replied.

"Whateva, dawg. Just stick to Live cuz that's about the only way you could ball anyway," Jamal joked.

Although he knew Jamal was only joking, Sylvio started to get weary of the wisecrack remarks about him not being able to play basketball as well as he could. Omar must have sensed the tension rising between his friends because he stepped in and propped his feet up toward the end of the couch.

"So, how'd that press conference go? Word on da street is that you a huge underdog in this fight," Omar said.

"I could care less what anybody has to say about my chances. At the end of the day, come fight night, I'mma settle all them bets once and for all," Sylvio said.

"Yeah, you got this. I mean, of course, I heard Maximo's a savage in the ring, and he broke some ribs in that ring, and even almost killed a dude. Sent him to the hospital for over three months. But, no pressure," Omar reminded Sylvio.

"Yeah, you talkin' about Hernandez. I fought that cat. He always had a glass jaw anyway," Sylvio said, while Omar snickered. "So, what you think, Jamal? You think I got a shot?"

"I don't know, man," Jamal said.

That response caused Sylvio to pause the game. "Hold up. What you mean, you don't know?" Sylvio asked Jamal, who started to shift uncomfortably on the couch.

"Man, forget about it," Jamal said as he restarted the game.

"Come on, man. Quit being an emotional ass bitch, and be straight wit' me. You think I got this, or what?" he asked testily.

"Oh, I'm being an emotional bitch?" Jamal asked, facing Sylvio.

"Yeah, you won't give me no straight answer," Sylvio replied.

"Ight, you wanna know how I think you gon' do in this fight? I think you'll have a better chance of winning if you drop yo' girl Valentina Cruz," Jamal said.

Sylvio looked at Omar incredulously, then followed his gaze back to Jamal. "You buggin' B. What does Val gotta do wit' any of this?"

"I said wasn't gon' say nothin', but since you took the fight, I'mma say it like this: yo girl's a hoe," Jamal said icily.

"What you mean, 'She a hoe?'" Sylvio asked as Jamal started to evolve from the laid-back guy to an irrational headcase in front of him.

"She's using you, dawg. Why you think she was quick to hook up wit' you?" Jamal asked.

"Because she wanted to, dawg. Where you goin' with this?" Sylvio said.

"There's a lot of things you don't know about Valentina. She probably came on to you, doin' some freaky stuff off rip. Then she be all ova you, and when it gets too hot, she starts trippin'. Before you know it, you mixed up in some cartel mafia shit," Jamal explained.

Sylvio turned to Omar. "Yo, Omar, you betta' get yo mans cuz he talkin' some crazy shit right now," he said, heatedly.

"Word, I don't know where he gets all this. Valentina looked like an average chick to me," Omar said.

"That's how it starts. She run game on you. Then when you become too attached, you start finding out stuff. And if you get too close…" Jamal's voice trailed off.

"What you mean 'if I get too close'? How you know all this about her?" Sylvio asked, before he came to a sudden realization. "You used to go wit' her, didn't you?"

"About two years ago, I was still ballin' with Syracuse, and some of my teammates went to a bar after the game. It wasn't no different than what we did after some games. Then some girls walk up to us, offering to do favors," Jamal said, putting up air quotes for emphasis.

"Most of my teammates had girls that they took to the nearby motel. My girl was Valentina. She was an escort, and I got caught up. One escapade later, I discovered the truth about her," he continued.

"What truth?"

"She's tied to the 85th Street Serps, a local gang. She was pimping people out for money, and if she wasn't paid, she sent her crew after you," Jamal replied. "They don't call themselves the Serps. They use a gambling ring as a front. The head guy of that gang was Valentina's boyfriend. On top of all that, do you know who the gang leader's brother was?"

Sylvio started to feel sick at the pit of his stomach. He had the feeling he knew what Jamal was going to say next, but the anticipation couldn't drown the next words that came out of his mouth.

"Felipe Maximo."

Chapter 17

Aside from the sounds of the video game in the room, there was complete silence. Even Omar, who had attempted to play peacemaker between his bickering friends, was speechless in the light of Jamal's new revelation about the current middleweight champion. Sylvio stood up from the couch. Video games no longer peaked his interest as he pondered over his predicament. Maximo was known to be a raw aggressive fighter that had unbridled rage, and it began to make sense to Sylvio. Then the fact that Jamal name-dropped Maximo as being the co-head of a dangerous gang didn't immediately faze Sylvio either. What made Sylvio angry was Jamal's decision to withhold the information.

"So that's why you dipped out of da club early. You saw her with me. You could've said something right there and then, but you ran yo ass up out of thea."

"Man, you know what happens to snitches. I don't know what world you livin' in, but I still stay in the real one. I ain't puttin' my ass at risk," Jamal said.

"Nah, you just gotta put me at risk." Sylvio felt a lump inside his throat like his stomach bile was pushing its way up his system. It was the sickest feeling he ever had—an overwhelming wave of nausea that he couldn't quell. If he won the fight against Maximo, he knew his crew was not going to let it slide. Sylvio was a boxer, but he wasn't delusional. He still lived in New York City, and although he probably wouldn't be in danger, he knew his family and friends would be facing the fear of gang retaliation. If he lost the fight, he would lose his shot at the middleweight crown, and he wouldn't be confirmed as a top-tier fighter.

It was his only chance to get a title, an award that had been so elusive and long sought-after for years, but could he now be pursuing the title at the cost of his loved ones? "I ain't got a choice, man! I issued the challenge on national TV, so I can't back out now."

"Is it worth losing everything?"

"Man, this ain't just about money, B. It's about my rep. I got people lookin' up to me. How's it gon' look if I punk out?"

"I don't know, dawg. But you gotta find a way to get yourself out this mix cuz it's bad business getting' mixed up wit' Valentina and Maximo. Straight up."

Sylvio glared at him. "Nah, you ain't leavin' me hangin'. Because of you, I got involved in this," he griped.

"Because of me?" Jamal was shocked. "So, was I the one that told you to date that chick? Was I the one that told you to take the fight? Stop brushing your issues off on me, homie. I ain't da boxer here. You are!" he added, raising his voice.

Sylvio had enough. He stepped up to Jamal, and the two young men stared each other. "Omar, you betta come get yo boy cuz he a minute away from gettin' his jaw bust," Sylvio said, balling his fists.

"Yo, come on, man. Let that shit go! Who cares whose fault it is? We boys, man. We all we got, feel me?" Omar asked.

"It don't look that way. It looks more like Jamal gon' dip out on us like he did at Apple Kim's," Sylvio said.

"I ain't droppin' nobody, but don't expect me to be in the same room with yo girl cuz she triflin'," Jamal said.

"Whateva, B. I'mma deal with her later, but you need to check who you loyal to," Sylvio replied.

"Who are you to talk to me about loyalty?" Jamal asked.

"I don't know. It wasn't my mama that was getting' piped by the community pastor," Sylvio answered, not realizing that the statement was a ticking bomb that would set Jamal off.

"Nigga, what? I'mma kick yo ass!" he lunged at Sylvio.

It took Omar all his efforts to hold Jamal back.

"Go ahead, Omar. Let him go," Sylvio said, enraged.

After Jamal stopped struggling to get to Sylvio, he turned back to Omar. "Yo, I thought we was boys, man, and you told him that?" Grabbing his sweater, Jamal took off, slamming the door behind him.

Omar looked at Sylvio. "Yo, I think you might've taken it too far, B. That thing with Jamal's mama was supposed to be confidential."

"Best if you hadn't told it to me at all."

"What if he right, though?"

"Come on, dude. You seen Val. Does she strike you as a project chick?"

"To be honest, I don't know, bro. A lot of these broads be playin' dudes nowadays. You need to ask her yourself."

Sylvio started to make his way out of the apartment. "I'll hit you up lata, B. I gotta clear my head," he said as he walked out.

I live for the fight game, but do I love it enough to risk everything?

After her nightshift was over, Valentina took the subway and bus back home. She tried calling Sylvio, but oddly enough, he wasn't picking up his phone. What's going on with him? Even if he was focused on a fight, he would still try to answer my calls.

She reached for the keys, all the while hoping that Sylvio wasn't cheating on her with another woman. After all, he was a high-profile athlete, and she knew that women would throw themselves at him. She knew it because she was one of those women at one point in her life until she got wiser and left the game. Many of her old peers, especially Pedro, loved to dangle the past in her face as a way of guilting her, but she was determined not to be fazed by anyone.

Entering the house, she flipped on the hallway light at the front door. As soon as the light came on, she saw Juan sitting on the living room couch by himself.

"Dios mio, you scared the shit outta me. I thought you weren't home yet. Where's Bruno?"

"I left him the car for the night. I got a lift back hea," Juan said. He then pulled out his phone and began scrolling, as if he was staring at pictures. "I wanna ask you something, mi hermana."

"Yeah, what's up?"

"How well do you know Sylvio Dominique?"

Valentina's heart skipped a beat. She didn't expect her brother to ask about Sylvio.

Apparently, he must've seen her surprised expression by the way his lips curled into a sly smile. "What happened? Cat got your tongue?" Juan asked as he showed Valentina pictures on his cell.

There, Valentina saw a photo of herself walking out of Apple Kim's with Sylvio, holding hands. One of Juan's friends apparently took the photo and sent it to Juan's Facebook profile with a post written above it that read, "I SEE YOUR SISTA STILL DIPPIN' IN DEM HIGH ROLLAS."

Valentina did not to show any emotion, but she was fuming inside. Don't people have a life other than spying on others? "Okay, that's me and Sylvio, and what's the big deal? We have celebrities walk in the club every day, and Sylvio was an old friend."

But Juan wasn't ready to let her off the hook. "You know, I thought the very same thing. I thought, 'maybe Valentina was just being nice to this guy...maybe walking him to his car, all of that.' Then I see this." He scrolled to another photo. This time the anonymous friend took a picture of Valentina leaving Sylvio's house at approximately 7:48 in the morning after one of their nightly activities, completely oblivious that someone was taking her pictures.

Unfortunately, Valentina had no clever comeback for the second photo. "I mean, correct me if I'm wrong, but I don't know a lot of old friends that leave each other's house at eight in the morning unless they were more than friends."

Valentina couldn't take her eyes away from the photos, but she was weary of having to explain her life away to him. "So, you hired someone to spy on me now? Why can't you just let me live my life?"

"Because I'm still your older brother, and I got the damn right to know where you been these past few months."

"So that means keeping tabs on me and getting your lowlife friends to take unwanted pictures of me? Yeah, that's real caring," Valentina scoffed sarcastically.

"Forget all that shit. I don't want you seeing that guy anymore. You hear me?"

"You don't have a right to tell me who I can or can't date. I'm a grown ass woman. I ain't gotta live my life dictated by you," she bit back.

"You still live under me! I'm the king hea!" Juan yelled, losing all cool pretenses.

"King of what? I still pay thirty-five percent of the rent around hea, so I think that gives me some say so on who I can date. You don't hear me sayin' nothin' when you drag yo ass back home after a night with some two-dollar hoes."

Juan got up and made a motion to slap his sister before changing his mind. "So, you're back in the game? Is that it?" Juan asked, raising an eyebrow.

Only Valentina knew what Juan meant by being "back in the game." She did not want to return to her former life of being a callgirl for anyone. "This ain't got nothin' to do with being back in the game. Sylvio's different."

"I ain't feelin' it. How you gon' date someone that's goin' against family?"

"What are you talkin' about?"

Again, Juan turned his phone screen for Valentina to read the latest sports news of the day. Although she tried to block it from her view, there was no denying what she just saw. "Maximo took the fight?"

"Of course, he took the fight. Did you think he was gon' let that tonto negro punk him live? Hell no. He took that fight. Remember what he did to Michael Karingas? You betta hope yo boy practices breathing through a tube cuz that's what's waiting for him after fight night,"

"Shut up, Juan!" Valentina ran out the house and began to walk as far away from there as she could.

She heard Juan calling for her to come back, but she didn't care. She was not going to sit around and hear her brothers insult her man. Frantically taking out her phone, Valentina dialed Sylvio's phone number. Why hasn't he answered my calls yet? Is he training that hard in the gym? He's never been too busy to call me. She hung up and dialed his number again.

This time, Sylvio answered the call on the third ring. "Hello?" she heard him reply, but right away she knew something was wrong. Sylvio always answered the phone enthusiastically whenever she called. This time his response was lifeless, almost hollow.

"Sylvio, what the hell? I tried calling you all day, and you ain't answered my calls. Are you training right now?" She was expecting Sylvio to explain himself or waiting for his excuse, but she received nothing of the sort.

"Is it true?" Sylvio asked, completely throwing Valentina off.

"What?"

"Don't play stupid wit' me."

Valentina sensed his rage building up on the other line.

"I asked you, 'Is it true?'"

"Is what true? What you talkin' about?"

"What you used to do before Apple Kim's, the 85th Street Serps, and Jamal? Is it all true?" Sylvio asked slowly.

Valentina closed her eyes, realizing the cat was out of the bag. Jamal must've told Sylvio everything.

"If I say that it is all true, does that change how you feel about me?" she asked,

"Yeah. It means I can't trust yo ass, Val. How come you ain't tell me you slept wit' Jamal before we met? Or how you know Maximo because you dated his brother? Why you ain't tell me none of that shit?"

"Sylvio, baby, I promise I was gonna tell you when the time was right."

"When? When were you gon' tell me about what you was mixed up in? Before or after my fight?"

"So, you're gonna fight Maximo, then?" Valentina asked as she attempted to change the subject.

Sylvio wasn't having any of it. "Stop dancing around the question. When were you gonna tell me that Maximo was gangbangin'? Or that Jamal was layin' the pipe on you? I thought being in a relationship meant keeping it a hundred between us."

"You have no idea what it's like to be trapped Sylvio." By the tremor in her voice, Valentina sounded as if she was on the verge of tears.

"Humor me," Sylvio replied mechanically

"After my papi's moving company went under, we struggled. I barely had two dimes to rub together at times, and I had to drop out of college to bring money in for my family. I had to hustle and do what I had to do. I met Pedro in school, and at first, he was a nice guy. We were cool at first, but that was before I knew who he really was. I had no idea he was a gang leader or a member of the Serps. I was naïve as fuck," she continued, sighing heavily.

"Pedro knew how to manipulate people to meet his bottom line. It didn't matter who he used or who he affected. He gave me the offer to work as an escort around the metropolitan area, and the money was good. I was pickin' em up faster than they own women, and I was finally making the money that I wouldn't have made if I was workin' a dead-end job."

"So, you preferred being a hoe and getting passed around by other men?"

"It's more complicated than that. My brothers were already being initiated by the Serps, so they moved out of Papi's house, and I went with them because I couldn't sneak around on my father anymore. My father was very traditional. Remember back when we were kids, you mentioned a desire to run away from your own father? I felt the same way every day, so finally, I got out. I couldn't let him see how I was living anymore," she sobbed.

Despite the anger Sylvio felt, he also felt a pang of remorse. "When did Jamal get in the picture?"

"He was just another guy. I had a thing for athletes, and it wasn't just about the money. It was their swagger, confidence, and of course, Jamal had a body most girls would kill for. So, one day I took my chance, and we had a moment. But while it was just sex to me, it was more than just physical to him. He got attached, and he was sending money to me almost every week, even after I stopped being intimate with him. Then we broke it off after Pedro and my brothers threatened him."

"Wait, hold up. Jamal was threatened by Pedro?"

"He's an asshole, but he has dangerous connections to the drug cartels, rival gangs, and clubs all around New York. Pedro ain't your regular gangbanger. He's a businessman. He knew how to make money and flip it to double for him. He changed the name of the Serps to Legarto Inc., where they laundered millions of dollars in gambling bets and investments from both Vegas oddsmakers and Atlantic City."

"Ain't that illegal?"

"All day, but Pedro doesn't give a shit. He's a self-serving bastard, and I wish I had never met him. But he's no worse than his brother—"

"You mean Felipe Maximo," Sylvio said, finishing Valentina's sentence.

"He's loco, Sylvio. Before he began boxing, he was the enforcer, kicking the ass of people who didn't pay his brother. I've seen where he's nearly killed people with his hands. His knuckles would be scarred as hell from years of beating guys to a pulp. It was only natural that he began boxing. But he can never hold his aggression back. I've seen what he can do, Sylvio, and even if you think I ain't worth shit now, I really do care about you, and I don't want to see you badly hurt."

Sylvio leaned against his wall as the startling revelations of Valentina's background spilled on the other line. What began as a simple anticipation for a title match became a gamble on his future and potentially his life.

But Sylvio was not wired to lose. He was determined not to be intimidated by any opponent, in or out of the ring. "I'm fighting him, Valentina, and I don't plan on losing. I don't care if you wit' it or not. I'm not gon' be punked out by anyone. If I gotta go out, I'mma go out swingin', and ain't nothin' you could say that's gon' change that."

For a few minutes, there was nothing but silence on the line. Then Sylvio heard Valentina sniffling again, still trying to hold back tears.

"So where does that leave us?"

"I gotta think about it cuz I don't know right now." With that, he abruptly hung up. Once again, it was him against the world, but he felt the weight of his doubt and distrust weighing him down.

I gotta release this frustration at the gym. Sylvio took his bags and left the house.

"What?" Jim asked in disbelief after Sylvio explained everything that Valentina and Jamal told him, while he was training. "Okay, that's it. I'll be right back." Jim left the ring and walked towards his office.

"Hold up. Where you going?"

"I'm calling Shareef to tell him to call this thing off."

"Wait, what? Nah, don't do that!" Sylvio leapt out of the ring and ran to stop his trainer.

"Sylvio, don't you see what's goin' on hea? Fighting anyone with gang affiliation is a huge risk, one that involves life and death. I'm not gonna let you be a sacrificial lamb for the sake of sport."

"Jim, don't call Shareef!" Sylvio shouted, causing the other boxers to stare back at him during their sparring sessions.

Jim had just reached the office door, before turning around. "Son, don't you know what this means? If you lose this fight, you lose your shot at a title. If you win this fight, his people's gon' come after you. This ain't rocket science. You're puttin' yo life on the line."

"And what about Bokavic? Didn't he put his life on the line? Or what about Hernandez, Chavez, or Brown? We put our lives on the line every time we step up in that ring."

"That ain't the same, Wolf. They didn't know about this guy's background. You do, and don't forget, I grew up in the streets. I know how the game works. Maximo's got streetcats out there bettin' on him. If they lose their money..." Jim's voice trailed off.

"I know, but I ain't goin' out like that." Sylvio walked over to Jim and put his arm around him. "Listen, Jim, I need that fuel now more than ever. You're the only one who believed that I would ever have a chance to be a champion. I need you to believe in me again, and be at my corner when this goes down."

After thinking it over, Jim finally conceded. "Okay, let's go for the crown," he said, heading back to the ring.

Sylvio eagerly followed. He trained with a sense of inspiration, elated that his trainer had not given up on him. He worked on speed, quickness, and footwork in the ring with Jim instructing him on every routine.

"You've fought fighters that were brawlers, and you've fought fighters that were quick hitters. This fight will be a combination of both. I've seen this kid Maximo fight, and with his combination of speed and power, he's gonna be a handful. He's gonna use his size to cut the ring off so he can get you trapped against the ropes. In the last few fights, you've been able to get away with hanging on the ropes, but it ain't gonna work this fight. Against a fighter like this, you gotta keep moving, and keep your hands busy. That's why Bokavic came close to beating him. Wear him out so he runs outta gas in the twelfth round."

After two hours of training, Sylvio showered in the gym locker room. After changing his clothes, he prepared to leave when his cell phone rang. Rebecca was calling him.

"Hello?" he answered.

"Sylvio, you need to come here right now," she said, and to Sylvio's surprise, she sounded frantic.

"What's going on? You want me to drop by Dad's house?"

"No, we're at Jamaica Hospital. His blood sugar level dropped, and he had a stroke. Hurry up and get here!" she said frantically.

Chapter 18

White rooms. Breathing tubes. IV packs. They were components for an environment Sylvio was unfamiliar with, and yet he found himself in his father's room with Rebecca, Simeon, and Jim. Jim had decided to accompany his protégé upon hearing the news of Sylvio's father. Weaving through the traffic on the Grand Conduit highway, Simeon reached the hospital shortly after six in the afternoon. When they arrived at the emergency entrance, Rebecca was already waiting where people were stirred by the presence of the famous boxer in the hospital.

Simeon had his work cut out for him after he parked the car, preventing fans or camera phones from getting a glimpse of Sylvio.

Sylvio promptly hugged his sister. "Where he at?" Sylvio said, frantically.

"He's on the third floor. C'mon," Rebecca led Sylvio and Simeon to the elevator. The hospital receptionist called out to Sylvio because he had not checked in.

"Excuse me, sir? Who are you here to see? You can't proceed unless you sign," she instructed.

"Ma'am, this is Jacques Dominique's son Sylvio. If you look at the sheet, you'll see that I've already signed his name," Rebecca said.

"Okay, very well. He can go, but the other gentlemen will need to stay here," the receptionist said, referring to Simeon and Jim.

"Listen, ma'am, wherever I go, they go, okay?" Sylvio started to protest.

"I'm afraid that's not possible, Mr. Dominique. Only immediate family members are allowed," she said.

Sylvio started to feel his blood boil, but Simeon said, "It's okay, champ. Go check on yo pops. I'll be down here, holding it down."

Jim also opted to stay in the waiting room. Rebecca nodded to Simeon to indicate that this was a good plan, and she and her brother took the elevator to the third floor.

"He's in Room 305," she said as they walked toward the end of the corridor.

"How did this happen? I thought you was gon' stay wit' him," Sylvio said.

"Look, don't put this on me, Sylvio. I couldn't stay up hea too long. I got a life in Philadephia, in case you forgot. I had to go back to work. He was taking his insulin shots before I left him. He probably failed to take his shots in the last few days. You should have been periodically checkin' up on him."

"Look, whateva. I don't wanna play the blame game right now. I got a lot goin' on too, and this was the last thing I needed to hear right now," he said, as they entered the room.

Jacques was lying in bed, his face gray and more sunken than the previous time Sylvio visited him. He was hooked up to the ventilator that was working on pumping oxygen into his body.

"Come on, Dad. Fight yo ass off, man. I ain't losing you, not now," Sylvio said through gritted teeth. His hands were balled into a fist, and he was tempted to punch anything in his way. A tear rolled down his eye, and he took one of his father's hands and held it tightly. The man whom Sylvio once feared growing up, the man who was the sign of anger and intimidation, was now reduced to a vulnerable shell of himself.

"If he pulls through this, we have to get him around-the-clock help," Rebecca said.

"You right," Sylvio agreed. If he makes it through this. If my father dies, I don't think I'm gonna function. Seeing his father fighting for his life couldn't have come at a worse time. But unbeknownst to Sylvio, he was at the cusp of being under media scrutiny. Sylvio heard a loud slam outside the room.

"What's goin' on?" Rebecca asked curiously, heading to the door. "Sylvio, there's a big guy out there walkin' like he possessed, and he got two other people with him. I've seen him before. Wait a minute. Ain't that the Dominican guy you're supposed to fight?"

"What?" Sylvio asked. He did not think there was anyway possible that Maximo was in the hospital, much less walking through the third-floor corridor. But before he had a chance to react, he heard Rebecca yell in pain as she was knocked onto the floor as the room door flew open.

Felipe Maximo, flanked by two other Latino men, laughed at the sight of Rebecca falling. Sylvio quickly checked on his sister, then turned to the men who had assaulted her.

"Ayo, is this the gamberro I'm supposed to be fighting next month? Sittin' hea cryin' like the puta he is?" Maximo said, as he and the other guys laughed in unison.

"What you doin' hea, man? How'd you even know where I was?" Sylvio asked Maximo.

"It was easy. I followed the teardrops," Maximo joked, laughing even louder.

Sylvio realized that one of Maximo's companions was recording the whole incident on his phone. It quickly became clear to Sylvio that Maximo was taping the event to post online to humiliate him. "You betta tell yo boy to stop recording this shit."

"Or what?" Maximo challenged. "I mean, you called me out on national TV, so I thought I'd return the favor."

"Not here, man. This ain't the right time," Sylvio said, wishing it didn't come out as a plea.

Maximo continued deriding his opponent. "I mean, if you're gonna cry, at least don't let the world see it."

"You gotta be a special kind of stupid to just walk up in here and clown a man who's visiting his sick father," Rebecca said angrily, standing up.

"Shut up, bitch!" Maximo said.

"Aye, that's my sister you talkin' to, you bean-burrito eatin' bastard," Sylvio walked towards Maximo with fists clenched. He didn't care if Maximo was in a gang or not. He was going to defend his family at any cost.

"I'm sorry. I take that back. She's my bitch," Maximo jeered, and Sylvio rushed to his opponent, wanting nothing more than to knock Maximo's teeth down his throat. Luckily, the orderlies and hospital employees came by to stop them.

"Gentlemen, you shouldn't be here. Please leave this floor before we call the police," they said to Maximo and the two men.

Snickering and speaking to his comrades in Spanish, Maximo then pointed at Sylvio, blowing a kiss at him and headed down the corridor.

 "Obviously, he was tryin' to get you rattled," Jim said.

It was a few days after the incident, and even in explaining the events that occurred at the hospital, Sylvio was still fuming with rage. He never had an issue with other fighters doing PR stunts to promote fights, but there was a time and place for those stunts. The hospital was the worst place for Maximo to ambush Sylvio. In barely twenty-four hours, the footage of the event had gone viral on every social media platform and had become the biggest story on sports talk radio and television. Some people believed Sylvio was right to swing and strike Maximo. Yet, Sylvio remembered what Jim taught him. He barely controlled his emotions.

"He think he slick, getting' away with that and broadcasting it," Sylvio replied. They were at the gym, where Sylvio was working on his power by hitting the heavy bag. "I'm still wondering how the hell he got up there." Sylvio punched the bag with a jab and hook combo.

"I don't know. Sim and I were downstairs in the waiting room, and he must have snuck in through the opposite door," Jim answered thoughtfully.

"But how did he know I was gonna be up there?" Sylvio hit the bag with more force than previously applied.

"Wish I knew. They said that boy got eyes all over the city."

"Yeah and with his connections, he could've had someone at the hospital who knew him and told him I was gon' be there."

Jim shrugged. "It's about as good a guess as anybody's. But let's forget about that. Keep yo eyes on the prize, Wolf. No distractions. Zero in on him. You see how he dissed you in public. You gon' make him pay for that in the ring."

They continued working on their combinations. After a few minutes of silence, apart from Sylvio's gloves hitting the heavy bag, Jim decided to address the elephant in the room. "So, have you talked to yo girl today?"

Sylvio continued punching the heavy bag, acting as if he didn't hear the question posed to him. "I don't talk to liars," he said, taking off his gloves to drink from a gallon of water.

"Technically, she didn't lie. She just withheld some information from you. Don't act like you neva done it."

"Nah, not like this. She dated a dude who was related to my next opponent, Jim. She didn't even bother to say nothin' when we first got involved. To me, that's about as bad as a liar. How do I know she ain't stickin' up for her ex?"

When Jim didn't respond, Sylvio started to take his headgear off and headed for the locker room.

"Where you going?" Jim asked.

"I'm done for today. Same time tomorrow," Sylvio confirmed as he walked away.

A few people were just leaving the locker room area, so Sylvio walked inside, expecting to be fully alone. However, when he turned on a lightswitch near the front of the locker room, he realized someone was sitting on one of the stools. The man was about 5'8" with black, slicked back hair that was neatly combed and greased. He appeared to be a middle-aged Latino man, and by the man's wardrobe, Sylvio knew he was rolling in cash. He had on four gold chains, and two of them were crucifixes.

It didn't take Sylvio long to find out that he was finally face-to-face with Pedro Quinones—Maximo's brother and Valentina's ex-boyfriend and pimp.

How many eyes does Maximo have out here in these streets?

"Sylvio Dominique, I got to say, it's a long time coming, but we finally meet. It's a huge pleasure and honor," Pedro said.

Sylvio rolled his eyes, knowing that Pedro didn't believe anything that came out his own mouth. He was laying it on too thick. Sylvio checked him immediately. "I wish I could say the same for you."

Pedro laughed. "Aw, so it's like that, dawg? I just came by to wish you good luck on the fight—" he started.

"Look, man, cut the shit. I ain't stupid, aight? I know about you and your brother, who paid me a visit at Jamaica Hospital the other day. I know you helped his ass get in there," he said.

Pedro's smug smile starting to disappear and a more stoic expression took its place. "You ain't got no proof of that, homes."

"What do you want, man? Are you here to talk me out of fightin' Maximo? Cuz I ain't goin' nowhere, and I won't stop till the belt's mine."

"Oh no, no, no...I ain't hea to stop nothin'. The fight's still scheduled as planned. Let me tell you, my brother can't wait to embarrass you once again by whuppin' yo black ass on Showtime. He's dying to break you," Pedro said grimly.

Finding it to be quite comical, Sylvio chuckled slightly.

"You think it's funny?" Pedro asked.

"Hell yeah. I think it's funny that Maximo sends his brother here to do all his trash talkin'. What are you, his bagboy or something?" Sylvio laughed.

Swiftly ignoring Sylvio's question, Pedro spoke in the same hollow tone. "I've seen you fight before, Dominique. You're not a bad boxer at all. You got style, power, and great footwork. But you ain't in the same league as Maximo when comes to ring awareness and straight raw aggression."

"You still ain't answer my question, homie. What do you want with me?"

Pedro appeared to be talking to himself as if he couldn't hear Sylvio ask him any questions. "I heard you and Valentina Cruz been fuckin'. That used to be mine one time, but you know what? A playa' respects another playa', so I let you do ya thing."

"Whatever, man, I don't need your permission on who to date. She left yo ass, remember?"

"You're naïve if you think Valentina's innocent. Lemme tell you a lil' something. Valentina has been on every avenue, every type of bedroom, and was open to doing anything when she was still with me. Did I pimp her out at one point? Yeah, but it was a business move. It was about raising money to kick off Legarto Inc. I run a multi-million-dollar conglomerate in underground Queens. We make money, and in return, we help our clients make money. It's living legit."

"Living legit?" Sylvio asked incredulously. "That's what you call it now? You garbage, Pedro. You ain't nothin' but a low level wanksta who played the system, and you never gave a shit about Valentina or anybody else. I don't even think you give a damn about yo own brother. It's all about the money to you."

"No shit, Sherlock. It's always been about the money. I thought you already knew. That's why most of our best clients always bet on my brother cuz they know he can deliver, and it keeps the money flow going. That's why I'm hea today."

"Why?"

"After negotiating with Shareef, I hear that both you and Maximo are planning to make over twenty mill this fight. That's more than any middleweight fighter has earned in their lifetimes. But I'm hea to give you a better offer."

"What offer can you give me that's better than what this fight's giving me?"

"I got boosters, pizzarias, the bodegas, clubs, promoters and bars and most of the other boriquas around the country betting on Maximo. After counting the spread, it tripled the deal that Showtime offered. You can make over sixty million dollars from this fight."

Sylvio wasn't convinced, and he was sure there was going to be a costly stipulation. "And how do I earn the sixty million?" he asked, although he already knew the answer to the question.

"It's very simple. Lose the fight to Maximo. Ensure that he keeps the belt, and the money's yours. No hassle, no backfees, no extra contracts."

"Fuck that!" This was the first time Sylvio was approached to lose a fight on purpose. Jim warned him about the dirty side of boxing, and now it was beginning to rear its ugly head. "You can take that deal and stick it where the sun don't shine cuz I ain't throwin' the fight. I'll die first before I throw anything."

Pedro confidently stepped forward to Sylvio whose fists were already clenched. Maximo would soon need a stretcher to pick his brother up if he provoked Sylvio any further.

"I see the hunger in your eyes. You wanna hurt me bad," Pedro mocked. "Lemme make this simple for you. You're younger than my brother, and as much as I hate to admit it, you're the one guy that actually has a chance against him. I've watched you train for weeks. I had people watch you train. Maximo's gon' bow out of this game soon, but you'll have plenty of chances to fight for the title."

"What's that supposed to mean?"

"You know what it is. Keep the fight interesting. Make sure he's up on points each round and no knockouts. Maximo wins in a split decision, or you can let him knock your ass out. It wouldn't make no difference to me," Pedro said, gleefully. "Look at it this way. When you lose, you win. You'll get sixty million dollars. You'll be comfortable and set for life. But if you even think about winnin' that belt, it's gonna cost me millions, and it's gonna cost you." Pedro's voice eerily deepened.

"Is that a threat? You ain't gonna do nothin'. They'll find yo ass and lock you up wit' da quickness."

"Who said it was gonna be me that's gon' bring the pain? I got people everywhere. The Serps are all ova, Sylvio—stores, supermarkets, and even employed at hospitals. How do you think Maximo found you?"

Pedro turned his back to Sylvio as he walked toward the locker room exit. "Yo sista's fine as hell by the way. I hear she's still at the hospital with your sick father. It would be a damn shame if something tragic were to happen to them because of her hardheaded brother, wouldn't you agree?" He snickered as he walked out, leaving Sylvio in the dimly lit locker room.

On the drive home, Sylvio's mind was running a thousand miles an hour. Pedro's threat was still fresh on his mind as he turned at an intersection. If he lost the fight, he would be looking at sixty million dollars. Although he was living comfortably, his level of comfort would no doubt increase dramatically, and he could bow out of the sport and be established for the rest of his days. But he knew if he lost the fight, he would lose a measure of respect in boxing circles, and he would not be able to challenge for the title for a long time.

Essentially, this was his only shot, and he only had one chance to make history. Winning the title would put his family in extreme danger, as he knew Pedro and his Serps would stop at nothing but to make his life a living hell, even if his family or friends were caught in the middle. Sylvio approached his driveway and could see two figures standing outside his house. As he shone his headlights toward the house, he saw Valentina Cruz with another woman he recognized as one of the dancers from Apple Kim's. It appeared that both were waiting for him, so he parked his car before stepping out to greet them.

"Hey Sylvio, I had my friend Passion drive me here so we can try to talk," Valentina said. Reminiscing on how the last conversation ended between them, Sylvio decided to give Valentina the benefit of the doubt.

"Yeah, we can talk. But before you start, I wanna apologize for the way I grilled you on the phone this morning. I was just pissed off cuz of all the secrets and lies, and I was outta pocket. My bad," Sylvio said.

To his relief, Valentina smiled and ran to hug him.

"Aw, look at ya, makin' up. That's so sweet!" her friend said, laughing.

"Quiet, Passion! We're having a moment. It's okay, baby. I'm sorry for not being upfront with you about my past, Jamal, or even Pedro," she said.

"Speakin' of Pedro, yo boy paid me a visit at my gym today," Sylvio said slowly.

Valentina's mouth dropped in shock. "Oh no, what did he want?" she asked.

"Well, he wants me to throw the fight and let Maximo win," Sylvio answered.

"What?" Valentina asked.

 "Yup. He said that if I lose the match, everyone that betted with his organization will earn back a lot of money, and Legarto Inc. will make over sixty million. He's offering to give me that money, if I lose," Sylvio explained. He saw clearly that Valentina was bothered by her ex-boyfriend's actions.

"What an asshole. He knows how hard you worked to get to this point," she said.

"Oh, it gets better," Sylvio replied sarcastically. "He said that if I won the fight and took the title from his brother, he's gonna kill my father and my sister."

Valentina put her hand over her mouth in shock.

Passion was unable to control her emotions. "What the hell? See, Val, I knew yo boy was crazy the moment I saw his narrow behind at Apple Kim's."

Valentina shook her head. "He can't do that. He can't just threaten you like that and just walk away. That's collusion and coercion. He can go to jail for that."

"Come on, Val. You know how gangs roll in this city. If you snitch, then yo family's gon' be in danger, too. Besides, ain't yo brothers still rollin' with him?" Sylvio asked.

"Yeah, but he went too far. Now you see why I broke up with his ass," Valentina answered.

Sylvio shook his head. "You was right, Val. I shouldn't have challenged him. I should've called it off earlier. What am I gon' do now?"

"I don't know. I still wanna get the police involved because Pedro been on that shady shit lately. But he'll get his, trust me. Sylvio, I wanna show you something, and promise me you won't tell anyone, okay?" she asked.

"Okay, I promise, but what you bout to show me?" Sylvio asked.

Valentina turned her back to Passion and asked her to roll her shirt up, revealing her bare back. Sylvio saw the emblem of the Serps, a tattoo of two snakes slithering up a light post with fangs blazing, as if they were ready to attack each other.

Chapter 19

"I always thought that was a dope tattoo," Sylvio said as Passion slid Valentina's shirt back down to her waist.

"Believe me, it's hardly just a fashion statement," Valentina said. "Everybody who was once a member or still runs with the Serps or Legarto Inc. has at least one of these tattoos. Pedro got about three of them himself, among others."

Sylvio vaguely remembered seeing the tattoo during moments where they were intimate, but he didn't think too much of it at the time. People got tattoos all the time, and Sylvio was no exception. He had a few tattoos too, including a picture of Muhammad Ali, one of his greatest influences. He also had a pair of boxing gloves, both on his right and left arms.

"Everyone who wore the tattoo of the Serps lived by one code. The code was abbreviated as AOO," Valentina continued.

"What does that stand for?" Sylvio asked.

"It means Avenge Our Own. The Serps used to be involved in a lot of gang wars over drugs, money, and territory. Most of those gangs are now gone, but instead of dismantling the Serps, Pedro just renamed them and started making deals with Las Vegas casinos and Atlantic City," she explained.

Sylvio was not a stranger to gang violence or gang influence. He remembered being a freshman at Richmond Hill and hearing about the death of a high school senior that got shot by the gang that previously occuppied the area, nicknamed M.O.B. for Money Over Bitches. Sylvio had friends who ran with M.O.B., and one of those friends during his time at Richmond Hill was Antonio Franks. An ex-member of M.O.B., Antonio was a star witness in the murder trial of the high school student. He testified in court despite the threats that he received from the ruthless leader of the gang. Sylvio never forgot the phone calls he received from Antonio, sometimes after midnight, expressing his fear that one day he was going to end up dead in the street for snitching on the members of his set.

Although Antonio's family was placed in the witness protection program, the emotional trauma never left him until they finally moved out of New York. By that time, M.O.B. was finally brought down by a special police task force. But they didn't go silently, resulting in one of the borough's deadliest shootouts. Many of the gangs dispersed afterwards, but a few still lingered around.

"How did I get mixed up in this shit?" Sylvio asked, rolling his eyes.

"You ain't the only one, Sylvio. Legarto, Inc. has given money from their illegal gambling ring to fund other businesses, one of them being Apple Kim's," she confessed.

"So that's why you work there. He was your plug to get you that job," Sylvio said.

"Yeah, but lookin' back at it now, I wouldn't have even wanted it that way. I wish I could take all that back," she said.

Suddenly, Sylvio's phone rang. He saw Omar's name flash through his phone screen. "Yo, what's up?"

"What's good, man? Yo, you busy lata' on?" Omar asked.

"Nah, I just came back from a workout."

"Yo, when you get a chance, meet me at the 'Ville," Omar said, referring to Brookville Park.

Sylvio looked at the sky. The nighttime was approaching. It would be pitch dark by the time he arrived at the park. Does he want me to come out and ball with him or something? "Aight, I'll be there in twenty minutes."

"Bet," Omar replied and hung up.

"Who was that?" Valentina asked.

"Omar. He wants to meet at the park," he answered.

"Okay, well I guess I'll see you lata." Valentina approached Sylvio and kissed him.

Her lips felt so warm and soft, sensations that he had not felt for weeks. "And I know what you gon' say," Sylvio said as he headed back to his car. "Don't fight Maximo, right?" he asked as he entered the car.

"Actually, I want you to go out there and kick his ass," Valentina said. "Don't worry. He ain't gonna do nothin' to me," she added, walking with Passion to her car.

When Sylvio arrived at Brookville Park, it was all but dark outside as the moonlight peaked from around the trees. He saw Omar dribbling and shooting hoops at the netless rim with another figure. As he approached the court, he saw that it was Jamal.

"What's up?" Sylvio asked.

Both basketball players turned around. Omar immediately smiled, but Jamal just stood with a blank expression on his face. Sylvio remembered that it wasn't too long ago that he nearly came to blows with Jamal in Omar's living room. Perhaps Jamal still harbored anger over the incident.

"Yo, what up, man?" Omar greeted as they walked toward center court.

"What's up, Jamal?" Sylvio greeted, holding out his hand for Jamal to dap him, but Jamal just stared at him.

At this, Omar couldn't stand the awkward silence between them. "C'mon, man, we boys. We go too far back to let this crap get to us, man."

Jamal finally broke a smile before finally dapping Sylvio. "What's up, man?"

"Yo, Jamal, on da real, my bad for what I said about yo moms. I was trippin', bro. Everything was copasetic one day. Then when you told me straight up what was goin' on, I gave you heat for no reason," Sylvio apologized.

"It's all good, man. I just knew what Valentina and her ex-boyfriend was about. I was just lookin' out for you," Jamal said.

"You was right all this time. Pedro and Felipe got issues, dawg," Sylvio said.

"I be tellin' you, man. But you could beat 'em. On October 14th, the belt's yours," Jamal said confidently, as Sylvio took the ball and dribbled beyond the three-point line.

"If I make this shot, I'm gon' be the middleweight champ," Sylvio said as he put up his shot with his familiar awkward release. The shot hit the side of the rim, and Omar grabbed the rebound, snickering.

"Stick to boxing, homie," Jamal laughed.

Feeling motivated once again, Sylvio attacked his training and preparation for the title bout. He was determined not to allow Pedro to intimidate him. With his focus back on track, Sylvio worked on agility, speed, blocks, and on improving his footwork. He also spent countless hours in the filmroom with Jim, studying the tendencies of his opponent.

"He's a hard hitter, that's for sure," Jim said as they watched Maximo's previous fights against Bokavic and Chavez again. They focused in on the Bokavic fight before realizing that Bokavic provided the blueprint on defeating Maximo.

"He goes for the quick knockout, and Bokavic is able to elude him and get him with a right hook to the body. That side is exposed all day long. Punish that right side early and often, and you got him where you want him. Throw some quick jabs to keep him off balance." Jim said.

"Yeah, but I have to get around his long reach," Sylvio interjected.

"Then we need to make his target smaller," Jim said.

A few minutes later, Jim tied a long rope from one gym post to another. He proceeded to instruct Sylvio on bobbing and weaving, ducking laterally from side to side. Although he began to feel the normal burn in his abs, back muscles, and calf muscles, his energy was at its peak as Jim continued to work on him.

One morning, Sylvio finished parking his car and was about to cross the street to enter the gym when a short white man approached him.

"Mr. Dominique, how are you today?" he greeted, and by the way he spoke, Sylvio noticed that he had a strong European accent.

"I'm good, sir. Thank you. Listen, I'm kinda in a rush, so I don't have time to sign autographs," he explained.

But the man waved his hand dismissively. "No, I did not come to ask for an autograph, sir. I wanted to let you know that my employer was interested in speaking with you," he said, pointing to a green SUV that parked up the block.

Sylvio was filled with suspicion and wasn't sure if he could trust the man. How do I know Pedro didn't send him to issue more scare tactics. Still, he followed the man until they arrived at the car.

"If you please, Mr. Dominique," the man said, stepping aside to allow Sylvio to open the back door.

Inside sat Rosjan Bokavic, dressed in a suit, his hair neatly combed to one side. He appeared to be in much better shape than the last time Sylvio saw him, which was inside the ring. For some reason, Sylvio was pleased to see him.

"Bokavic, how you doin', man?" Sylvio shook the hand of his former opponent.

"Very vell, thank you. I hope I found you in good spirits," Bokavic replied in his strong accent as Sylvio entered the vehicle.

Sylvio suddenly recognized that the man who led him to Bokavic's vehicle was one of his cornermen. "Hardly," Sylvio replied. "But how you holdin' up, bro? Lookin' more toned since the last time I saw you."

"Yes, I've been eating more plant-based meals, and I've cut meat out of my diet," Bokavic replied.

Sylvio was surprised to hear Bokavic speak nearly perfect English, since he barely muttered a word when they fought. "That's what's up. So, what brings you round my neck of the woods?"

Bokavic's smile dissipated, and he lowered his voice to a whisper. "I came to warn you, Dominique. I know you are preparing to fight Felipe for the middleweight belt. But soon before the fight, you're going to receive a visit from his brother, and he's going to try to convince you—"

Sylvio knew where he was going with the conversation. "—to lose the fight?" he finished.

Bokavic confirmed by nodding his head.

"I know. He came to see me a few days ago and said he was going to pay me sixty million to lose the fight," Sylvio said.

"And then if you refused, did he threaten to hurt your family?" Bokavic asked.

Just as Bokavic had done before, Sylvio nodded to confirm his plight. But it didn't make sense. How would Bokavic know anything about it unless he was directly involved? "They came to see you too, didn't they?"

"Yes. His brother offered me twenty million dollars to lose to Maximo," Bokavic confessed. "It wasn't an accident that I lost that fight. If you watch the tape, you'll see I was keeping up with him the whole fight. In the final round, I could have knocked him out, but I didn't."

"And he ended up winnin' on points, didn't he?"

"Yeah, I held myself back. But I thought about my family, Dominique. My family came all the way from Croatia to watch me fight, and they don't know how life is here. I have two sisters and a brother, and whenever I fight, they come into town to visit. I couldn't let anything happen to them."

"So, you took the money to protect your family. I can respect that. But we can't keep letting Pedro get away with that shit. Something's gotta be done about this."

"Something can be done. You can do what I wasn't able to do. You can beat him."

"Yeah, but then what if he comes after my family?"

"Protect them. Make sure you keep your team close by them around the clock. If you beat Maximo, you would be making history. They're doing everything to make sure that don't happen."

"Not that I don't appreciate it, but why are you tellin' me all this?"

"Because the belt belongs to someone who earned it by being the best, and I think you are the best right now."

"Appreciate that, money."

"Besides, if you win da belt, it makes it easier for me to get my chance at it," Bokavic smiled as the two men shook hands, and Sylvio prepared to exit the car.

"Remember what I told you, Sylvio. Good luck." Bokavic closed the door, and his driver pulled out of the parking spot to immerse into the Queens traffic.

October 14th. Fight night. After a sleepless night, Sylvio finally rose out of bed. Normally before most fights, he would contend with his growing anxiety and fear. But on this day, he felt nauseous because he knew this fight would not be just a regular fight. There was immense pressure from his fans to win the fight, along with pressure from Maximo's camp to throw the bout. After a long night where he just stared at the ceiling for hours, Sylvio remained adamant that he would not lose the fight on purpose.

He owed that much to Jim, Kevin, Kyle, Gary, Omar, Jamal and the other members of the Wolf Pack. He also owed it to Valentina to prove to her that he was not intimidated by her ex-boyfriend and his threats of death. So Sylvio was determined to be prepared for any confrontation. On the night before, he'd called Simeon and asked him to stand guard outside his father's hospital room.

Miraculously, a few days earlier, Jacques had awakened from his diabetic coma. Although he was disoriented, and he couldn't move the right side of his body, he was alive. Slowly but surely, the hospital staff worked to strengthen Jacques's motor skills and movements. He still slurred in speech, and his skin was still haggard, but he was grateful whenever his son dropped by to visit him.

Rebecca returned to work in Philadelphia, but every week she would drive back to New York to visit her ailing father. Sylvio knew that she was also on Pedro's radar and understood how imperative it was to ensure her safety.

At first, Sim disagreed with Sylvio upon leaving his client. "You sho' bout this, boss? Without me, who's gon' watch yo back?"

"I've neva been more certain in my life. Just keep an eye on my father and my sister for now, even after the fight's over."

Although Simeon didn't ask why Sylvio requested last-minute security detail for his family on the day of a fight, he was no stranger to the streets. Without a second thought, accepted the assignment.

The boxing weigh-in was scheduled at two in the afternoon, so Sylvio packed his shorts and his athletic wrap, which bore Dante Shaw's picture. After a couple of hours, Kevin arrived with Kyle and Omar, and they rode together to Madison Square Garden, the venue where the middleweight championship fight was scheduled to take place. While they waited in morning rush-hour traffic to Manhattan, Sylvio's phone rang.

"Hey, baby, how you feelin'?" Valentina asked after Sylvio answered his phone.

"Numb as hell, but I'm ready," he replied. "It just sucks that it had to be a member of yo family."

"Pedro and Maximo ain't my family anymore. They think they run things around hea, and it's about time someone knocks some sense into them."

"I guess I'm just the man for the job. And after it's over, I'm comin' over to see you, aight?"

"I'll be waitin'," she cooed in her best seductive voice.

After hanging up, Omar eyed Sylvio curiously. "You still sho' you can trust her?"

"No doubt," Sylvio replied before drifting off to sleep while watching the tranquil view of trees, power lines, and buildings.

Both fighters arrived at Madison Square Garden shortly before the scheduled weigh-in. Scores of reporters, journalists, pundits, and radio personalities were in attendance. Jim had already booked his room along with rooms for the remaining members of the Wolf Pack at the nearby Marriott Hotel. He met with Sylvio in the room where the WBC official scale was set up.

"How you feelin', Wolf?" Jim asked his fighter.

"Ready to work," Sylvio replied.

"That's what I like to hear. Let's shock the world today like Ali did," Jim said.

No sooner did he make the comment did the doors open, and Felipe Maximo walked in followed by members of his entourage, including Pedro, his trainers Marcos Paz, Roberto Perez, cornermen Dana Carros, and other young men of Dominican descent. Entering the room, they rambunctiously yelled, "Campeon! Campeon!" and swaggered their way to the stage.

Sylvio and Maximo glared at each other from across the scale. Maximo's eyes were set in his famous wide-eyed glare that normally frightened the regular man, but Sylvio did not back down as he stared back at him in anger. He had not forgotten the stunt that Maximo had pulled at the hospital, and apparently, neither did Maximo's handlers.

When Sylvio approached the scale, one of Maximo's men yelled, "Papi, papi!" while contorting his face to pretend to cry. That drew laughter from Maximo and his team as they referred to the viral video of Sylvio hunched over his father's bed at Jamaica Hospital.

"Ignore 'em, Wolf. Don't let em' get to you," Jim said.

Sylvio heeded his advice and internalized it.

But it already reached the boiling point with Omar. "Ayo, if yo mans knew what was good for him, you'd tell him to shut the hell up before I really give him something to cry about!" he said to Maximo, standing up for his friend.

"Screw you, you lil' black parasito!" Maximo replied. "That's why all you do is hang on to this loser cuz you ain't got a life of yo own."

"What you say, you lil' punk ass bitch? You ain't nothin' without dem gloves on, playa. I'd like to see you step in da hood and try that fake tough guy shit and watch yo ass get dealt wit'!" Omar yelled.

Maximo started to head to Sylvio's side, but Sylvio stepped in before Maximo could get close to his friend. "You got something to say, bring it up in the ring with me. You fightin' Sylvio 'Wolf' Dominique, not Omar," Sylvio replied, stepping between Omar and Felipe. "Whatever you got to say, we gon' address that in the ring, you feel me?" he told Maximo, ending the confrontation.

After both fighters met the weight requirement, the only option left was settling all bets in the ring.

A deafening roar could be heard from outside the locker room as fighting time approached. Sylvio expected Madison Square Garden to sell out because he knew that his title fight with Maximo was going to be the hottest ticket in town. He was going to perform in a venue that held over twenty-four thousand people—the highest attendance ever for a middleweight championship fight. Jim helped Sylvio with his wrap, which bore his late son's name and corrected the padding before putting on his gloves.

Sylvio himself was fighting through emotion, but not because of the match. A few minutes earlier, Jim suggested Sylvio to change his boxing shorts. Instead of his normal signature black trunks, Jim had bought Sylvio customized trunks that were blue with a red trim. In the middle of the trunks was a strange image resembling palm trees and cannons. It was not until Sylvio took a closer look that he realized the trunks were emblazoned with the Haitian national flag.

"When you go out there and fight, you don't represent just us, you represent your country, your nationality, and your culture. Go out and show 'em what Haitians are capable of," Jim said, and in an impulsive moment, Sylvio hugged his trainer before changing his trunks.

After Sylvio's gloves were fitted, Jim took out weeks-old newspaper editions and flipped the pages toward the sports section. He showed

Sylvio the predictions of sports analysts and reporters, and not one of them had Sylvio emerging victorious. A few even predicted Sylvio would be knocked out by the taller, more experienced Maximo within three rounds.

As the referee came to give the five-minute warning, Jim turned to offer his fighter more motivation. "Do you hear how loud they are outside? The anticipation of two gladiators ready to fight each other? Starting now, I want you to clear your mind. There's nobody out there right now. It's just you and him. Zero in on him, and focus on the task at hand. All the anger you feel from him disrespecting you and the media predicting your downfall, you pack that anger into every fist. Channel it in every jab tonight. I want Maximo to be hit by dynamite each time. Even if they don't believe in you, I believe that this is your time. You are going to make history tonight. The only person that can defeat you is yourself. Erase all doubt, fear, and paranoia. Replace it with intelligence, confidence, and perseverance. People think they are watching a champion defend his title, but I'm looking at a champion who's ready to take his throne. Let's go," Jim finished as Gary, Kyle, Kevin, and Omar hyped up the grand speech.

With that, Sylvio's robe was placed around him, and before long the deafening roar increased as Sylvio walked the long corridor making his way out into the arena upon hearing his name announced as the challenger.

With Jorge Quintero's "300 Violin Orchestra" playing loudly upon his entrance, Sylvio made his way to the ring. His sights were zeroed in on one person already there. Maximo's robe was already removed, displaying various tattoos on his chest and back. Immediately, Sylvio saw the symbol of the Serps tattooed on both Maximo's right and left arms.

Both fighters were now in the ring and in their respective corners. The referee called them to the center of the ring where he reinforced the rules, included but not limited to rabbit punches, kicks, or striking after an opponent has been knocked down, which would result in immediate disqualification.

"Touch gloves, gentlemen," the referee ordered.

As Sylvio touched Maximo's glove, the champion said, "Those shorts are shitty, like your country."

The fighters went back to their corners. Though he was enraged, Sylvio knew it was a tactic, and he eagerly anticipated the bell. A few seconds later it rang, and the moment finally arrived as Maximo and Sylvio circled each other with their gloves up, both waiting for an opening.

Jim had warned Sylvio that Maximo was the master of pacing himself in the ring. If he pressed too early and often, he would use up all his energy reserve too soon. Nonetheless, Sylvio threw two jabs toward the body, but none of them connected. Maximo had extraordinary hand speed, and Sylvio had to work double time to keep his hands up to block Maximo's straight jabs flying in as fast as arrows.

Toward the end of the first round, Maximo connected by faking a jab with his left hand. Then using his speed, he hooked with his right and caught Sylvio with a jarring right hook at his side. Sylvio winced in pain and instinctively tried to counter with two hooks of his own, but they were easily blocked by Maximo. He then countered with a left jab to Sylvio's head as the bell rang, ending the first round.

Jim's expression, as well as the expressions from the rest of the Wolf Pack, spoke volumes. Sylvio knew he lost the first round. Hitting the stool in frustration, he sat down.

"Okay, Wolf, breathe. You're doing fine. You just tight right now. You're fighting right into his hands. He's dictating the speed and the pace right now. We've got to slow the pace down by tiring him. Work his ass around the ring, make him use more energy, and then when it's time, unleash on him," he advised Sylvio.

Suddenly, Sylvio's eyes darted to the crowd. He didn't know if it was by instinct or accident, but he noticed Pedro sitting ringside behind his brother's corner, smiling from ear to ear, thoroughly enjoying the fight. But Sylvio knew the other reason he was so jovial. His smirk said a lot. Make sure every round goes like this, and we won't have any problems. My brother still holds on to the belt and you get paid even though you get your ass kicked.

At the start of the second round, Sylvio got up from his stool and began working his jab again. Maximo was blocking each one of them, but he kept his distance with his long reach. Sylvio knew the secret to beating Maximo was finding a way to evade his reach to get to his body, just like he did with Bokavic. Unlike the Croatian boxer, Maximo moved quicker and was more athletic. The second round ended as both fighters failed to inflict any damage.

"Sylvio, you're stalling right now. Maximo's flank is wide open, and you have yet to take advantage of it. It's the third round. Now is the time to press the attack," he said.

As the bell rang to begin the third round, Sylvio was more aggressive, digging down with uppercuts and wide hooks in hopes of getting Maximo against the ropes. Finally, he succeeded in getting Maximo against the ropes. The flank was opened, and Sylvio connected hard with a right hook. He knew it hurt Maximo because he slightly bent over in pain, and he heard a short grunt. As Maximo doubled over, his temple was exposed, and Sylvio threw a left and connected again, knocking Maximo off balance to the canvas. The Wolf Pack whooped in celebration. Sylvio saw Pedro looking uneasy out of the corner of his eye.

Growling in rage, Maximo stood back up and decided to press the attack and threw a flurry of jabs that forced Sylvio to constantly duck and block, but he couldn't block all the hits. Maximo connected with Sylvio's nose, just as the bell rang. Lights were popping in his head and Sylvio's vision started to blur, and he saw crimson drops dripping from his nose onto the ring.

"Get him on the stool, now!" he vaguely heard Jim say as the cornerman frantically sat Wolf down.

It took the full sixty seconds to stop the nosebleed. After a swig of water, Sylvio was back in the center of the ring with Maximo. For the next four rounds, both fighters swung at will. Sylvio started to implement his bobbing and weaving method, frustrating Maximo by forcing missed jabs and hooks. Still, Sylvio was unable to get to his body.

By the seventh round, Maximo was panting from exhaustion and unable to contain the oncoming locomotion that was Sylvio "The Wolf"

Dominique. Sylvio started to gain the upper hand when he ducked a wide left hook by Maximo and responded with a hook and jab combo. Maximo's cheek vibrated under the crushing blow, and his legs buckled. But he was still on his feet.

"That's the way to fight, Wolf!" Jim exulted as they sat Sylvio down at the end of the round.

Maximo stared across the ring at his opponent, searching for signs of fatigue, but there was none. Sylvio was intent on chopping down the tree, and he was not going to let up.

In Round 9, Sylvio made the mistake of gambling when he attempted to hook right to the body. Maximo side-stepped, avoiding the punch and throwing a hard right at Sylvio's rib cage. A sharp, indescribable pain shot up Sylvio's rib cage. He thought he might have imagined it, but he heard what sounded like a small crack. Wincing in extreme pain, his left cheek vibrated as Maximo's glove found its mark. Sylvio hit the floor, but as the referee began the count, he was back on his feet to the roaring sound of the crowd.

After the referee checked him, Sylvio glared at Pedro. Your family's goin' down tonight. I ain't goin' nowhere. Sylvio let off a flurry of jabs and hooks at Maximo, connecting on a few and opening a small cut above Maximo's left eye.

Round 10, both fighters were clearly exhausted and started to lose their stamina, but they were relentless and searched for the final blow that would effectively end the bout. But the bell rang, signaling the end of the round.

"Two more rounds, son. Fight's even right now, but it looks like you have the slight advantage. Keep at him. He's ours," Jim said as the bell for the eleventh round rang.

Both fighters rested before coming back at each other a minute later. Maximo was the first to connect with a shot that sent Sylvio's head slightly snapping back. Sylvio responded with another jarring uppercut and two body shots.

With only thirty seconds left in the round, Sylvio could hear the voice of Jim in his head. "Attack now!" With Maximo exhausted and throwing empty jabs, Sylvio threw a right hook to Maximo's exposed cheek that finally dropped the Dominican contender.

The referee began his ten count, and it was apparent that Maximo, who had never been knocked out in his career, was not going to be able to get back up. The referee finished the ten-count, and the fight was over.

Sylvio raised his hands in victory, but not before pointing at a stunned Pedro ringside, yelling, "Ain't no price on respect!"

Jim ran toward his protégé, tears running down his eyes as Gary and Omar shouted, "That's how we do it! Put on for the Zoe nation!"

The crowd cheered as Sylvio was awarded the middleweight championship belt for his tenth-round knockout of Felipe Maximo. At last, he was champion. Walking over to his corner, Sylvio smiled as he handed his belt to Jim Shaw, the man who had prepared and groomed him for this very moment. "This is for you, Jim. Thanks for taking a small, skinny boy from Queens out of obscurity to tell him that anything is possible."

Jim had never recieved any belts during his boxing years, and here was his student, finally at the mountaintop. "Thank you, son," he said as they made their way back to the locker room.

"So, what's next, champ?" Omar asked as they entered the confines of their room.

"Sleep, for about twelve hours. Then I'mma go see my girl. Matter fact, I need you to drop me off at her place," he replied.

Although confused at the strange request, Omar obliged to accompany the new middleweight champion during his visit to Valentina's house.

Chapter 20

Tires screeching as he rapidly turned at an intersection, Jamal drove nearly 65 miles an hour, weaving his way around cars through multiple lanes. Time was precious, and he didn't know how much time he had left before he reached Queens Hospital Center. Only a couple hours ago, he was lying in bed asleep when he got a call that he never imagined he would receive. A frantic Ashley called him, and in a couple of sentences, his world crumbled. As he drove through Forest Hills and through the turnpike, the conversation replayed back and forth in rotation through his mind.

His phone vibrated so much that it awakened him from his sleep, and before he could get the word "hello" out, Ashley dropped the bomb.

"Jamal, you need to come to Queens Hospital right now! Omar and Sylvio's been shot!" she yelled frantically.

"What?" Jamal was stunned in disbelief. It couldn't be true. Either he was in the middle of a joke or a terrible nightmare. He had to wake himself up. "What you mean, 'Omar and Sylvio's been shot?'"

"They've been shot, Jamal. I don't know who did it, but they're in bad shape. You need to come down hea right now. Omar's mama is already on her way and Sylvio's dad, sister, and trainer are already here. Please hurry up!" she pleaded before the call dropped.

Still dazed as if he was in the Twilight Zone, Jamal threw on some clothes and made his way towards the ER. Thirty-five minutes later, he parked in the public lot then rushed inside through the urgent care unit entrance. After minutes of searching, he found Ashley wrapped in her coat and Omar's mother and father in the room too.

When Omar's mom saw Jamal, she ran forward to hug him in hopes of consoling him.

"Where is he?" he asked frantically.

"He's in emergency surgery right now, but they said he lost a lot of blood. It's touch and go," Patty Keaton said.

Jamal could tell that she had been crying. The tears had already dried on her face. "But he's gon' be okay, right?"

Omar's father, Stanley Keaton just shook his head in uncertainty.

"He'll pull through, right?" Jamal repeated but still received no answer. "What about Sylvio?"

"He's hangin' on too, Jamal," Ashley replied.

Jamal stared out the waiting room window. "This don't make no damn sense," he said to Ashley. With his grief slowly transforming into rage, Jamal gritted his teeth and clenched his fists. "I'mma find whoever did this."

Soon as he uttered those words, Valentina stepped into the hospital, accompanied by Juan and Bruno. Suddenly, Jamal's anger zeroed in on the siblings, and he sprinted towards them. "YOU! It's yo fault!" he yelled, pointing at Valentina, as he charged at her and her brothers before being held back by Stanley and Ashley.

Causing a stir in the waiting room, the orderlies warned Jamal that if he didn't control his temper, they would ask him to leave or call the police. But Jamal wanted nothing more than to rip Valentina and her brothers to shreds.

"Jamal, please calm down. Valentina had nothing to do with this. She was the one who called 9-1-1 after hearing the shots," Ashley explained.

"Yeah, she set him and Omar up! I knew this girl was toxic from the moment I saw her," Jamal said angrily.

"I ain't set nobody up, Jamal. I didn't know what was about to go down. I swear to God," Valentina said.

"Yeah well, I'm sho' they knew what was up," Jamal replied, pointing at Juan and Bruno.

"Chill out, bro. When we got to the crib, we were warning Valentina that the Serps were comin' to do Sylvio Dominique and whoever he was with. We know who blasted yo boy and the champ, man," Juan said.

"Yeah, it was the crew that you run wit'. I ain't stupid, B.!" Jamal yelled.

"Sir, I won't warn you again to keep your voice down or take it outside. Otherwise I will be calling the police," the orderly said.

"Shut up!" Jamal yelled at the orderly.

"Son, calm down. Believe me, I wanna find the bastard who did this to my boy, too. But we've got to wait to see what happens. Maybe, he'll pull through," Stanley Keaton said.

Jamal marched away from the waiting room and out the hospital door to try and calm himself down.

After two days of unconsciousness, Sylvio finally opened his eyes. All he could see was darkness at first, and he still believed his eyes were closed. After blinking twice, he attempted to move his arms and legs but quickly discovered that he could move either. He felt numb in every part of his body except for an excruciating pain in his lower stomach. The last memory he had before all went dark was him and Omar walking through the streets at night and them seeing car headlights as if it was driving on its own in slow motion with the windows tinted. Then he remembered a hand protruding out of one of the open windows with a .45mm gun. He was warning Omar to run before the shots fired. Then Sylvio remembered feeling a piercing pain in his midsection, the feeling of skin and flesh ripping and fluid pouring out of him before all went black.

As he made a slight effort to turn his head sideways, Sylvio saw he was hooked up to various machines. One machine, he recognized as the EKG, was green and displaying jagged lines across the screen, validating that he was still alive. His heart was still pumping, and oxygen was being filtered through his oxygen CPAP mask. He overheard doctors outside his ward.

"Yeah, it's a good thing we got that bullet out of his torso. He lost a lost of blood…"

"Absolutely. He's extremely lucky. I wish I could say the same for the other one."

Sylvio made steady movements to sit up in his bed. Omar. They had to be talking about Omar. Then the harrowing realization hit him. Sylvio knew if he was incapable of avoiding the bullet, Omar must have been struck as well. Omar was shot because of him. It was his fault. He was right all along, as well as Jamal. Valentina, or her brothers, must have set him up to win the fight versus Maximo and tipped off the Serps. Now they were paying for it with their blood.

As he struggled to sit up, a female's voice said, "Jim, he's comin' around."

Rebecca approached the side of Sylvio's bed and smiled at her brother. "Hey, big jerk. Welcome back."

Sylvio was unable to speak because of the oxygen mask over his nose and mouth, but he nodded his head and stroked the back of his sister's hand as a sign he was okay. He then realized Rebecca had slept in his room, and judging from the larger silhouette, he knew his father was in there also. And Jim was seated at the foot of his fighter's bed. Standing up to approach Sylvio, Jim walked to his bedside, and immediately Sylvio knew he must've slept overnight as well, judging by the dark circles and bags under his eyes.

Eager to speak to his trainer, Sylvio lifted his left hand to remove the oxygen mask, but Jim advised against. "Whoa, not so fast, champ. Take it easy. You've had a rough couple of days. Hell, you've had a rough week," he said, laughing.

Gesturing to Rebecca to remove the oxygen mask from his face, Sylvio finally spoke. "I must be the first boxing champion in history to get shot a day after winning the belt."

As weak as his voice was, Jim instructed Sylvio not to waste energy talking. "I'm so sorry, Sylvio. I feel as though this was my fault. I should've been there with you that night. Watching you fight for survival here opened old wounds. It was like I was watching my son die all over again." Jim wiped away a tear.

Despite his trainer's warning, Sylvio was determined to console his mentor.Carefully pulling the mask off, he said, "Jim, this wasn't yo fault. I was stupid. I went out into gang territory, thinking I could run things because I was champ. All I did was paint a bigger bull's-eye on my back."

"Why wasn't Sim and L.A. with you that night?" Jim asked, lowering his voice to a whisper.

"Because he threatened Rebecca and Dad. I had to make sure they were protected," Sylvio replied.

"Wait, what? Who threatened me and Dad?" Rebecca asked.

Without answering, Sylvio asked, "Where's Omar?"

Jim and Rebecca turned to face each other, and the room fell silent, except for Jacques, who was steadily snoring.

Sylvio suddenly felt sick. Their silence was deafening but was saying a lot. "Where's Omar?" he repeated as Jim looked at him in his eyes.

"Sylvio, there were three bullet shells found on the scene. One hit you in your torso, but the other two hit Omar. One hit his kidney, and the other struck his neck, hitting the carotid artery," Jim explained slowly.

As Jim spoke, the hot tears flowed down the sides of Sylvio's face as he came to terms with reality. Omar was gone.

"The doctors worked on him as hard as they could, but he lost too much blood, and there was nothing more they could do," Jim finished, but the damage was done.

Sylvio turned away from Jim and Rebecca. Burying his face in his pillow, he sobbed loudly in anguish.

Recovery proved to be the toughest opponent Sylvio faced throughout his career as he continued to heal from the gunshot wound to his stomach. Throughout the day, the doctors who performed emergency surgery on

Sylvio explained how extremely lucky he was to survive. On more than one occasion, they'd operated on gunshot wounds in similar areas and were unsuccessful, often due to the bullet rupturing a major organ or the patient enduring too much blood loss during the procedure. Nonetheless, the doctors informed him that had it not been for Valentina's quick 9-1-1 call, they might not have been able to save his life.

But this information offered very little comfort to Sylvio. While Valentina's emergency call saved his life, it couldn't save the life of his friend. Sylvio was forced to confront the harsh reality that Omar died because of him. He had to cope with the fact that he led his friend to his death. Omar was not obligated to be outside with him that night. He didn't have to accompany Sylvio to Valentina's house, but Sylvio knew that his victory against the previously undefeated Maximo would bear repercussions.

His stunning knockout of Maximo was not lost on Pedro. He lost millions of dollars on his bet, and Legarto Incorporated had to answer to various angry businesses and corporations. With the threat of Legarto Inc. being under investigation for money laundering, illegal gambling, and embezzlement, Pedro was furious, and as a result, he had to order a hit on the man who publicly humiliated him.

With his bodyguards watching his family members, Sylvio needed someone to accompany him to Valentina's house without being detected, so he entrusted Omar to go with him. At first Sylvio believed that Valentina helped the Serps by luring him over to her house. What initially began as an oil massage turned into a night of intimacy, and with Sylvio's guard down, she could have alerted her brothers or any other Legarto employee who was an actual member of the Serps.

But Valentina, after being greatly relieved that Sylvio survived the shooting, expressed her sorrow at Omar's death and how she regretted not calling the ambulance sooner to potentially save his life. Sylvio listened to Valentina. Although eventually he realized that Valentina had no part in the drive-by shooting, he remained suspicious of her brothers until she explained that her brothers had been on their way home to warn her that Sylvio was in grave danger. They apparently knew Sylvio was seeing Valentina, and they knew that Pedro was none too pleased about their relationship.

Along with the fact that he watched his brother get defeated for the first time, it caused Pedro to be extremely unbalanced in his fury and rage. Bruno Cruz was one of the men who was inside the Legarto headquarters when he overheard Pedro threatening to kill Sylvio and offering to pay over two million dollars for the hit.

After all the facts were revealed, Bruno and Juan walked away to give their statements to the police, and there was no doubt that Pedro would be facing charges for his role in Omar Keaton's murder. But Sylvio knew there was yet another player in the deception game. There was no way Pedro would have known he was going to be at Valentina's house on his own. He knew someone was watching him or had infiltrated his camp, but he just couldn't figure out who the Benedict Arnold was.

Later that day after Valentina left his bedside, Sylvio received a visit from Gary, Kyle, A.D., and Angie.

"Man, you got a lot of love hea. You must think you da man now," Angie joked as she poured over thousands of get-well cards that were sent by Sylvio's fans.

"What you talkin' bout, Angie? I've always been the man," Sylvio laughed.

Angie walked over to Sylvio and kissed him on the forehead. "Don't get too down on yo self, homie. You'll be back on yo feet in no time," she reassured him.

"Appreciate that, Angie. Hold it down at the gym for me. When I ain't there, you the beneficiary Wolf," Sylvio said, smiling slyly.

"Wait, what? What you mean, 'beneficiary'?" she asked.

"Well, you know what a female dog is, so you can roll wit' that. I wasn't gon call you da 'B' word myself, but...." Sylvio started joking before Angie playfully hit him on the arm.

"Lame ass. Wait till you get back. I'm sparring yo ass next," she laughed.

After Angie left, Gary said, "Ight, stay up, boy. We waitin' on da return."

"You already know," Sylvio replied. After receiving encouraging words from A.D. and Kyle, they both were about to make their way out of the room when Sylvio said, "Yo, Kyle, lemme holla at you for a minute, dawg."

"Aight, Wolf," Kyle said.

A.D. left and Kyle walked back to Sylvio's bedside. "Yo, I noticed after the Maximo fight, you dipped out. I ain't seen you since. You good?"

"Oh yeah, I couldn't stay. A brotha had to handle some business back in da crib, you feel me?"

"Oh yeah, no doubt," Sylvio said.

"But I showed you love after da win, though," Kyle interjected as he dapped Sylvio again with his right hand.

Suddenly, Sylvio's eyes fell on Kyle's arm, and that's when he made a stunning discovery of a tattoo with two snakes intertwined, slithering up a pole that had the street number eighty-five on it. "Yo, that's a dope tattoo, son," he told Kyle.

"Appreciate it, dawg. Had that shit done last week, it's healin' up now," Kyle replied, completely oblivious that Sylvio regarded the tattoo as nothing more than a cowardly, worthless, piece of body art that wasn't worthy of contaminating one's arm, especially when it was drawn on traitors.

"That's dope," Sylvio repeated. As he looked Kyle in the eye, he saw no sign of remorse or regret.

Instead, Kyle was in a jovial mood, acting as though he wasn't responsible for Sylvio lying in the hospital bed at that moment. He just continued to act natural.

"Aight, dawg, I gotta bounce. Get back up so you can get back in that ring," Kyle said as he left.

As soon as Kyle walked out of earshot, Sylvio slammed his fist as hard as he could on the side of his bed. The friend he'd grown up with since elementary school and the one person who was present at every boxing match he'd fought, turned out to be the very same person that betrayed him and Omar. Furiously, Sylvio turned around in his bed and struggled to fall back asleep, staring at the inside of his linen sheets.

Longing to be left to his thoughts, Sylvio informed the doctors that he did not want to see any new visitors in his hospital room, apart from Jim, his father, and Rebecca. He also extended an invitation for Jamal, who had yet to visit him. According to Valentina, Jamal was so traumatized with Omar's death that he left the hospital, despite entreaties from his friends and Omar's teammates from the Dyckman Park Summer League. Sylvio understood why Jamal may not have wanted to visit him. He may have very well thought that Sylvio had a hand in Omar's murder. Whatever the reason may have been for Jamal's departure, he hoped that Jamal didn't sink in deep trauma and depression.

Another day passed by as Sylvio began rehabilitation. Doctors initially feared that the bullet fractured his spine and affected his motor skills and mobility, but they were relieved to discover that it missed his spine. Nonetheless, due to the length of time Sylvio was laying in bed and heavily medicated with morphine and other painkillers, he had to perform several range-of-motion movements taught to him by a physical therapist. Sylvio made a personal guarantee to himself that by month's end, he would be able to walk and run normally, but he knew he was far from ready for a return to the ring. Sylvio was also pleased that while the doctors extracted the bullet from his body, they also managed to fix one of his ribs that had been fractured during his fight with Maximo.

After a full night's sleep, the next morning Sylvio was awakened by a hand softly patting his chest. With a groan, he finally opened his eyes and saw a face that he never expected to see.

With her soft touch, Anne Dominique smiled at her son. "Cherie, you awake?" she asked, beaming widely.

Sylvio blinked twice at the woman who addressed him just so he could make sure that he wasn't dreaming as her facial features came into view. But Sylvio was less than thrilled to see her since the only thing he remembered was the back of his mother's head as she walked away from him and her father nearly twenty years ago.

"No, I'm still asleep," he replied with an edge to his voice, until he heard his father say, "Sylvio! That's your mother you're talking to!"

Rebecca had walked back into the room and turned on the light, and Sylvio finally saw his mother in full view. She was short with her gray and black har tied in a bun behind her head. Her lips were thin, and she wore a green and blue colored sweater.

"Sylvio, how are you doing, my son?" she asked as if she had been involved in his life for the past eighteen years.

"I'm doin'," Sylvio replied coldly. He knew his father didn't approve of his attitude toward his mother, but at that moment, he didn't care.

"When I heard that someone almost killed you, I knew I had to come as soon as possible. I know I'm late, but I had no money for travel. I'm sorry," she said.

"Why now?" Sylvio asked.

"What do you mean?" Anne asked, clearly confused.

"You're too late, Mom. Not only are you five days late from when someone tried to kill me, but you're eighteen years late," Sylvio continued.

"Sylvio, come on," Rebecca pleaded. "She came all this way from Philly to see you. This is the first time we've been together as a family."

"Yeah, and we're doing this family reunion in the damn hospital when she could've visited me many times before. Where was she during my elementary years? Where was she during junior high and high school? Where was she to clean my cuts, cook dinner, buy Christmas gifts, or any other time? I'll tell you where—she was nowhere to be found. She was out living the life in Philly and left us hea in the dirt."

Tears began forming in Anne's eyes.

"But it's okay, Mom. I was doin' just fine without you. It's a shame that you wait until I get shot, and you finally decide to leave your great life and see how your son's doin'," he added.

"Sylvio, that's enough," his father said. Although Jacques was weak because of his diabetic condition, he still attempted to calm his son down.

"No, Dad, that's not enough!" Sylvio shouted at his father, who was immediately silent. "I ain't a lil' kid anymore. Since I was four, I've been reliving that day when Mom walked out on us. Since then, my life's been a living hell. I've had to survive kids in school, your beatings, and the fact that my own mother didn't care enough to visit, and she thinks she can erase all that by one visit to the hospital?"

"Sylvio, please forgive me. I know I was wrong to avoid you and your father all those years. I shouldn't have stayed away as long as I did," Anne said, but Sylvio had his back turned to her, pulling the sheets back over his head.

"It's a little too late for apologies, Anne," Sylvio said, while his whole family stood in shock after hearing him address his mother by her first name.

Anne gently patted her son's shoulder and left the room.

"Okay, Dad, maybe we should leave Sylvio alone," Rebecca suggested as she helped her ailing father to his feet, and they left the room.

Walking down the block after three in the morning, Sylvio turned to Omar. "Look, dawg, I'm sorry I dragged you out here, man. It's just that what I did tonight—" he started to explain, but Omar shook his head.

"It's all good, man. I know it was about respect. For what it's worth, I glad you ain't lose on purpose cuz you inspire millions," he said.

But Sylvio didn't feel like a role model. He felt guilty because he knew Pedro would be out to get him or his family, and Omar was oblivious to it.

"I look at Ashley carrying my son, and I'm thinkin', 'who does he have as a role model to look up to?' It ain't too many cats out hea grindin' like us," Omar said.

"True that. So, you already know that you havin' a boy?" Sylvio laughed.

"Yeah man, we went to to the doctor yesterday, and she confirmed it's a boy," Omar said proudly. "Now technically, I wasn't supposed to tell you that cuz she wanted to have a big gender reveal and all that extra shit, but I don't care. You're the first to know cuz you like blood to me, man."

"Congrats, B.! Bet you he gon' grow up to be an ill balla like his daddy," Sylvio replied, laughing.

"Hopefully," Omar laughed. "But even if my son don't eva play ball, I want him to change the world. If he wants to be a scientist, a doctor, or an explorer, I'll support him in whatever he wants to do. But someday, I wanna get him out of here. I don't want him to be exposed to the gang life. I don't want him struggling like me. I want better for him. Believe me, one day, I'mma get my family out of here where my son will have a chance to thrive."

"I feel you, man. I'm wit' it," Sylvio replied. "If Valentina does turn out to be the one, I would want the same thing for us. Maybe I'll give her a shorty too, who knows?"

Omar laughed. "You heard it hea first. After me, you gon' be a father next, and finally it's gonna be Jamal, in that order. All our kids gon' be playin' in their playpens, and we'll be like the Huxtables."

"You already know. But I ain't gonna expose my child to this boxing game, especially if I have a son. I'll teach him to defend himself when the time comes, but I want my son to use his mind to solve his problems. Damn, I sound like my pops," Sylvio said, as both men laughed for what would be the final laugh they'd share together.

After his afternoon physical therapy session, Sylvio returned to his room alone, reflecting on the final conversation with his friend before he met his untimely end. Omar had plans of getting his family away from Queens and dreamed of a brighter future for his son. In a cryptic way, the more Sylvio thought about the conversation, the subtle hints were given to him that Omar might have already known he was in danger. From the question he asked about throwing the fight, to his reflective conversation about his son's future.

Could it be possible that Omar knew he wouldn't be alive much longer because of his association with Sylvio? He hated riddles and whether Omar knew about his fate wasn't important anymore. Sylvio went back into bed, deeply depressed. He attempted to sleep until he heard a knock on his door.

"Go away," Sylvio answered, and it was silent for a few seconds. But the door opened, upsetting him. Believing the intruder to be Jim or his family, he turned around, only to face a strange man that he had never seen before.

The man stood at about six-feet-four with a muscular frame with a bald head and a black beard with specks of gray. Wearing a Polo collar shirt that was tucked inside his gray slacks, he smiled at Sylvio.

"Mr. Sylvio Dominique, I presume?" he asked, and Sylvio's fear heightened.

Pedro might have sent another hitman to finish the job, but Sylvio wasn't going out without a fight. Sitting up on his bed, raising his fists he asked, "Who are you?"

The man extended his hand to shake Sylvio's. "Reverend Michael Hillman, but people call me Pastor Mike. I've heard quite a bit about you, brother."

Sylvio, who was still suspicious of his new visitor, shook his hand. He recalled hearing Pastor Mike's name swirling in controversy nearly ten years earlier. "Yeah, I've heard about you too."

"You mind if I sit here?" Pastor Mike asked, gesturing to a chair across the room that was previously occupied by Jacques.

"Yeah, whateva'. I mean you're already in the room," Sylvio replied, secretly hoping that he wasn't going to get any type of grief counsel. He wasn't in the mood for someone to hold his hand to repeatedly tell him that everything would be alright. "I don't mean to be rude, Pastor Mike, but how did you know I was here?"

"Well, a certain mutual friend of ours, Mr. Jamal Samuels, asked me to come visit you. Apparently, he knows you're going through a rough time."

"How's Jamal holdin' up?"

"He's coping with it the best way he can, but it's gonna take some time. Jamal and Omar were friends since grade school, so his passing hit him real hard. But with time and prayer, he'll be okay."

Sylvio hung his head and tried to close his eyes, but no matter how hard he squeezed them, they couldn't prevent his tears from falling.

"Hey, look, son. You have no reason to feel guilty."

"Nothing against you, pastor, but you're the last person in this room to be talkin' to me about guilt."

Pastor Mike didn't seem fazed by the partially rude comment. Perhaps, he was aware that Sylvio alluded to his past marital infidelity. "You'll be surprised how many times I've heard that, and it's been almost ten years since my incident. But just as I've learned to forgive myself, and my wife has learned to forgive me, I had to understand that God forgives when we ask Him for forgiveness in earnest humility. I'm not going to sit here and pretend like I was perfect, but I'm assured in my walk with Christ, and I know that when I read His Word, and I draw close to Him, I receive new confidence, and that's what I want to give you."

"How you gon' give that to me? I've never gone to church too much, and when I did as a kid, it didn't do anything for me. I don't wait on a God to get me right. I go out, and I get mine. That's the way it's always been."

"And that's how it was when you decided to visit your girlfriend after winning a fight that was rigged for you to lose, knowing the danger that you would put yourself and those around you in."

Sylvio's temper started to rise. Even though he was right, this pastor was infuriating him, and he'd only been in the room for four minutes. "Man, what you know about it?"

"Sylvio, believe it or not, I was an athlete too. All the way through high school, I was one of the most highly touted quarterbacks in the tri-state area with a chance to go to college on scholarship. But I made some poor decisions, and I ended up missing my opportunity to play at the next level. Do I regret it sometimes? Yes, but our decisions shape who we are and who we decide to be in the future. Life is not about demanding respect from everybody. People will fail you, and they will turn on you, but at the end of the day, do you have self-respect?"

Sylvio opened his mouth to reply, but he was at a loss for words.

"Think about that. There's self-respect, and then there's self-pride. Self-pride, when misguided, can lead to vanity and selfishness which leads to our demise. Self-respect is knowing what you're worth and what you can do to improve yourself and others."

"What if you don't have either? What if you were on top of the world, only to realize that your mother never wanted you, your friends betrayed you, and you gambled somebody's life and lost?"

"One of my favorite verses from the Bible is found in 1 John 1:9, and it says, 'God is faithful and reliable.' If we confess our sins, he forgives them and cleanses us of everything we've done wrong. We don't have to be a perfect saint. We don't have to pretend that we have it all together or that we come from a perfect family. We just have to be honest with ourselves and with God, and when we talk to him, He will respond and light our true paths," he said, before giving Sylvio his card. "Anytime you wanna talk, you can call me."

Chapter 21

Walking down the stairs of his three-story home in uptown New York, Pedro lit his Cuban link cigar and made his way to the living room area. A different array of meals was set on the dining room table. He had bottles of Moet and Alize' set between every five plates. In total, he had over fifty table placements prepared. Pedro was expecting company from his colleagues at Legarto Incorporated along with new faces of those being inducted into the organization.

Unbeknownst to many, except a select few, Pedro ran the gambling operation in the basement of his home. This unique location was designed to throw off the scent of law enforcement and federal officers. Pedro figured out many years earlier that police suspect low-end locations whenever the subject of underground gambling was brought up, but nobody would suspect the basement of a Victorian home. As he settled in for the evening, he heard a knock on his door.

"Yo, Raul, get the door!" he bellowed to his assistant, and Raul quickly answered it.

"Who is it?" Pedro asked from his couch as he turned toward the door.

"It's Kyle Green," the visitor replied.

Pedro stood up from his chair and greeted Kyle, shaking his hand proudly. "I know you've just become a member of our committee two weeks ago, but I wanted to thank you for your tip. It saved me a lot of trouble, and I managed to sleep soundly."

"Glad I could be of service. But I didn't come for a social meetin'. I came to claim my money. Where's it at?"

Pedro smacked his head to indicate he forgot about their arrangement. "Oh yeah, the money. What did we agree on, a hundred grand?"

"A hundred and twenty grand."

"That's right. You know I'm bad wit' numbers, brotha. Forgive me. Raul, pay the man," Pedro ordered, and his employee went to the safe located in the basement and returned with a check.

"There you go, brother. A hundred and twenty grand, per our agreement. It wasn't easy negotiating with you though."

"Yeah, well it wasn't easy turnin' on fam, but I'm bout the cash, and at the right price, I'd turn my brother ova."

"There's something I can't quite wrap my finger around though."

"Yeah, what's that?"

"Why'd you sell out yo boy that you was tight with for years? Seemed like a pretty good dude until he pulled that shit at the fight. You're damn near his right-hand man. Why?"

"I wasn't Sylvio's right-hand man. Omar was. I rolled wit' him cuz I knew he was in the box office. When he started makin' bank, I had to follow da' money. But I had my money on Maximo. Since I lost my bet, he became an enemy to me too."

"So, you ain't got no hard feelings about 'em getting' blasted?"

"It's the code of da streets, right?" Kyle shrugged.

Pedro led Kyle into the dining room area, where he saw the table set up for a grand dinner. "I'm inviting some associates over for a business dinner tonight. Feel free to hang around for that."

"Nah, man, I gotta bounce. It was great doing business with you."

Pedro did not intend to let Kyle leave empty-handed. "Yo, at least have a drink wit' me, brother," he said, walking over to take one of the bottles at the far end of the table. "I got that Alize' on deck. Shit's smooth." he added, gripping the wine bottle by its neck.

Eventually Kyle gave in, accepting a drink as Pedro poured a glass for himself and a glass for his guest. Raising the glass, Pedro said, "To the return of Maximo as middleweight champion and the death of those who stand in his way."

"Here, here," Kyle replied as he took a sip of the wine. Enticed by the rich flavor, he continued drinking, emptying the glass. "You weren't playin' man. This is smooth," he said.

Pedro nodded in approval. "Appreciate it, Kyle. Not too many guys show a taste for fine drinks. Welcome to the good life. In addition to my pay, allow me to give you the rest of the bottle on the house," he said, after sealing the lid.

"Appreciate it, man."

"No doubt, homes," Pedro said, walking Kyle to his front door. He watched Kyle pull out of his driveway in his Camaro and head for the freeway.

Now I can finally relax. Pedro sat back down on his couch.

But five minutes later he heard his front door open. It was Maximo, returning home from visiting his mother and father in the Bronx. Since his humbling defeat to Sylvio, Maximo had stayed out of the public eye.

"Yo, Max, que pasa, homes? How's Mama and Papa?" he asked, but Maximo ignored his brother's questions.

Staring intently at Pedro, he asked, "Is is true?"

Pedro looked at Maximo, puzzled. "What you talkin' about?"

"Don't avoid the question, Pedro. You better answer me now! Did you, do it?"

His brother suddenly became shifty-eyed, taken aback by the impromptu interrogation. "Did what?"

"So, you gonna keep on acting like you don't know what I'm talking about?" Maximo slammed a copy of The New York Post down on the coffee table. On the cover of the paper, the lead story title read: NEWLY CROWNED MIDDLEWEIGHT CHAMP SHOT IN DRIVE-BY.

"Don't lie to me! I know how you operate. This story said that Sylvio and his friend were shot close-range from a black Mazda. Sylvio survived, but his friend died. So, I'll ask you again, did you order the hit?"

"What if I did?" Pedro replied, weary of the questioning. "You were the undefeated champion. You had all the juice. We had sponsors, endorsements, bettin' lines, and TV deals all lined up, and we lost it all because of him."

"No, it was because of me. Pedro, I lost the fight to a better boxer. He was a competitor like I was a competitor, and at the end of the day, it's part of the fight game. It wasn't worth killin' over."

"Money is worth killin' ova!" Pedro shouted. "If you think otherwise, you're just lyin' to yourself. All of this shit revolves around money."

"This ain't about no rival gang steppin' on Serp territory anymore, Pedro! There's levels to this shit now. Don't you get it? What, you expected me to stay undefeated forever? What you did was murder. I used to be on this with you, but that was before I became a pro and before I became champion!"

"That chump came and took it all from us. He knew what was on the table, and he ignored it," Pedro replied irrationally, without realizing he provided more information than he intended.

Now his brother finally came to the sudden realization that his opponent was asked to take a dive. "What do you mean, he knew what was on the table?"

Pedro turned his back to his brother.

"No, don't you turn yo back on me! I will beat yo ass right now if you don't answer me straight," he warned.

Silently, in fear of his larger brother, Maximo watched as Pedro turned back to face him, guilt written on his face.

"Look me in the eye and tell me you didn't offer Dominique money to throw the fight," Maximo said, and before long, police sirens could be heard approaching the house.

Pedro's fear heightened as the sirens grew louder. Maybe they'll pass by. Maybe those sirens aren't for me. Those comforting thoughts were dashed when he heard a car door slam outside and a knock on his door.

"Pedro? This is the NYPD. We have a warrant for your arrest in connection to the murder of Omar Keaton," a deep voice boomed from outside.

Pedro made a dash for the back door to escape, but Maximo tackled him from behind, holding him in submission with a chokehold. When he realized that his crime had caught up to him, Pedro looked at his brother from underneath his arm. "So, this is how you repay family? By snitchin' to the cops?"

"No, I ain't the one who made the call," Maximo said, as he coerced his brother to the door, opened it, and watched as police handcuffed his brother.

Chapter 22

The funeral service for Omar Marquise Keaton was held in the Rock of Jacob Baptist Church in Richmond Hill, New York. Just a few days removed from the hospital, Sylvio was not originally scheduled to be discharged from the hospital, as he was still recovering from his wounds. But the doctors observed the rapid improvement he made in physical therapy, and he was determined not to miss the burial of his friend. As a result, the doctors grudgingly discharged him, which allowed him to attend the funeral.

Accompanied by Simeon, Sylvio arrived at the church at 10:26 in the morning. The casket bearing Omar's body was placed in the center of the church for viewing before the start of the service. The church was packed with various mourners, and Omar's classmates from middle and high school as well as his basketball teammates were among those in attendance. His mother and father sat in the front row along with Jamal's mother and father.

Upon arrival, Omar's mother asked Sylvio to be one of the pallbearers. Other pallbearers included Jamal and basketball teammates. Sylvio recognized two of them from the Dyckman Summer Jam where he previously watched Omar and Jamal battle on the court as they often did back in their childhood.

During the viewing, Sylvio walked up and saw Omar lying in the casket. He looked peaceful, like he was asleep, free from the excruciating pain he suffered in his final moments. *Your suffering's finally over. If only you could see the love people had for you, bro.*

Sylvio couldn't control his tears from spilling and while he wiped them from his cheeks, Jamal came up to him and reassuringly patted him on his shoulder. "How you feelin', champ?"

"I don't know, man. I don't feel like I've won anything right now. He should still be hea wit' us."

"I know," Jamal agreed. "I be staring down in this box, lookin' straight at him, and it still hasn't hit me that he's gone. I ain't had no brothers or sisters growing up. Omar was my brother. We've been through a lot together."

"I'm sorry, dawg. I didn't know him as well as you did, and it hurts me that I couldn't save him. I should be lying in this box, not him."

"Nah, bro, don't even think that. God kept you alive for a reason. Never forget that," Jamal said as they both sat in their respective seats.

When the service began, Pastor Mike Hillman began his eulogy for Omar and expressed witnessing Omar's growth as he would often attend the church and participate in youth functions with Jamal. He also expressed how much work was left in decreasing violence in the neighborhood.

Omar's parents soon took to the pulpit and spoke glowingly about their son.

A few other keynote speakers were Jamal and Ashley before Shania McClain, Pastor Mike's daughter, spoke of Omar's participation in her wedding as a groomsman to her husband, Trevor. Then local recording artist Andrea McAfee, also known as Adia, sang a musical number so touching that there was hardly a dry eye in the building.

After the keynote speakers and the song, Pastor Mike asked, "Is there anyone else who would like to say a few words reflecting on the life of our dear brother Omar Keaton?"

Sylvio looked around him to see if anyone else would walk up to the pulpit. There were no volunteers. He initially did not plan to speak at Omar's homegoing service, but a feeling gnawed away at him. Whether it was his conscious or otherwise, it was convincing him that he should step up to the pulpit to speak on his friend. You were there that night. If anyone should send him off, it should be you. Before Sylvio knew it, he was walking past rows of seats, and as he stepped up to the stage, Pastor Mike shook his hand and stepped aside to allow him to step into the pulpit.

Right away, he regretted his decision. He had severely underestimated the vast number of people in attendance, and his knees started to shake. Being a boxer, he had fought in venues with thousands of people. Madison Square Garden alone had over thirty thousand people in attendance when he fought Maximo, more than triple the attendance at Omar's homegoing service. But it was a different environment than the ring, where his adrenaline and the task of overcoming his opponent took precedence over his fear of crowds. He was now facing a different kind of pressure with all eyes on him. He could feel the stares.

"Hi, my name is Sylvio Dominique," he began nervously. "To many of you, I'm known as Sylvio 'The Wolf' Dominique, which is my boxing persona. It's a character that you see me in whenever I'm facing someone. Everyone knows 'The Wolf.' He's brash, relentless, fearless, and driven. Few people knew who the real Sylvio was. Omar was one of those few," he added, looking at Omar's parents, who were grieving openly.

"I've known him since seventh grade at I.S. 139, and I realized right away that this was a different dude. He was mad smart. I remember every year when we did them science fairs, and we had to get partners to make science projects. I would try to get Omar as my partner, but Jamal would always beat me to him," he confessed, which drew laughter from those in attendance, including Jamal.

"We didn't become best friends till high school though, and that was when he was a beast on the court. When I look at myself as a boxer and him as a basketball player, I see someone just as driven as myself on the court, and he not only pushed himself to be the best, but he pushed others to be the best, including myself. He inspired me on so many levels, and I know I can never repay him for the impact that he had on my life." Glancing to his right at the front pew, he saw Shania sitting with Trevor and their one-year old daughter, Loree.

"And even though we spent some time apart, when he went to college, and I began my pro career, once we reconnected, it was like we never left.

The same vibe was there. He was excited about his chances to be in pro basketball and excited about being a father," he said, as Ashley, who was four months pregnant, burst into tears and had to be comforted by Omar's cousins and uncles.

"And even though those things were taken away from him, I remember speaking to Omar for the last time, and his words really made me think that we have to be the change for our kids. We gotta do better to make the world a safer place for them. And although, he's gone now, I want to do my best to carry on the legacy that Omar left behind. Rest in peace, brother," he said, as the audience clapped. As Sylvio stepped down from the stage, he shook hands with the grieving family before making his way back to his seat.

After a final prayer, the time came for the burial. Sylvio, Jamal, and the other pallbearers carried the casket that bore the body of the late friend and father and one of Queens' children to the hearse. The funeral procession ended at the Edward D. Lynch Funeral Home on Queens Boulevard, where Omar was finally laid to rest.

As Sylvio watched the casket being lowered into the ground, he was approached by Andrea McAfee, the woman who sang at the service. Two individuals that had lost loved ones in similar tragic circumstances, stood side-by-side. That was a beautiful speech you gave today," she said.

"Thanks. That song was beautiful too," he replied.

"Thanks. I know you're probably sick of hearing it, but believe me, I know exactly how you feel. It always hurts losing someone so early, but the Lord heals. It's just takes time," she reassured him.

"I know," he replied.

"It just gives me comfort that somewhere out there, my sister and Omar are waiting for us," she said, before walking away to comfort Omar's family.

In the weeks that followed, new developing stories unfolded, beginning with the trial and conviction of Pedro Quinones, who was charged with conspiracy to murder, the selling of illegal weapons, illegal gambling, and embezzlement.

Two Dominican men, Carlito Lagares and Arturo Deimer, also members of the 85th Street Serps that pulled the trigger on Sylvio and Omar, were charged with first degree murder and aggravated assault with a deadly weapon. Aided by Juan and Bruno Cruz's testimony, the police were able to track the license plate tag of the vehicle. It was registered under Pedro.

Juan confessed in court that Pedro had originally asked him to carry out the hit on Sylvio, but at the last moment, he feigned an illness and left the compound. After convincing Bruno to leave, Juan drove back home to warn Sylvio that danger was near, and his cover was blown by an informant who recently became a member of the Serps. With the evidence presented, the state had enough to lock Pedro for more than twenty years. But on the final day in court, new information was revealed.

A week before the trial, a pedestrian crossing above an overpass saw a wrecked Camaro rammed into the bridge wall. The driver of the vehicle was unresponsive, and the witness called 9-1-1. But the motorist fell into a coma on the way to the hospital and died in the hospital room. Two days passed before the deceased motorist was identified as Kyle Green.

After traces of depressants were found in his bloodstream, the coroner revealed that Kyle was drugged before taking the wheel of his car and was unconscious while his car continued to speed over sixty miles an hour before ramming into a bridge abutment.

According to Raul during his police interrogation, Pedro secretly laced a bottle of Alize' with a mixture of sleeping pills and other depressants. He knew Kyle was owed money for revealing Sylvio's whereabouts, so he began plotting Kyle's demise. He gave Kyle a sip of wine, with the knowledge that he only had a matter of time before he'd feel the effects of the drugs. With the new revelations, Pedro was charged with murder in the third degree, and his prison time was extended from twenty years to life.

With Pedro's imprisonment, Legarto Inc. was shut down, and the Serps disbanded, scattering throughout the tri-state area. Although he didn't forgive Kyle for the betrayal, Sylvio felt the impact of Kyle's death because of their shared history throughout the years. Bereaved of two friends, Sylvio found himself preparing to make another speech although he knew it wouldn't be as heartwarming as the funeral.

He sat with Jim in the locker room of the Prudential Center in New Jersey, the site where he fought Kenny "Kamikaze" Brown. It was a venue that was near and dear to Sylvio. The fight against Brown started the path toward the middleweight championship, and it bore a special significance and place in his boxing memory. Adjusting his tie, Jim walked up to Sylvio.

"Okay, the press is out there ready for you. Are you sure you wanna do this?" he asked.

"Yeah, I'm sure," Sylvio replied.

Jim patted Sylvio's shoulder, and they both walked out into the conference room, where more than eighty reporters, photographers, and sportscasters waited for him. Looking through the crowd, Sylvio saw the only person that made him smile. Valentina Cruz and her brothers were attending the press conference that Sylvio scheduled for the day.

Various questions flew out at Sylvio as he headed to his seat. "Sylvio, how are you feeling now?"

"Are you ready to get back into the ring?"

"Are you announcing your next opponent?"

"Who are you going to defend your title against?"

The PR specialist informed the reporters to wait until Sylvio sat down to address the crowd.

How do I start this? This ain't easy for me to do. After a couple of minutes of clearing his throat, Sylvio decided to speak, knowing the time was right to make his stunning announcement. "Good afternoon, everyone. I'm happy to be back on my feet again, and I'm very thankful for the opportunity to hold this conference. In light of recent events, after much discussion between myself, my family, and my trainer, I have decided to retire from middleweight boxing."

There were several gasps of shock from the members of the press.

"But Mr. Dominique, you're only twenty-two years of age, and you have not hit your prime as a boxer yet. What led you to this decision?" a reporter asked.

"I'm glad you asked that, sir. I've always been my own self-motivator, and I always had self-pride. These two were my greatest weapons, moreso than my fists ever were. I made many mistakes in my life, both inside the ring and outside, due to my self-pride. It almost cost me my life, and it cost me my friend's life. I'm not making any excuses for it, but I'm hoping that I can change the narrative for others. In order to do this, I must shed myself of that self-pride, and I must use the tools that were given to me to motivate others. As a result, I had to come to this very tough decision."

"So, what are your plans?" another reporter asked.

"I will use the earnings from my title bout and with financial assistance and investments, I plan on building and opening a community center in my neighborhood of Richmond Hill, New York. It will give kids the opportunity to flourish and to keep them out of the streets," Sylvio replied.

"Don't you think that's why you're obligated to continue fighting? To inspire the next generation?" a third reporter asked.

"Who said I had to keep fighting to inspire the next generation? A wise man taught me how important it was to use our minds rather than our fists," Sylvio replied, winking at his father, standing with the help of a walking cane, accompanied Rebecca and his mother at the back of the conference room.

Jim added, "This is a venture that I will fully support Sylvio on. As his trainer, friend, and mentor, I will do whatever it takes to help his dream become a reality. Say what you want about him, but Sylvio 'The Wolf' Dominique has worked his way to the top, and he earned the belt. In my eyes, he has already accomplished more than most people will in their lifetimes. If he sees a boy that needs encouragement, I don't see nothing wrong with him offering that encouragement to someone else."

After a few questions, the conference ended, and Sylvio stood up to make his way through the throng of reporters. Valentina and her brothers waited for him. After shaking hands with Bruno and Juan, Valentina asked them, "Can you give me and Sylvio a couple minutes alone?"

"No problem, Val. Bruno and I are about to get a bite to eat, anyway," Juan replied, walking to the complimentary gourmet meal in the next room.

With the reporters still in a frenzy over Sylvio's surprise announcement, he walked away from the press and outside the arena with Valentina.

"Man, you gave every sports channel something to talk about all day," she said, staring back inside the conference room.

"Yeah, I guess I did," Sylvio shrugged. "So how you feel about datin' another average dude? Probably not yo cup of tea, huh?" he asked, laughing.

Valentina looked at Sylvio incredulously. "Boy, you need to sit down somewhere. You ain't getting' rid of me that easily," she replied, as she leaned forward and kissed him.

For a moment in time, they were in their own world, and there was no greater joy that Sylvio felt than knowing that Valentina would remain with him even after stepping down from boxing. The feeling was magnified when Juan and Bruno expressed their support for Sylvio to resume dating their sister.

"I gotta show you something," Valentina said after they stopped kissing. Reaching into her bag, she pulled out a letter.

After reading the letter, Sylvio realized that it was an institute acceptance letter. "Yo, you got in?" he asked her as he read the letter.

"No doubt! You lookin' at a new student of the New York Film Academy," she replied proudly.

Sylvio knew how much Valentina loved acting. Being accepted at one of New York's prestigious drama institutions was the pinnacle for her. "Congrats, that's dope! Soon, I'mma be watchin' all yo movies on the big screen!"

"All thanks to you, baby. You believed in me," she said, hugging him. "So how are things with you and your mom?"

"You know, just takin' it one day at a time. I've started catching up with her again, and I've learned to forgive her. I don't think we can fill an 18-year gap in three weeks, but we're tryin'. Hopefully, we can build some type of trust."

"What about Jamal?" Valentina asked.

"Well, he was just invited to a tryout for a team in the Euroleague. My bet is, he'll probably make the team and stay out there. But I know he wants to play in the NBA."

"I know he'll get there one day," Valentina replied. As they continued walking, Sylvio couldn't help but reflect on the arduous task that awaited him in building a safehaven for his community.

Six Years Later

"How much farther is it?" Tracy Ellis asked impatiently as Jamal Samuels turned at an intersection.

"We only about a couple blocks away, baby. Sit tight," he replied.

"I wish you'd let me cut yo hair. You look raggedy," Tracy laughed, as she lovingly caressed her boyfriend's short curly afro.

Although Jamal was out of the country for nine out of twelve months, they had been in a relationship for over three years. Jamal was a member of the Greek team Olympiacos, which was a part of the Euroleague. Although he flourished on his new team and made more money overseas than he did at any other point in his career, he still held out hope that he would play in the NBA.

Back in town for a month, he'd received a call from none other than Sylvio Dominique, inviting him to visit his new community center that had just celebrated its grand opening a few months earlier. Finally, Jamal and Tracy arrived, and they marveled at the futuristic design of the community center. Built in the intersection between Woodhaven Blvd and Atlantic Avenue, the center had its own parking deck next to the building and a huge sign above the entrance that read, "SDCC." After parking in the deck, Jamal and Tracy walked inside the center and stared in awe at the vast number of kids, between ages seven and eighteen.

"Yo, Jamal, what's good?" Sylvio greeted him at the front door.

After giving dap to his friend, Jamal introduced him to Tracy.

"So, what does SDCC stand for?" Tracy asked.

"It stands for the Shaw-Dominique Community Center. Yo, lemme give you a tour of this place. It's dope, huh?" Sylvio replied as they walked the corridors of the first floor.

"Yeah, man. It's bigga' than I expected. I know this had to cost a grip," Jamal replied.

"Yeah, but with a few financial investments and takin' on a business partner and co-owner, who owns fifty percent of this, we made it a reality," Sylvio said.

He took them on a tour of the first level that included a physical wellness facility. Next to the facility was a boxing gym. Jamal stared at the sign above the entrance to the boxing gym. It read "Dante Shaw Boxing Gym."

"This is my favorite spot right hea," Sylvio said as he guided Jamal and Tracy through the gym.

Jim was working with two boxers as they sparred in the ring. Sylvio's old friend A.D. was working as a trainer in the facility, practicing drills with a seventh-grade boxer.

"Let me show you the second floor," Sylvio said as he took them out of the gym and upstairs. They walked into what appeared to be a computer lab and saw five students working on technology simulations on the Internet.

"We got programs and small courses for kids in junior high and high school looking to study technology and CISCO systems," he said.

The adjacent room was as vast as a high school band room with four rows of chairs in the back and a small platform stage in the front. The room was empty, but Sylvio explained, "This is is where we teach our drama courses through the week. Many of our teachers are professionals who worked within the New York City Public School System. Although we charge $250 for membership in this center, a huge sum of those profits goes to the professors. Consider it extra income that they don't get from the city."

"I hear that," Jamal agreed.

"Yeah, sometimes Valentina stops by and gives our kids acting tips," Sylvio said.

"That's what's up. How she doin', by the way?" Jamal asked.

"She's doin' good, man. She just finished studying at the New York Film Academy, and she already started auditioning for some movie roles. You ain't seen her in that new Apple commercial last week?" Sylvio asked.

"She was in a commercial? Get outta hea!" Jamal laughed.

"Dead-ass, son. Look it up. They might've put it on YouTube by now," Sylvio said. "But lemme take you back down to the first floor cuz there's one more part of the center that I wanna show you."

But before he guided them downstairs, Valentina appeared from the bottom of the stairwell. "Hey Sylvio, they're hea."

"Who's hea?" Jamal asked curiously as they followed Sylvio downstairs and toward the front door.

A young woman stood behind the door, looking around as if she was surveying her surroundings. She was holding her five-year-old son in her hand.

"Let 'em in, Val. Show 'em around," Sylvio said, and Valentina greeted the young woman as she walked into the center.

"Is that who I think it is?" Jamal asked.

"Yeah, it's her, and that's her son, Cory," Sylvio replied.

Ashley saw Sylvio and Jamal from the other end of the hall and smiled, waving her hand. Cory was occupied with his toddler tablet.

"Baby, you know her?" Tracy asked.

"Yeah, she's a widow of a friend of ours who passed away about six years ago," Jamal replied.

"Oh my God, that's awful. That poor boy, growin' up without his daddy," Tracy said remorsefully.

Sylvio once again felt the pang of guilt. But he quickly dispelled the feeling and introduced Jamal and Tracy to Ashley and her son. "God, he looks so much like him. That's definitely lil' Omar Jr. right there," Sylvio said. "Okay, now that everyone's here, lemme show ya'll a surprise. I think ya'll are gonna like this part of the center," he added as he led the group to the back of the center.

Finally arriving at their destination, they reached two double-doors. Opening them, Sylvio flipped the light switch, and the indoor basketball court lit up. There were six hoops, four at half-court size and a full 94x50 court with a basketball hoop on each side.

"Yo, this is off the chain!" Jamal said in awe.

"Check out the hardwood," Sylvio said.

Jamal stared down on the hardwood court. On each end of the court, the words "Omar Keaton Court" were emblazoned in scripted calligraphy with a huge basketball drawn at halfcourt.

"I was thinking about doing some type of Pro-Am League with some of New York's best streetball players. It would be an honor if you were to stop by and play in the very first pickup game on the Keaton Court," Sylvio said to Jamal.

"Man, if I get some time off in the future, it's a bet," Jamal said, dapping Sylvio.

"Cory, look! This court is named after Daddy!" Ashley told her son, who looked around.

Although Sylvio knew Cory was oblivious to the significance, he had a feeling that he would one day play basketball on his father's court.

Suddenly, Jim called out to Sylvio from the hallway. "Yo, Sylvio! Got someone out hea that wants to meet you."

While the family still marveled at the court, Sylvio excused himself and made his way back to the front of the center with Jim alongside him. He arrived just in time to see a rangy, six-foot man dressed in Nike apparel walk into the community center, flanked by his entourage. The last time Sylvio laid eyes on the man was a week ago from his television screen, celebrating his win over current top ranked middleweight contender Jermaine Dodson.

"Ain't that Barry Taylor?" Sylvio asked.

"Yup. He sure sprouted, didn't he?"

Sylvio remembered Barry from the days back in the Steel Glove Gym. Barry, a regular at Steel Glove, was a short wiry kid, barely sixteen at the time, and he would often spar with the other older boxers and trainers. Now he had built muscle, and with Sylvio out of boxing, he felt that it was his time to be champion. Since Sylvio's retirement, many contenders won the crown but were unable to maintain the top status.

Maximo never recovered from his loss, and when it was revealed that his brother was involved in fixing fights and other illegal activity, he lost all credibility and was ultimately ostracized from the division.

As a result, the belt was held by a wide variety of boxers, including Sylvio's old rival Rosjan Bokavic, who won his title bout over the top contender of the time, Santana Gutierrez. Bokavic held the belt until he was finally defeated, and then it landed in the hands of Jermaine Dodson, until a few nights ago when young Barry Taylor pulled off the upset by winning the title bout and snatched the middleweight crown.

Sylvio watched the fight, and it was no question that Barry would have been a formidable opponent for him, had he stayed in the game.

"Yo, Barry, what's good, champ? Welcome to the SDCC," he greeted the current champion, but he wasn't met with the same courtesy.

Barry rudely ignored Sylvio's outstretched hand. "So, this is where you been hidin' all along, B.?" Barry's tone was more than arrogant.

"Hiding? Ain't nobody hiding, bro. This is just me giving back to my community," Sylvio replied.

"Nah, this can't be why yo ass dipped out. I know you ain't go out just for this," Barry sneered, looking around.

Man, this guy's feelin' himself a lil' too much. Reminds me a bit of myself.

"Aye, show some respect, dawg. He from our block," a member of Barry's entourage said.

"Man, this joker ain't from our block. Nobody from our block wins the title belt, then quits like a punk-ass bitch," Barry replied.

"Look, Barry, why you care 'bout what I decide to do in my life? You da' champ now. Shouldn't you be celebratin' somewhere?" Sylvio asked.

"Yeah, I'm the champ. But I still gotta walk around the Hill, and I keep hearin' cats runnin' their mouths, talkin' bout I'm good, but I ain't no Sylvio Dominique. 'He the true champ.' I want my respect in my hood," Barry replied.

Sylvio realized that people still considered him the true champion, even after retiring at twenty-two. Barry's ego demanded greater respect from his counterparts, and he would stop at nothing until he shut his doubters' mouths.

"Look, Barry, I've been in yo shoes, okay? I know what it's like to have nobody give a damn about you. I know what it's like fightin' battles every day. You got a chip on your shoulder like I did before I was champ. That'll drive you to greatness, but if you let it consume you, it'll destroy you."

Barry couldn't understand what Sylvio was telling him. Barry walked up to Sylvio until they were nearly nose-to-nose. "Sounds like a challenge, boy. Destroy me, then. Right here, right now, come out of retirement, and fight me for this belt," he said, goading Sylvio.

Then there was complete silence in the center. The trainers and the boxers at the boxing gym stepped out to witness the commotion.

"Nah, it ain't happenin'. I told folks I was done with the fight game," Sylvio said.

"Then you a bitch, and yo mama's a bitch too," Barry responded.

Sylvio, who started to walk away, turned around and walked back. Barry had struck a nerve. "Okay, I tried to be cool wit' you, but you ain't lettin' up, so I'mma tell it to you like this: I ain't comin' back to pro boxing, so you can sit down somewhere wit' yo psyche game. I ain't wit' it, and I have kids in this center. Keep causing trouble, and I'mma have you thrown outta hea."

As the other members of the community center walked back into the gym, Barry continued calling Sylvio out. "Oh, is that a boxing gym that ya' walkin' into? Me and you gon' settle this right hea right now. All I need is one round, playa. I bet I knock yo ass out in one round. We gon' settle this once and fo' all...no press, no promo, no cameras," Barry said, taking off his championship belt that had been around his waist. He headed for the Dante Shaw Boxing Gym.

"Okay, I can't take anymore of this, Sylvio," Jim said after watching Sylvio get berated by Barry.

"You heard that fool? I ain't got nothin' to prove to nobody," Sylvio said.

"No, you ain't got nothin' more to prove to anyone, but you gon' have to humble this man by showing him why they used to call you 'Wolf' six years ago."

"So, what are you saying I should do?" Sylvio asked, although he had a feeling that he knew what the answer would be.

Jim reached into his athletic duffel bag and pulled out a pair of red boxing gloves, giving Sylvio the same answer he gave him nearly twenty years earlier at the age of nine.

"Box."

THE END?

ABOUT THE AUTHOR

"Marc A. Beausejour"

Marc A. Beausejour was born on July 28, 1987 in Queens, New York to Haitian parents Jean and Lineda Beausejour. He discovered his passion for writing at the tender age of twelve, with poetry becoming his initial artistic expression. Beausejour showcased his poetic talents in various school talent shows and poetry reading events during his time at North Cobb High School and later at Kennesaw State University after moving to Kennesaw, Georgia in 2001.

Throughout the years, Beausejour continued to hone his craft, writing poems for diverse occasions such as weddings, funerals, and church events. In 2011, he took a significant step by self-publishing his first book, "Words on High," a compilation of spiritually inspired poems from his formative years. Building on this success, Beausejour released his second poetry book, "Rising Higher Than Ever," in 2015.

In the same year, he ventured into a different literary landscape by writing and publishing his first urban novel, "The Preacher's Web." This gritty morality tale marked a departure from his earlier poetic works, showcasing Beausejour's versatility as an author. Expanding his literary horizons, he created the *BlackCyrano* series, demonstrating a wide-ranging creative skill.

While continuing to share his literary work on blogs and social networks, Beausejour remains committed to his education and promotions, earning his associate degree in marketing management from Chattahoochee Technical College in 2018. As a multifaceted writer, Marc A. Beausejour continues to captivate audiences with his words across various genres and platforms.

ALSO BY, AUTHOR

"Marc A. Beausejour"

Title: The Preacher's Web | Publisher: SHE PUBLISHING LLC | ISBN: 978-1-953163-91-2 (paperback) Publication Date: February 2024 (*Second Edition*)

Set in the heart of the city, "The Preacher's Web" unfolds a gripping narrative of former All-City quarterback turned pastor, Mike Hillman, whose dedication to preaching love and forgiveness in Queens, New York is challenged by the return of an old friend seeking revenge. Amidst a community grappling with the scourge of drugs and gangs. As Mike puts his reputation on the line to testify for a young man accused of murder, the story converges with the adolescent struggles of Jamal Samuels on the basketball courts of New York City.

Now, standing at the crossroads of faith, family, and societal challenges, Mike faces a pivotal choice. Will he risk more than his reputation to uphold justice and fulfill his role as a public servant and father? The pages of "The Preacher's Web" beckon you to explore the complexities of morality and redemption. Can Mike Hillman rise above, or will he be consumed by the web of his past?

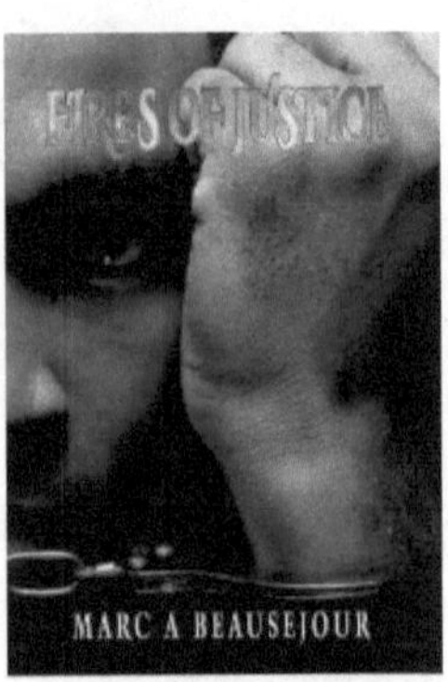

Title: Fires of Justice | Author: Marc A. Beausejour | Publisher: SHE PUBLISHING LLC | ISBN: 978-1-953163-93-6 (paperback) | Publication Date: February 2024 (*second edition*)

English professor Levell Thomas is ecstatic when he receives the opportunity to teach in a metro Atlanta high school. A native of Queens, New York, Levell moves to Georgia with his family and as they settle in their new home, Levell meets his neighbor, a mysterious girl named Raven Roberts. Despite being underaged, she doesn't hide her desires for Levell and pursues him relentlessly. Levell refuses her advances but would soon pay dearly for his decision. The spurned teenager accuses Levell of assault after a physical confrontation and Levell is found guilty in the court of law. Detective Isaac Sands leads the investigation to expose a plot of false accusation and imprisonment in a race against time. Will Sands help prove Levell's innocence by finding the conspirators, or would he put himself in harm's way?

"The controversies confronted, stirred, and then addressed in this story have no choice but to awaken you to new perspectives that might not have ever crossed your mind. Readers, all I can say is be prepared to feel the fire that Beausejour has ignited in this suspenseful masterpiece!"

—D.A. Goodwin, author of The Offender I Once Defended

Title: Adia's Ballad | Author: Marc A. Beausejour | Publisher: SHE PUBLISHING LLC | ISBN: 978-1-953163-92-9 (paperback) | Publication Date: February 2024 (*second edition*)

From the author of "The Preacher's Web", this coming-of-age story explores the life of young Andrea McAfee who struggles to cope with the tragic murder of her older sister. Then a chance opportunity lands Andrea into the music business where she shares a bond with other artists in the hip hop industry and learns she has more in common with them than she realizes. As Andrea immerses herself deeper into the life of recording, touring and partying as Adia, the new R&B princess, she begins drifting away from her family and her loved ones as her star rises too fast for her to absorb. With fame corrupting her relationships with those she loves, will Andrea find the inner peace and closure she seeks, or will she succumb to the draw of money and celebrity?

Title: Split Decision II - The Comeback | Author: Marc A. Beausejour | Publisher: SHE PUBLISHING LLC | ISBN: 978-1-953163-95-0 (paperback) | Publication Date: February 2024 (*second edition*)

After Sylvio Dominique's sudden retirement from middleweight boxing following a close brush with death, the former champion hangs up his gloves to continue running the Shaw-Dominique Community Center in Queens, New York. When Sylvio's hometown rival and current middleweight champion Barry Taylor; asks him to help train for his title defense against new contender and former MMA fighter Jun Zhang, Sylvio agrees to the proposition. But Taylor is defeated handily, and when Sylvio suffers a tragic death in the family and the center struggles financially, he makes the decision to return to the ring. Meanwhile, his girlfriend, Valentina Cruz find success as an actress and her relationship with Sylvio begins coming apart at the seams. Sylvio's trainer, Jim Shaw is reluctant to help Sylvio, as he finds himself struggling with his own personal demons. Jun Zhang then challenges Sylvio to fight him for the crown. As he prepares for his toughest ring battle yet, can Sylvio and Jim find the fortitude to emerge victorious while putting all their struggles behind them?

Title: Street Retribution | Author: Marc A. Beausejour | Publisher: SHE PUBLISHING LLC | ISBN: 978-1-953163-96-7 (*paperback*) | Publication Date: February 2024 (*second edition*)

New York City attorney Edward Reed harbors a secret. He was once known as Antonio Franks, a member of M.O.B., the most dangerous gang in Queens, New York. He was also the key witness in the trial that exonerated another ex-gang member, David Anderson, when he was falsely accused of murdering his girlfriend, Loree McAfee. But years later, both men's lives are in danger, as other former gang members are slain under mysterious circumstances by a femme fatale, prompting rumors that M.O.B.'s ruthless gang leader, Tadarius Hill is seeking revenge on those that turned on him and his organization. Will Edward and David survive the bounty, or will they fall victim to the code of the streets?

Title: Divine Vengeance | Author: Marc A. Beausejour | Publisher: SHE PUBLISHING LLC | Publication Date: COMING SOON!

After the murder of David Anderson, LaToya Richardson awaits her day in court while attorney Edward Reed receives a warning from Tadarius Hill, the gang leader of M.O.B. and sexy femme fatale Tina, who gives him an ultimatum. Realizing that he cannot use conventional methods to combat the tactics of his former gang, Edward pulls out all the stops to prevent Tadarius from wreaking havoc in the city. LaToya's son, Chris adjusts to his new home and new school while staying with David's family. Andrea McAfee's relationship with her boyfriend Quentin comes apart at the seams as lust and infidelity threatens to tear the couple apart. Can Edward, Chris, and Andrea summon the strength amidst the chaos in their environment to secure their futures?

www.ingramcontent.com/pod-product-compliance
Lightning Source LLC
Chambersburg PA
CBHW060814190726

48285CB00002B/658